THE MAN FROM MOROCCO

Tom Walsingham Mysteries
Book Seven

C. P. Giuliani

SAPERE
BOOKS

THE MAN FROM
MOROCCO

Published by Sapere Books.

24 Trafalgar Road, Ilkley, LS29 8HH,
United Kingdom

saperebooks.com

ISBN: 978-0-85495-796-5

To Svitlana — together with her family, her brother at the front, her students, and her people, and all of Ukraine. To their courage, their strength, their hopes.

ACKNOWLEDGEMENTS

Many thanks go to Lyn Crisp of the Chideock and Seatown Community Website for the cider-houses, to C. G. Machin for the trees among several other things, and to James Grant for making me aware of the *Sources Inédites de l'Histoire du Maroc.*

Thanks, as usual, to the wonderful librarians at Baratta, and to my little band of listeners and cheerers-on: Rosie, Milla, Pip.

CHAPTER 1

3rd of January 1589, Richmond Palace

One didn't fault an allowance of travelling money — least of all one so generous — but Tom Walsingham still raised an eyebrow as he weighed the two fat purses in his palm.

"Twenty-five pounds, seven shillings in all," John Cardenas explained, high forehead creasing in calculation. "Mr. Secretary's own orders. We're not quite sure how many of them you'll be shepherding — and besides, a Moorish ambassador... Who knows what you may need to pay for?"

Well, then... Tom slipped the purses inside his sleeve, where they sat uncomfortably heavy. If Sir Francis Walsingham, Queen Elizabeth's principal secretary and spymaster, foresaw the need for that much money, it was hardly reassuring. As Sir Francis's kinsman, and his trusted agent these past ten years, Tom knew enough to wonder at just what lay before him.

Through the small writing room's glazed window, he frowned at the first light of dawn fingering its way among the palace's forest of turrets and ornate brick chimneys, and then looked back at Cardenas. "I still would like to have you come along, John," he sighed. "What do I know about Morocco and Moroccans?" Which was foolish — for Cardenas may be half Spanish, but he had grown up an Englishman in England. As Sir Francis's secretary for Spanish matters, he might know about the dealings of England and Barbary — but then, so did Tom. "I saw more Moors in Kit Marley's play last month, than in my whole life!"

"Well, so did I — and if the Moors are anything like that, how you'll travel discreetly, I don't know!" Cardenas's full moustache and pointed beard always seemed like a boy's disguise when he laughed. "Come, come, Mr. Thomas, the only advantage I have is better Spanish, but I've taught you, haven't I? And I'll gladly leave to you the Sultan's envoy and all the rest." He sobered at once. "For one thing, if there's a Spanish spy among them, what would I do with him?"

"Little question of *if*, is there?" Only last summer the Sultan Ahmad al-Mansur, King of Morocco, had taken the sinking of the Spanish Armada as a sign that England might make a worthy ally. Ever since, England and Morocco had been groping their wary way towards an alliance — and now the Sultan, regarding Catholic Spain as the very devil, had sent his ambassador to the Protestant Queen Elizabeth. He'd sent him with offers of friendship, alliance, money and assistance against Spain — or so claimed the merchants of the Barbary Company who had brought about this mission — and bragged of it a good deal. And Sir Francis Walsingham wanted this treaty very much. "Put yourself in the shoes of Philip of Spain, John: wouldn't you want to know?"

The Spaniard — they called him that in jest at times — tilted his head, lips pursed. "Very much — and, in my own shoes, I don't know that I'd know how to smoke out the spy." From among the papers on the writing table, he took a packet tied with a silk cord. "Your papers, Mr. Thomas — but truly, how can you tell?"

How, indeed? Not an hour earlier Tom had discussed the matter at some length with Sir Francis — his great cousin haggard with ill-health and worry. It could be one of the Moors, come all the way from Morocco; it could have been anyone on the ship; it could be anyone who'd accosted the party after storms and ill-luck had stranded them in Ireland first and Cornwall later…

"Discrepancies, mostly. You look for those and hope they lead somewhere." Which wasn't much, but it held true of murderers and spies alike. Ignoring Cardenas's dubious look, Tom took the packet — the official, much-sealed letter identifying him as Mr. Secretary Walsingham's man, out on the Queen's business, to be used with discretion — and tucked that in his sleeve as well. "But, I'll say, I very much wish to God they'd made land in Falmouth, instead of touching half the known world's coasts."

"If you believe that Dunne," the Spaniard said, mouth thinning into a line.

"You don't like the man, do you?" Not that there was much to like about dour, gruff, taciturn Bartholomew Dunne, who had ridden in the day before, exhausted and half frozen, bringing tidings of the ambassador's coming — and very sparing with his words. Cardenas had taken against him from the first moment.

"If he'd come to Mr. Secretary first, then I'd like him a little better," he groused — for, he'd found out, Dunne's first call had been with the Barbary merchants in London.

"Well, his master is a Company man, and one who takes orders, rather than gives them. Henry Roberts does not count on Sir Francis for his livelihood."

Not that this seemed a cause for indulgence to Cardenas. "Roberts is not even a merchant! What was Lord Leicester thinking, plucking one of his soldiers out of Ireland, and making him his agent in Morocco?"

That had been … what? Four years earlier? Five? Tom remembered only too well the earl's greedy glee over his newfangled Barbary Company. "He was like a child with a new toy, back then."

"A costly toy — and chancy!" The Spaniard shook his head. "And now that Leicester is dead, what will become of it?"

"As long as it brings about this treaty…" Tom began with a shrug — and then stopped. "But no, that's not true. Pray that the Barbary Company prospers, John — for Sir Francis doesn't just want the treaty. He wants the alliance to last."

"Then pray that the fine merchants learn where to look for direction!" was the belligerent retort. "And Henry Roberts with them."

Bless John Cardenas — a very clever fellow, but still young enough, and new enough at the game, to mislike the notion of anyone not regarding Mr. Secretary above all others. Then again, it was one of Sir Francis's qualities that he inspired such loyalty in his men — Tom first and foremost. He glanced at the window: the frost flowers on the glass panes were turning silver.

"I'd better be on my way." He gathered his sword-belt from the windowsill, and fastened it on, the weight of the rapier settling comfortingly on his hip, the parrying dagger at his back. When he adjusted the silver-encrusted hilt, it was nearly a caress.

"Why, look at that!" Cardenas leant close to peer at the fine swept hilt, extending a forefinger towards the vine pattern on the knuckle-guard and barrel-shaped pommel. "Italian, is it?"

"Italian, yes."

If the Spaniard hoped for more, he was facing disappointment. The elegant rapier had been Frances's New Year gift — and nobody must know that Sir Francis's widowed daughter was Tom's beloved and that she loved him back. *You must carry it always*, she'd whispered, dark-grey eyes alight, as she'd fastened the fine scabbard to her cousin's belt. *I want to think that, when you are in danger, a part of me faces it with you.* And she'd closed her fingers around the hilt as he'd kissed her... He blinked out of the remembrance to find that he'd been smiling to himself, and that Cardenas was studying him — Jove rain on all lovelorn dreamers!

"Haven't we squandered enough time?" he grumbled, hoping to cover the blush he felt creeping up his neck.

"You'll let me borrow that beauty for a bout, one of these days, won't you?" Utterly unoffended, Cardenas blew out the candles in the two-branched holder and led the way out, stopping only to lock the doors to his small, borrowed study, and then that of Sir Francis.

Kitchens, sculleries and stables, the underbelly of Richmond Palace, would be already astir in this beginning of dawn. In this wing, though, where the Privy Councillors and their people had their lodgings, only a few servants moved about, swift and silent, to light fires and empty chamber pots. None of them spared a glance for Mr. Secretary's men — who, by common knowledge, never slept and were about at all hours. Tom's mind was still on Frances as he and Cardenas made their quiet way through the cold greyness. Had she ever spoken like this to her husband, before poor Sidney left for the Low Countries to find his death in battle? She'd liked him well enough — but loved him? Surely *he* hadn't loved her half enough... And there he went again! Let Sir Francis never know what a wool-gathering halfwit he had for a kinsman — and much less just what sort of wool he gathered instead of putting his mind to the matters of Morocco, and Spain, and Portugal.

And then, as though conjured by the thought of Portugal, a lilting, carrying murmur sounded from behind. "Mr. Thomas, is that you?"

They stopped, both knowing the voice at once. Dr. Roderigo Lopes, the Queen's Portuguese physician — and quite a few other things beside — was of those men born for the stage or the pulpit, blessed with a vast, burnished voice that he knew to make as thunderous or as soft as he pleased, and with a tall frame and a kindly face. How could one meet Dr. Roderigo, and not be reassured?

At present, though, when he reached them, the one candle his large-shouldered young servant carried showed little that was reassuring in the physician's manner. Tom was alarmed at once.

"I come from Mr. Secretary's room," Lopes began — and then stopped, touching Tom's arm briefly. "No, he's no worse than when you left him. He sent for me to discuss King Antonio, given the juncture."

It was almost comical, the way they all three sighed — Tom, Cardenas, and Lopes — and even the young servant winced. This was how most in England reacted at the mention of Dom Antonio, Prior of Crato, prince of questionable legitimacy, and exiled pretender to the throne of Portugal — now under Spanish rule. Most, at least, of those who knew of the gentleman's pretence, and of his beggarly stance. All amusement fled, though, when an unpleasant thought struck Tom.

"They never also sent word to him, did they?" he exclaimed. Not even the Barbary merchants could be this witless. They must know, they must have been made to see that, much as the Sultan wanted Spain out of Portugal, it must all go by way of the English Crown?

Dr. Lopes raised both palms and both black brows. "I don't think so — not the Company, at least. But even if they haven't, what of the ambassador himself? He'll have orders to make

14

contact with the King — letters and offers. So, Mr. Secretary says, if you could sound out the ambassador, Mr. Thomas — with the greatest prudence, you understand — and glean something of his intentions…"

"Or his actions, yes." And wasn't this most interesting? For Tom had discussed all of this with his cousin. He would do so, he promised, most prudently. He thanked the physician for his trouble, and they exchanged grave bows.

"Godspeed, then, Mr. Thomas," Dr. Lopes wished. "But you've no candles! Let my scrivener light your way to the stables. Lucas…"

The lad at his elbow stepped eagerly forward, and the candle's flame flickered on a keen, swarthy, boyish countenance, ill matched to his sturdy frame. His brown eyes crinkled in disappointment when Tom said there was no need, for it was almost light already.

Which wasn't quite true, but enough that he and Cardenas had no trouble finding their way to the nearest staircase and descending it at a good clip.

They were two flights down before the Spaniard laughed softly. "Well, well! What would you wager that His Honour didn't send for the good doctor at all?"

"Oh, he may have — he wasn't well when I left him," Tom said. "As for running to tell me things I already know… With the fuss he made to play go-between for Mr. Secretary and Dom Antonio, now he has to make himself important on both sides."

"And talkative on both sides, too?"

Tom considered for the briefest moment as they reached the door to the stable yard. "Oh come! There may be money and state to be had in this matter of Portugal — but Dr. Lopes knows where it will come from." And what the price would be if he crossed Sir Francis in this of all matters…

They rushed across the yard into the stables — cavernously huge, and dark, but for the lanterns hanging here and there — and a groom directed them to where Nick Skeres, Tom's servant, waited with three saddled horses and Tolly Dunne.

There was no other word for it: the two men were sulking, each to himself. Stocky, curly-headed Skeres, who was called the Minotaur for a reason, was whistling through his teeth, making a great show of checking straps and buckles. Dunne, a lanky, harsh-faced former soldier of thirty or so, stood with his arms crossed, head thrown back to squint up to where, at some lighter time, he could have seen the tall, truss-beamed roof.

"Are we ready?" Tom asked sharply.

There was a double "Ay, Master" — followed by a mutter of "Been for a while" from Dunne.

"What's that, Dunne?"

"Ready when you want, Master," the soldier said.

He said it with such a slow drawl that Skeres stepped around the horses, chin jutting and shoulders bunched, muttering, "Do I trounce 'im, Master?"

Oh, Jove! "No, you don't," Tom snapped. "And that's enough, from the both of you!"

"And have a cheerful journey, Mr. Thomas," murmured Cardenas.

Had he wanted cheer, Tom would have stayed in Paris — or else in Cambridge, to read Latin poetry all day — but this didn't mean he liked to ride with two surly brawlers.

"I'll say it once more, Dunne: I've no need of a guide — still less one so tired he'll slow me down. You stay behind and follow at your pace."

Not that it had worked before — and why should it work now? In fact, Dunne set his face in a stubborn scowl.

"I ain't tired, Master. Capt'n Roberts said to ride back at once, so riding back I am." He tugged on his horse's lead as proof of his intention. "And if you want no guide, or it's just me, that's your own business, Master — but I was never Leicester's man: I'm Capt'n Roberts's." And with that he walked away, leading his horse, ready to take off alone.

However, Tom called to him, "And what's Lord Leicester got to do with it?"

"Mr. Secretary's men are done trusting Leicester's, ain't they?" Over the horse's saddle, the soldier glowered at Skeres. "Been done for some time!" Clicking his tongue in disgust, he stalked out.

And trust the Minotaur to blather! But did he show repentance under Tom's baleful glare? Why, not in the least: he planted both fists on his hips and rumbled, loud enough for the whole palace to hear, "What did 'e expect, when 'is master turned against 'Is 'Onour?"

Only the Earl of Leicester was dead now, and Roberts had been long away from England, and might have thought little of the falling-out between Mr. Secretary and the earl — or even not known about it at all. Now, just to make things easier, he was going to think himself distrusted on principle — and to mistrust in turn.

"Will you ever learn to keep that plaguey mouth shut?" Tom growled at Skeres. Snatching his horse's reins from the lad, he hastened out to the yard after Dunne, before the soldier rode off on his own.

CHAPTER 2

Three days later, Tom was hunched in the saddle, narrowing his eyes against the flurry of fat snowflakes and the greying afternoon light. He could hardly feel the reins through his thick gloves, and surely the soles of his boots had changed into slabs of ice.

"If your master has a grain of sense, Dunne," he ground out through chattering teeth, "they'll all be huddling by the fire in some roadside inn! What's the next village? Whether we find them or not, we're stopping there." He cursed when his hired sorrel snorted out a great cloud of vapour, dancing away from the ice-rimmed rivulet of nameless water — not that he could blame the poor beast. Had it been for him, Tom would have turned around and gone back to Bridport. But Tolly Dunne, at his side, shook his head like a restive mule.

"And I'm telling you again, Master: the Capt'n is dead set on making good time. As long as there's daylight, he'll be going."

Tom squinted. He could barely see a dozen yards ahead, and the grey gloom was so flat that it threw no shadows across the knee-deep snow. "Daylight, you call it!" he muttered.

When Dunne shrugged, a layer of snow was dislodged from his cloaked shoulders. "The Capt'n will," he said, and pushed his horse ahead, to skittishly splash across ice and black water.

"Only to the next village, Dunne!" Tom called, spurring the sorrel to follow.

Behind him, Nick Skeres was voicing bitter thoughts. "Mite late for that, ain't it? Seven weeks to get out of Morocco, and now 'e frets!" the lad groused, not even bothering to keep it low. But then, Skeres had said the same to Dunne's face more than once since the day they'd left London, and would have told him worse and more often as they pushed their miserable way along the West road, if Tom hadn't quelled him. In truth, he rather agreed with the lad, and at that moment, chilled to the marrow, with the wet snow seeping through his cloak, he had half a mind to let Skeres warm himself with ill humour, as long as it didn't flare into fighting.

It was the Minotaur's grimly pleased air — for truly, the lad at times read him far too well — that made him straighten in the saddle. "Oh Hades, enough! At the next place with a roof, we stop — but until then…"

"Ay, ay — not a peep out of me," Skeres rumbled, glowering at the pommel of his saddle.

"Nor afterwards, mind — not if it's to needle Dunne. I've had enough of —"

"Mr. Walsingham!"

Dunne's call seemed to come from far away, softened by the curtain of snow — but the soldier was just a little ahead, where the road curved around a rising of the land, standing in his stirrups and pointing.

"There!"

Tom nudged his mount a few steps forward, to follow the pointing finger in the grey-white distance. It wasn't easy to reckon the distance to a large, crooked elm rearing like a ghost by the road. Under it huddled a number of cloaked figures and horses, black against the snow.

"Are you sure? Why have they stopped out here?"

In answer, Dunne simply trotted ahead. "Master Roberts!" he hailed at the top of his harsh battlefield voice. "Capt'n!"

The reckless fool! What if it was a gang of highway robbers? Calling to Skeres, Tom hastened to follow, loosening his rapier in the scabbard — for all the good it would do him, when he could hardly feel his fingers.

But he would need no blade, after all: one of the figures moved away from the group, resolving itself into a man in a dark cloak.

"Is that you, Tolly?" he called. "Sink me — but I'm glad to see you, lad!"

He waited, squat and still as a tree stump, until the horsemen were by him, and then he pushed back his hood to show a jowly, raw-red face that seemed too old for the thick, brown mane of hair. He could have been of any age between forty and five-and-fifty.

A hand on the neck of the dismounting Dunne's horse, the man blinked up at Tom through red-rimmed eyes. "I'm Roberts of the Barbary Company," he announced.

"Thomas Walsingham. Mr. Secretary sent me to meet you." Tom slid off the saddle more stiffly than he'd have liked, and frowned at the very small clutch of men under the elm. "The Moroccan ambassador?"

From Roberts's weary hum, one wouldn't think there was great joy to find in the company of ambassadors. "There," he said, jerking his head at the wretched-looking figures. Not half a dozen of them were muffled in dark cloaks and huddling together. Surely that could never be...?

"But where's the retinue?"

Roberts flourished a gloved hand. "*There*," he repeated.

Which was how Tom knew himself for a poetical dolt. Not that he'd truly expected Kit Marley's kings of Africa, jewelled and swathed in silks, the dozen dark-skinned guards with pointed helmets and scimitars, the glint of gold and steel, the scarlet turbans — not *quite*...

"But —" He stopped short of blurting out that those ghostly scarecrows shivering in the snow looked nothing like a Moorish sultan's envoys.

"Didn't Dunne tell you?" Roberts asked.

Tom glared sideways at the soldier. "Not half of what there was to tell — and I'll want to hear the tale when we have a roof over our heads. Now introduce me, Mr. Roberts, if you'd be so kind."

Seen close, the Moors were even more mysterious, silently waiting in their thick cloaks of brown and black and pointed hoods. Tom counted three men and the smaller figure of a boy. A fifth fellow, sitting by himself at the elm's foot, must have been Roberts's servant, for he wore a green, round hood of English make.

"*Señor* Raìs," Roberts announced in rough Spanish, with a stiff little nod to one of the dark figures. "This is Mr. Thomas Walsingham."

Wasn't this a little short, as introductions went? The addressed man stepped forward, tall, hawk-visaged, with a pointed beard and tired but searching eyes. Bowing a little deeper, Tom summoned his best Spanish. "Servant and kinsman of the Principal Secretary to Her Highness Queen Elizabeth, Sir Francis Walsingham. On behalf of my master and of Her Highness's Privy Council, I'm sent to meet, welcome, and escort Your Excellency to London."

Heaven be thanked for Cardenas's tutelage: the Raìs made no sign of incomprehension. Instead, he nodded in turn, touching a hand to his chest in a gesture of impressively noble grace.

"*As-salaamu 'alaikum, ya Sayyidi* Tomàs Ulsingam," he greeted. The Arabic words and even the mangled version of his name glittered in Tom's mind like all the silk and jewels in Marley's play. It was almost a pity when the man shifted to Spanish.

"Peace be upon you, and God's mercy and blessing, *Monseñor* Tomàs Ulsingam. I am Marzuq Rais, the appointed voice of His Sharifian Majesty, Sultan Ahmad al-Mansur, by God's boundless grace the King, as you would say, of Morocco and Fez. In you, beside your noble self, I thank your illustrious master and kinsman, and your luminous sovereign lady, and her venerable councillors."

Oh, the most fluent and poetical Spanish it was — and Tom floundered. What did one say to such flowery compliments? And should one correct the honorific that, whatever it was in Arabic, was too much for a private gentleman in Spanish? Tom bowed again, deeper.

"Thank you, *Monseñor*," he stammered. Were they going to trade bows and thanks under the snow until Lady Day? Why, oh why hadn't Sir Francis sent Cardenas? Was it amusement that glinted in the Moor's dark gaze? It was surely wariness from the three other Moors... Well, Roberts seemed the sort to have accustomed these people to English briskness — and they would appreciate some English practicality. "May I suggest that we find shelter? There is a town little more than a mile ahead."

Marzuq Rais's smile made the lean face younger and less hawkish: the man couldn't be more than one or two-and-thirty. "Ah, this makes my heart glad, *Señor*! As my good friend *Señor* Roberts will tell you, my people do not thrive in your English winter."

A gesture sent the ambassador's men scurrying, sudden and nimble. So after all it hadn't been solemnity making statues of them, but the held breath of chariness.

The horses were fetched — four mounts and two pack animals. Roberts's green-hooded man was helped to his feet and hoisted up, wheezing and awkward, behind one of the Moors.

"Have you had trouble?" Tom asked of Roberts, who stopped with his foot in the stirrup to harrumph.

"Trouble — ha!" He spat as he hauled himself into the saddle. "I pray it's really just a mile to this place, you say?"

With a notion that it would be quite the tale he'd hear once in Bridport, Tom mounted, traded raised brows with Skeres, and turned his horse into the thicker and thicker snowfall.

A brackish wind from the invisible sea was spinning the snow in whorls, and dusk was closing in by the time they arrived at the Boar's Head in Bridport. It was a small, worn-looking house with little in the way of stables — and, to see the two innkeeper sisters and their scant people, one would have thought Tom's party a savage horde storming the place.

Nine men and a dozen horses, God-a-mercy! But didn't they run an inn? So they did — but truly, how long had it been since even one single traveller had spent the night? And now they were to put up *nine men and a dozen horses*?

And that was before Mrs. Peters's sister discovered that half of those nine men were no Englishmen at all.

"Moors!" the sister squealed, after peering around Tom's shoulder into the depth of the passage, where Marzuq Raìs and his pageboy stood with Roberts, hoodless and blowing on their hands. "Save and deliver, Beaton — they're *Moors!*"

"Quiet, Bridie!" Mrs. Peters ordered, and took a peep of her own. "We've seen Moors before, Master," she announced when she was done. "Sailors at the harbour, not sleeping under a Christian roof."

Bless the woman with hot water! Yanking off his gloves, Tom did what he should have done from the beginning, and flourished his papers. "Well, the gentleman is a Moorish lord with his servants," he said, "travelling to London on a most important errand."

Beaton Peters stole a doubtful glance at the two — and Heaven knew they had no lordly air — but there was no ignoring the seals on Tom's paper. In no time at all, Tom, Roberts, Marzuq Raìs and the boy were ushered through a screened passage and into a hall with a low trussed ceiling and a fireplace large enough to roast a calf. The hearth was empty, and the hall — which had perhaps been part of a statelier house at some time — cold as Cocytus.

"At least we're out of the snow," Roberts sighed, as he lowered himself onto a bench with the stiffness of a day in the saddle.

Tom apologised to the ambassador, promising that a warm chamber would be provided — not that he knew for sure — and waved away the sturdy maid who gaped from the passage door. Marzuq Raìs was gracious — but, he said, he and his men needed first a place to pray, for it was late for *Maghrib* already.

They pray to their God many times a day, no matter where they find themselves. It was the sort of thing one read about, and now had become a matter to arrange in a provincial inn, where the people already thought they were harbouring the devil...

He was floundering again. Tom's heart sank: this was going to be a long chain of flounderings all the way to London, and what opinion would the ambassador form of Mr. Secretary's people? It was small relief that the ambassador seemed, for the most part, amused.

"We'll be discreet, *Señor*, I promise," he said, lips curling into a half smile. "*Señor* Roberts will tell you that we've learnt to be. All I ask for is a room to ourselves and a pail of snow to melt."

Snow to melt? He'd ask later, Tom decided, and went in search of the innkeepers. In the kitchen he found Roberts's green-hooded fellow, huddled on a stool by the fire, coughing and shivering, and Bridie Peters busy chopping herbs — hopefully for supper. Her sister was seeing to the chambers, she said, and as for the snow, there was only too much of it —

She stopped short when the angry cries erupted — incomprehensible, and so furious that even the sick man looked up. Tom hurried to the passage to find Bartholomew Dunne and one of the Moors shouting at each other in Arabic, with Skeres adding his own English noise.

Even in the dim green glow of a rushlight, the veins stood out on Dunne's bullish neck like cords — and the thin Moor barked back, stained teeth bared and fists tight.

"What's this?" Tom demanded in English first, and then in Spanish.

"There's no place to sleep in this rat-'ole!" Skeres shouted over the unabated stream of Arabic from the ambassador's man.

Only when Tom shouted for silence did the fellow quieten, eyes glittering.

"Dunne, you understand him?" Tom asked.

The soldier shrugged. "Hakim, here, wants the one good room with the fireplace all to his master — and the Capt'n and us all can go hang ourselves."

Which, Tom supposed, wasn't entirely wrong, Marzuq Raìs being a royal envoy. But then, so was Roberts — or at least he had been, for his tenure as the Queen's ambassador was finished, and the Barbary Company surely ranked lower than a Sultan? Still, he turned to the seething Hakim.

"It's hardly yours to decide, fellow," he said in slow Spanish — to which the servant only glowered.

"Please you, *Sayyidi*." The rumble came from the door to the stable, where the third of the Ambassador's men had come to stand. A black turban framed a domed forehead, much creased and sparsely bearded cheeks, and one deep-set eye, the other being covered with a strip of cloth. "He has no Spanish, *Sayyidi*."

"Ay — or so he says!" Dunne warned in English. "Mind him, Mr. Walsingham — mind 'em all, for they're sly dogs and heathens." And then he rounded on Hakim in halting Arabic and, Tom was sure, proceeded to translate the insults for him.

It was of a piece with the rest that Hakim should take a menacing step towards Dunne, and Dunne one towards the Moor. And see if Skeres, for all his dislike of the soldier, didn't step to his side.

"Do I trounce the Moor, Master?" the lad growled.

"No, Skeres — you don't!" For good measure, Tom pushed back Dunne. "Nor do you." The one-eyed fellow hadn't moved a muscle when Tom addressed him in Spanish. "What is your name?"

Head tilted sideways, the man gave a half-bow. "Farras al-Awar, *Sayyidi*."

"Well, Farras al-Awar." Tom's tongue stumbled around the unfamiliar syllables. "Nobody will fight. Tell your fellow."

The Moor spoke half a dozen Arabic words to Hakim, whose answer made Dunne bark out a laugh.

"Didn't I tell you he's a shameless dog? He says, if it's not his to decide who sleeps warm, then whose is it?"

Oh, Lord give patience — and give help too, while he was at it! "Mine," Tom announced. Wasn't he the one with the much-sealed paper? He shouted for Mrs. Peters — not much caring which one answered — and found he'd had no need to shout at all: the two sisters had been eavesdropping from the kitchen door. When they bustled forward together, the maid who had been behind them all but fell into the passage, and the stable boy with her. Did these people know how to do aught but gape?

When questioned, the sisters said that they indeed had one chamber with a fireplace — well, two — no, one — in truth...

"Two, if we sleep in the garret, Beaton," Bridie Peters said, glowing with importance. She dropped her voice for her sister's ear — but not so low that Tom didn't hear. "There's great gentlemen, and that poor man all sick with the cold. Must they sleep above the stables?"

Mrs. Peters's mouth worked as she scowled at Moors and Englishmen alike. "Well, then!" she groused at length. "Two chambers, each with a big bed and a pallet. For the others, it's either the floor or the hayloft."

For all of which, Tom had no doubt, he was going to pay handsomely in the morning. Meanwhile, it was a relief to translate it for the one-eyed man, who listened with his head tilted.

"Now see to your work — all of you — and I want to hear no more arguing!"

"Yes, *Sayyidi*." With another of those grave nods of his, al-Awar steered the sulking Hakim to the stables, followed by the stable lad, while the three women hurried away, murmuring among themselves.

Well, they were giving the Boar's Head enough to gossip about until Doomsday.

"'Eathens — the lot of them!" Skeres exploded, the moment they were alone in the passage. "Why you didn't let me give that mangy dog what for, Mr. Tom, I don't know."

All Tom lacked now — the Minotaur pugnacious... "Because, Skeres, these heathens are on their way to meet the

27

Queen — or their master is, who won't be happy if the Queen's men trounce his people for no very great reason. And the same goes for you, Dunne. Does Mr. Roberts like it that you call the Moors names in their tongue?"

"'Tis just…" Dunne blew out his cheeks. "You don't know what they called us back there, Master. Sometimes they'd smile and call me son of a dog, and all the rest with it, thinking I wouldn't understand. I picked up the tongue so that I'd knew when to knap a nose or two."

Which must have done wonders for Roberts's diplomacy. "And so that, when you insulted them back, they'd know."

Tolly Dunne jutted out his chin most fiercely. "I'm an Englishman, Master. When I tell a man what's his, I do it to his face!"

And hear Skeres's grunt of approval — proof that a common foe will make friends out of enemies.

"Well, you'll both restrain yourselves until we reach London." Tom glared at both men and dismissed them. Only as they went each his way did it occur to him to ask Dunne, "What is … sa-hee-dee?"

The soldier chuckled grimly. "You've fared well enough, Master: they say *Sayyidi* to mean lord."

There was a reason why the fireplace in the hall looked unused — or perhaps it had been neglected for so long that the blackbirds had made their nest in the chimney. Be that as it may, it spewed great clouds of smoke, so much of it that the air stung the eyes and throat when Tom joined Roberts. Wisely the man had chosen a table at some distance from the hearth to sit and sulk by himself, while the Ambassador rested after his prayers and the servants scurried to and fro with much ill-humoured clattering.

"Is it always like this?" Tom asked, lowering himself onto the bench at Roberts's side. Lord — but he was cold.

Never moving a finger, gaze fast on the sickly flames across the room, Roberts huffed. "The praying, you mean? Or folks ogling us like we're the devil? Or the men at each other's throats? Yes, always like this since we made land in Cornwall. The days we spent in Ireland after the shipwreck were much worse." He darted a sour glance at Tom. "Not that Mr. Secretary's folk like us much better, eh?"

Pinch Dunne — but no, the soldier was bound to tell his master. Pinch Nick Skeres, rather. "That rascal of mine seldom thinks before he speaks," Tom sighed. "There used to be some rivalry between Mr. Secretary's men and those of the earl. It never mattered much — and it surely doesn't now."

A grunt. "Ay, ay... And His Lordship thought he was doing me a good turn, when he sent me to Morocco!"

What a cheerless fellow! But then, perhaps he had reason. Tom leant back against the wainscoting and watched as the maid bustled by to set two steaming pots in front of them. She sloshed a bit of warm wine as she did, but never mind. Dropping a half-hearted curtsey, she ran away to watch the far more interesting Moors. Ah well... Curling his chilled fingers around his pot, Tom savoured the scent of wine and sugar.

At his side, Roberts just stared down at the table, lips pursing and unpursing as he braced himself for the interrogation.

Why make the man wait, after all? "Dunne told me about the shipwreck." Tom kept his voice low. "What he didn't say is that you were decimated in it."

"The shipwreck!" Roberts hunched forward, eyes glinting. "The shipwreck wasn't half of it! We sailed from Santa Cruz — Agadir, they call it — on the second of November, and ever since we had naught but foul weather and torment. Such storms as were never seen, the old hands said. Sails torn, men washed overboard, a mast-yard thrown to the deck...." He looked away. "There were men crushed to death, and others injured who sickened and died. And then the storm drove us all the way to Ireland. You know where the Corkaguiny is? Dunmore Head?" He spat the names the way he would sour quinces, and held up his left hand, fingers splayed and crooked. "When God made Ireland — on a bad day, I'm sure — he gave it a foot with five claws scratching westward, so that decent Christians would be warned." He wagged his forefinger. "This here is Dunmore Head, where we were wrecked. Others died there, yes — and some were wounded and stayed behind when we found passage on another ship. Then another Moor grew sick on the crossing from Ireland, and died just after we made land in St. Ives, on New Year's Day."

A door slammed somewhere, and Tom twisted around in the chair in time to see the stable boy and Farras al-Awar hurrying past the gap in the screen. When he sat back, Roberts was studying his wine, turning the pot round and round.

"How many of you sailed from Santa Cruz?" Tom asked.

"Nine."

"And seven are left?"

"Six. Marzuq Rais, his pageboy, that scoundrel Hakim, and one of the guards. With myself and Tolly Dunne, that makes six out of nine."

"Seven," Tom insisted. "What of that fellow in the green hood?"

"Harker? Or I think that's his name. No, he's not one of mine. He's a notary's clerk or something, out of Exeter. We'd just come across him when you found us, limping along the road on foot, half dead. Thieves had robbed him, poor devil, taken all his money, his horse, his dagger. Couldn't leave him there to die, could we?"

For that Tom only had a half-hearted shake of the head, for his mind was on those six men still alive out of nine. "And no one from the first ship stayed with you?"

"Rats, all of them!" Roberts's mouth twisted. "The *Consent*'s captain, half the gunners and the merchant factor had died at sea, together with eight hands or so, and a dozen more drowned at Dunmore Head, the sailing master among them. When the ship was lost, the boatswain said… You know what sailors are like; he said it was ill luck to sail with Moors, and they wouldn't do it again, even if they had a ship — which they hadn't, for the *Consent* was past hoping for. I found another ship, a tub it was, and they stayed behind, one and all — God give them their deserts among those Irish savages —"

"And nobody else has travelled with you since? Followed you from St. Ives?" If Tom had hoped to cut short what promised to become a tirade, he was disappointed, for Roberts turned to him, red-faced with anger.

"And who'd travel with us, pray?" he blustered, slamming the pot on the table. "The Company never bothered to give me a man — never, since the day Lord Leicester, rest his soul, dragged me away from Ireland. Alone as a stray dog, that's what I've been for three years and a half — with Dunne and a servant lad for household, and all at my expense! And now, with what I've had to endure, with all I've lost, they send a … a…" He waved wildly at Tom. "They send a *boy* to question and teach me!"

"But be quiet!" Jove rain on the man! Tom leant forward to grab Roberts's flailing arm and hiss, "Mr. Secretary sent me, I tell you — not your Company — and he sent me because…" He stopped to release the becalmed Roberts and peer around.

The passage looked dark, but chatter and rattling came from the kitchen and from the chambers. To be safe, he drew closer to whisper, "Mr. Secretary has reason to believe there may be a Spanish spy in your party."

Roberts took a great breath and let it out slowly as he sat back. "A Spanish spy!" he mouthed.

And this fellow had been for three years the Queen's ambassador in foreign lands! Tom stopped himself from snapping, and explained instead with what patience he possessed, "It must have occurred to you, Mr. Roberts, that Spain would give much to know about the Raìs's journey?"

"Of course it has!" Roberts growled, with the ill humour of one who had given the matter no thought and was caught at it. "But I would have observed a Spaniard —"

The noise of steps from the passage stopped him short, and Skeres came to stand on the threshold with an air of great severity.

"You want me, Mr. Tom?" the lad called, but his glower was on Roberts. Had he heard the man's outburst? Even on being told that all was well, he lingered, going to the fireplace and pretending to busy himself with the fire. The Minotaur protective...

Recovering his pot, Tom sipped the lukewarm wine. "It wouldn't be a Spaniard of necessity," he said. "Lord knows we have enough Englishmen taking King Philip's coin."

"Well, I don't!" Roberts leant forward, both elbows on the table. "And Tolly Dunne has been with me nigh on ten years, in Ireland and in Barbary — so these Englishmen you can leave out."

And this Tom was ready to let pass, at least for the moment. "What of the Moors, then? Not really Marzuq Raìs himself — but the others?"

Roberts studied the depths of his wine as though the answer must lie drowned there. "Hakim has no Spanish, for what it's worth — nor young Khalid, but he's just a boy. The guard, though... They have some heathen name for the likes of him: taken as a child and converted, would he, nould he. The Sultan has plenty of those in his army — and many are Spanish-born."

Yes, the man's Spanish had sounded easy. "It could be," Tom said. Not that the spy would need much Spanish to inform Don Bernardino de Mendoza, King Philip's devil of a spymaster — nor would he show it if he spoke it well. Or else... "What of the three who died, though? It would be a great chance if Mendoza's man were lying dead at the bottom of the sea."

Roberts considered. "One was my servant, a good lad but dull-witted. For the guards I can't rightly —"

High-pitched, and ragged, and sudden, a scream pierced through the man's words and the quiet noises of the inn, and ended in a crash. There was a heartbeat of the deepest silence, and then the cries broke out. Tom found himself in the screened passage before he knew he'd leapt from the bench. He ran straight into one of the maids, who was carrying a candle, and the other pushed past, coming from the kitchen.

"It was outside!" she cried over her shoulder.

Tom followed Mrs. Peters. He hadn't observed before that a huge door stood at the far end of the passage, and the innkeeper was tugging at one of several bolts.

"We never ... use it..." she panted between tugs.

"Here, let me." Tom applied himself to the bolt. It was clogged with rust, but yielded a little, and then the guard Farras al-Awar was there to help — thin-lipped in the fitful light.

Between them, they threw the door open against a gust of sharp wind. It snaked in, full of snow, and blew out the maid's candle.

"Fetch a lantern!" Tom called over his shoulder, and stepped out into the calf-deep snow, the chill seeping through his wet boots and his doublet. Everyone else was spilling out of the door, and at once Bridie Peters stumbled at Tom's side with a lantern, coif gone and grey hair blowing. When Al-Awar took the lantern from her and raised it high, the yellow light danced on a fence, on a stretch of white, uneven courtyard. Above, it touched the inn's half-timbered back — the low hall, the taller building of the chamber and, hard by it, two winter-bare trees. And under one of these trees, amidst a ruin of broken branches…

"Lord-a-mercy!" cried Mrs. Peters, as she clung to her sister.

Al-Awar stepped forward to illuminate a figure lying sprawled on the ground, the cloak spread around it like the wings of a shot bird. Snow was already gathering on the black folds, and on the slack, knobby face.

The guard knelt by the body and murmured in Arabic — some prayer, perhaps, just as the boy Khalid pushed his way to the front and gasped, "Hakim!"

CHAPTER 3

Roberts, Marzuq Raìs with his hand on the green-faced boy's shoulder, the sisters, the coughing man, the stable lad carrying the lantern and the round-eyed maid — all but Dunne, who'd been sent to find an open window upstairs in the chambers — crowded around as al-Awar and a grumbling Skeres carried the body inside. They were all so quiet that Tom could have sworn he could hear the bones grinding horribly in the body's broken neck — until Beaton Peters placed herself before the doorway to the hall and raised objections. "You're not laying him in my hall!" she announced, chin jutting and arms crossed.

It should come as no great surprise, perhaps. Poor Mrs. Peters, invaded by Moors, and now finding herself with a dead one on her hands! But then... "Where else, Mistress?" Tom asked wearily — and wished he'd put it some other way when the innkeeper began to list each room she owned.

"Nor in my chambers, either, and you're never thinking of the kitchen, Master. And the horses will sicken with fright if you put a dead man in the stables..."

"There's the cellar..." Bridie Peters began through her sister's litany, but she went no further, as an urgent knock came from the street door. All fell quiet, except for the maid, who whimpered — though why she should...

"Is it likely to be the constable?" Tom asked when no one moved.

"The constable!" Mrs. Peters snorted. "Last Judgment wouldn't drag that one out of his bed on a night like this."

"It'll be the neighbours," the groom said, "asking what's the racket."

All they lacked now! A gaggle of good citizens nosing around... "Whoever it is, Mistress, say that one of your guests hurt himself, and it's nothing to worry about. Tomorrow we'll see about the law."

Not that Tom relished the prospect — but what was one to do with a dead foreigner? As Mrs. Peters bustled away to deal with yet another invasion, it occurred to Tom that Roberts had done this before. Before he could seek the man's counsel, someone tugged at his sleeve, and he found Bridie Peters considering him.

"Put him in the hall for now, Master," she said. "I'll mind my sister."

Bless the woman! Tom waved at the two bearers, and they moved into the hall, awkward with their shared burden, followed by the pageboy and the innkeeper.

The moment they were gone, the stable lad closing the procession, Tom sought Roberts again and found Marzuq Raìs instead.

"Excellency," he said, nodding deeply. "A terrible accident. He fell from a window, I think?"

The Ambassador spread both palms. "I would think so. He was readying the chamber. But, *Señor* Ulsingam, you understand, we must bury the poor man — before the next sunset, as our faith commands."

Before the next sunset, Tom dearly hoped to be well past Dorchester, and he began to say so when a clamour of raised voices cut him short.

What now? Tom rushed into the smoke-filled hall to find al-Awar growling in Spanish at Skeres, the boy chattering in high-pitched Arabic, and the body half stretched on a bench, with its legs thrown helter-skelter, and the cloak hanging open.

"Your man all but dropped the body," Bridie Peters announced amid Skeres's loud protestations that he'd just stumbled.

"Cuds-me, 'tis dark as a wolf's gullet in 'ere!" the lad cried — and promptly tangled himself again in the hanging cloak, just as al-Awar was rearranging the body on the bench. Amidst more exclamations from the two Moors, something slipped from the sash around the body's waist and fell with a muffled clink. A purse. Al-Awar made to pick it up, but Skeres was faster and snatched it up clumsily, spilling a stream of coins that fell tinkling and glittering onto the flagged floor. Many coins.

"Cuds-me!" the lad exclaimed. "They're well-paid, these Moorish servants!"

"Leave it, Skeres," Tom ordered, and the lad surrendered the half-empty purse to the Ambassador.

Marzuq Raìs poured the remaining coins into his palm: coins of different sizes and thicknesses, most of them gold. At least twice as many lay strewn on the floor. "I never knew that he was wealthy," he said, and then spoke to his two remaining servants in Arabic. Both raised their chins and clicked their tongues.

"That means *no* with them," Roberts said from where he stood by the door — which Tom took to mean they hadn't known of their fellow's abundance, either.

But there was something to the coins... Tom bent to pick up a couple of them and brought them close to the lantern: the gold one was larger and thicker than an angel, and foreign-looking. Instead of a ship, the Christ inside an almond-like shape glimmered on one side, and on the other a haloed saint handing a banner to a kneeling man. The large silver one was no shilling, either, with an inscription around a winged lion reading: *ducatus venetus.*

"Do you pay your people's wages in Venetian coin, Excellency?" Tom asked, and was surprised to see the Rais hesitate.

"No ... or I should say..." He fingered the coins in his palm and looked up, frowning. "In truth, Hakim had not been my servant for long. I do not know how he was paid before."

"But it's an unusual sum for a servant to possess?"

"Well beyond common wages — but who knows? He might have taken all he owns on this journey. Venetian money is not uncommon in Morocco."

Nor was it in Spain, for that matter. "But, you say, you didn't know the man well."

"I did not, *Señor.*"

"He came into the Ambassador's service in Santa Cruz, not long before we took ship," said Roberts, stepping close to finger the coins in Tom's hand and those the Rais held. Behind him, hunched on a bench, sat the sick man, Harker, eyes glittering with fever as he observed them all.

He watched as young Khalil picked the coins from the floor, sliding them carefully back into the purse, and Farras al-Awar murmured in Arabic to his master, and jumped a little when Dunne appeared on the threshold with a candle.

The soldier beckoned to Roberts with an air of such secrecy that Tom hastened to join the two.

"What is it?" he asked.

Dunne looked at his master first, and waited for a nod before answering, "The women upstairs are all a-pother. They say the garret window's open, and there's a bundle of their things."

So Hakim hadn't been readying his master's chamber, after all. Leaving Skeres to watch the Moors, Tom followed Dunne and Roberts. They had barely reached the stairs when Farras al-Awar came after them — so much for Skeres keeping watch.

"*Sayyidi.*" The shadows played on the guard's strangely skewed face. "We need water and cloth to wash the body, and a shroud, as our faith commands. Would you please ask the innkeeper for these things, *Sayyidi?*"

Bridie Peters took the requests well enough, if rather breathlessly — especially once Tom assured her there would be compensation for it all, and for the inconvenience. Her sister, Tom suspected, would have been more intractable.

Mrs. Peters was certainly angry when he, Roberts and Dunne joined her up in the garret. Rising from one of two cots, she pointed at the small window that gaped open, its wooden board propped against the wall, the pegs strewn on the floor.

It made for a small hole enough that Tom had to wedge his shoulders cornerwise to lean out.

"That Hakim was narrow-made," Roberts said behind him. "Not that you're very big yourself. Mind you don't go his way!"

A sound caution, Tom thought, for it would be all too easy to topple out while peering outside. What would the Moor have seen, though? A deep murk whirled all around, blowing ice flakes that stung brow and cheeks. After a short while, though, as Tom grew accustomed, the blackness was relieved, just barely — or rather resolved into different shades of gloom by some faint reverberation of the snow. One could tell yard from houses, and make out a denseness below that had to be the trees; above, the lines of rooves and eaves and chimneys stood out against the swirling sky. Clinging to the window's jamb, Tom stretched upwards, groping the wall until his fingers brushed wood — the overhanging eaves. Yes: by kneeling or standing on the sill, a nimble man could heave himself over the roof, and from there…

"God's bones — but have a care!" cried Roberts's voice, and rough hands grabbed Tom's legs and doublet, and he found himself hauled back inside, shuddering and a tad winded. Had he truly risked a fall?

"Hakim wasn't as deft as he thought," he said, not quite steadily — to which Roberts snorted that ay, there were quite a few like that.

"And quite a few who aren't honest!" Having been ignored for long enough, Mrs. Peters brought to the fore her grudge again. "See, masters!" She tugged open a bundle that lay on the other cot, revealing a well-polished pewter plate and a pair of candlesticks. "These he took from the chamber downstairs. A thief, that's what he was!" *And you brought him into my house*, hung unsaid, but plain as day in her purse-lipped manner.

There was a hum from Dunne. "Never liked the fellow one whit. Didn't I tell ye, Capt'n?"

"Ay, Tolly, so you did — often enough." Roberts clapped his man's shoulder. "And that explains the purse."

Well, not all of it, perhaps — and not the Venetian ducats. But the shillings, and perhaps even the angels… "I take it you aren't missing any money, Mistress?" Tom asked.

And see how Mrs. Peters startled. "Why, no…" Her eyes slid sideways as she thought of some hiding place, surely — one she wouldn't check while they were around. Ah well, who could blame her, after the night she'd had?

They left her to her checking then, Dunne only staying behind long enough to wedge the board back into place. They were halfway down the stairs before Roberts spoke — and it was with some relief.

"So we know where he fell from — and why."

But did they? Tom stopped at the foot of the stairs, observing the doors on either side — one to the lower chamber, the other, standing wide open, to the kitchen. And from the kitchen, one reached the passage…

"Why didn't he just go out via the stables or the street door?" he asked, more of himself than Roberts, but the man answered all the same.

"Everything's well bolted up. And besides, he would have crossed the kitchen. There would be people."

And everybody had been going around and carrying things — but… "Yes, he must have feared someone would stop him. Still, why run at all?"

"Why do thieves run?" Roberts shrugged. "He had his booty."

"What he had, Roberts, was a purse of gold and silver — with which he could have gone whenever he wanted. Why risk his neck for a sackful of pewter? Easy to sell, I'll grant you, and less likely to be marked than foreign gold — but when one looks as foreign as he did…"

Roberts opened his mouth to answer and closed it again, staring at Tom, his brow darkening slowly as the notion occurred to him. "You never think…?"

For all that no one was around, Tom lowered his voice to a whisper. "Not being caught by the man from London strikes me as a fair reason for many hazards."

"Devil seize him! But then, the plunder upstairs?"

"If he's a thief, we won't suspect him of being a spy, will we?" *But I have.* Tom wished he hadn't sounded so impatient and condescending when Roberts's scowl deepened again at being lectured by a man half his age.

It was a good thing that, right then, Dunne came trotting down the stairs, grumbling that the shrew upstairs had made him move the cots too.

Back in the smoke-filled hall, al-Awar and the boy had finished their washing, and they were now shrouding the body with such solemnity that Tom paused on the threshold, unwilling to disturb the rite. Even Skeres, playing guard by the fire, stood quite still for once.

If only it could be so easy … but Tom very much doubted that. "I don't reckon we can put him in the graveyard?" he asked of Roberts.

The man lowered his chin. "At sea we made do. Back in Cornwall, we had to find a fellow who'd let us do the burying in his field — not that he did it out of the goodness of his heart, mind."

Of course not. *Who knows what you may need to pay for?* Cardenas had said — although he might have hardly had burials in mind. Tom sighed to himself. Even discounting the delay, how did one go about bribing folks to have a Moor buried in their fields? "Let's hope Mrs. Peters knows someone amenable. And if she doesn't, the constable will…"

There was more humming. "Are you sure you want the law, Mr. Walsingham?"

"Am I sure…?" Tom stared at the man. "Why, no: let's drop the corpse in the nearest sandpit and ride on!"

"Back in Cornwall, it took nearly two days."

Marzuq Raìs's instructions came back to Tom's mind. "Mustn't it be done within the day?"

"And weren't the Moors mad with the waiting! But what with the lord of the manor, the law, and the vicar squabbling over what's proper and whose trouble it was… And in the end we still had to do it at night, mind, for otherwise folks would come and throw stones."

Oh, better and better! How would the Sultan of Morocco like the way his envoy was treated in England? Come to that, how was Sir Francis going to like an envoy who arrived in London already offended?

But, Sir, it was either bury the man on the sly, or rouse the whole town against us — and either way would insult the Ambassador, for all that the dead man had been a Spanish spy... If he had truly been — and this, too, must be discussed with Marzuq Raìs. Oh, Jove! Tom pinched the bridge of his nose, and wished he hadn't when Roberts patted his arm.

"Heed me, lad. The Raìs will be the first to want it done nice and quiet."

And in that, at least, Roberts was proved right when the Ambassador came to join them. He had changed into a light-coloured robe, with silver trim at the neck and wrists and down his chest, and over it a cloak of the deepest black. He looked even more foreign and severe.

"Were you told, *Señor* Ulsingam, of the burying in Cornwall?" he asked, fingering his small black beard. "It was done much against the demands of our faith, back then. I trust that this time it will be different."

His dark eyes travelled to Roberts, who only shrugged, and then back to Tom — the one with the much-sealed papers.

"You are aware, Excellency, that *it* can only be done differently outside of English law and custom?"

Another of those slow, grave nods. "As long as Hakim ibn Ayyub is laid to rest by the next sunset." Marzuq Raìs held Tom's gaze for a moment longer, and then went to rejoin his people, his cloak billowing behind him.

"And wouldn't you think him the Emperor of Fez himself!" Dunne grumbled, only to be silenced, not very sharply, by his master.

"Well, Mr. Roberts, you were right — and we'd better do it before dawn, rather than sunset." Tom watched the three Moors across the hall. *Ye Moors, and valiant men of Barbary...* Limned in gold by the lantern's light, murmuring in Arabic over the shrouded body, they made as arcane a sight as he'd ever seen. "Now to find a bit of land."

And this was how Tom found himself in a strip of field outside of Bridport, late at night, shivering under the snow. He stood side by side with Roberts, a little out of the way while Farras al-Awar, Dunne, and Skeres dug up the frozen ground by the glow of a lantern. Marzuq Raìs had chosen the place beneath a hawthorn shrub, bare but for a few red berries, and made much of the way the grave should lie.

"Even dead, they must be facing towards some holy place of theirs," Roberts explained, like one deprecating some great stubbornness. "They must —" He was cut short by a coughing fit that had him hawking and spitting. "See? Morocco has ruined my health for me," he rasped, just as Marzuq Raìs ordered the diggers to stop, and the three men climbed out of the hole.

"Will it be deep enough?" Tom couldn't help imagining the sisters' heirs, someday, ploughing the field and coming across the shrouded bones — or, worse, a pig digging up the body.

"They'll have their rules for it, I'll warrant," muttered Roberts.

And if they had, it would be an insult to impose a deeper hole — or at least unseemly.

As Tom hesitated, the body was lowered, and Skeres and his companions began to fill the grave, and it was too late to do aught but hope for Hakim ibn Ayyub to enjoy a long and undisturbed peace under the hawthorn. Did this count as a prayer for the dead? Was it Christian charity or wasted thought to pray for a Moor who had died unbaptised? Tom wondered between shivers as the Ambassador bared his head and stepped in front of the grave, with the guard and the boy on either side, and began some sort of litany, raising his hands or bowing at unfathomable intervals.

The afternoon's fat snowflakes had turned into stinging needles, and the wind had grown sharp with the salt of the nearby sea. It blew the tails of the Moors' cloaks like sails, the sight of it enough to chill a man's marrow. Oh, for a warm place and some mulled wine — although right then Tom would have contented himself with the inn's bleak and smoky hall. Why, even a chance to stamp his feet would have been welcome. When Dunne and Skeres joined their masters, and Skeres, puffing and hissing and rubbing his arms, asked whether they'd be at it all night, Tom lacked the heart to chide him too much.

At last the men were done. They walked away from the grave, loose clothes billowing around them — the boy with the lantern, then the Ambassador, and the guard last — in a procession that wasn't less stately for being comprised of three men. Marzuq Raìs stopped before the Englishmen and bowed.

"Thank you, *Señores*," he said, touching a hand to his heart. "I have no purse on me, *Señor* Roberts, to recompense these two good men…"

None too happily, Roberts handed his own purse to the Raìs, and the Raìs gave a coin each to Skeres and Dunne, then bowed again to the men's masters.

"May God reward your forbearance," he said, "and the assistance you lent to what must seem barbarous to you."

"Honouring the dead can never be barbarous, *Monseñor*," Tom answered — and at once wished he could take it back. It was as good as saying that all the rest was indeed outlandish nonsense. Marzuq Raìs accompanied yet another nod with some quiet Arabic and walked past with his attendants.

And then, Sir, I insulted the Ambassador at his servant's grave... Tom looked at Roberts, but it was Dunne who explained, "Called for his God's blessing upon your head."

Hardly the answer of an insulted man — and Fates be thanked for that! Tom let out his breath in a small white cloud.

"'E ain't bad, for an 'eathen," Skeres conceded, fingering the coin in his palm — which must have been a rather generous vail to move the Minotaur to such magnanimity.

When the two servants followed the Moors, spades over their shoulders, Tom fell into step with Roberts.

"He'll take back his blessing when I tell him that this dead man they honoured was a spy."

Roberts turned sharply. "Tell him? Why tell him, now the man is dead?"

"If he had a spy in his retinue, don't you think he should know?"

"Provided he doesn't know already..."

This made Tom stop short and grab the man's arm. Had Morocco wasted more than just Henry Roberts's lungs? "Mr. Roberts, if the Sultan's ambassador himself is in Spain's pay, then we're deep in trouble — you, I, Mr. Secretary, the Privy Council, and the Queen herself! Do you have reason to suspect...?"

"Reason ... no!" With a harrumph, the man shrugged free. "Never you mind me, Mr. Walsingham. It's winter muddling my old head. I'm on such tenterhooks to bring the Rais to London — and now you talk of spies, I see them at all corners, is all." He took two strides, stopped, then strode back. "But truly: what will he think if we go about calling his people traitors? What if he takes it in snuff?" He made a helpless gesture. "It was four years of penance, over there. To come home now, and to have sent it all a-waste..."

Because the others had walked on with the lantern, it was too dark to read the man's face — but there was no mistaking the disquiet in his speech. Could he truly expect, though, that the matter of a Spanish spy would be ignored?

"I'll be careful," Tom promised — and he could have sworn that Henry Roberts wasn't much reassured.

It was late and snowing hard again by the time they made it back to the Boar's Head. Beaton and Bridie Peters were still up, and very uneasy with what had been done in their field. They soundly cuffed the stable boy who asked if the Moors had called up the devil — but the thought must have crossed their minds, because they were much appeased when Tom said it had all been as sober and pious, in its way, as any Christian burial.

"Still," he added, considering the groom's unwholesome eagerness, "in your place, I'd keep that poor man's death a secret for a while. It was a good, generous thing that you did — all of you — but not everyone would understand. Say that one of us injured himself, but not so badly that he couldn't leave with the rest."

A discretion that, for all their eager assurances, Tom knew he'd better buy generously — bless the well-filled purse! Only while he was wishing the household a good night did he remember that he had questions to ask. Oh, but Roberts was right, and this cold muddled a man's wits... It was a good thing that the sisters and their servants smelt a chance for more vails in his curiosity.

Had any money been filched, after all?

The sisters both said that none had.

Had any of them seen Hakim sneaking up to the garret?

There was much shaking of heads.

"He was goin' about, Master," the groom said. "We all were. I saw him when I brought the palliasses."

"Where?"

"On the stairs, comin' down from the room upstairs."

"Did he have a bundle?"

The boy scratched at his head as he thought. "Can't say, Master — what with the palliasses and all. But they was all carryin' and fetchin'."

"He had none when he came to the kitchen," said Bridie Peters. "That was soon after you arrived. He walked in as I was warming some wine for that poor sick fellow of yours, and started barking away in tongues." She spread her hands. "I told him to speak God's own English, but he just went back where he'd come from."

"Upstairs, for sure!" The elder sister cut in. "To filch my plate, and Bridie's candlesticks! Not that I saw him, for all that I was up and down the stairs with Gocey, moving our things to the garret, weren't we, girl?"

The maid pursed her lips and sniffed. "Goes to show the fleet-footed thief he was!"

Or else it went to show that he hadn't been doing his thieving at that moment — but that Tom kept to himself. And, after learning that the sisters' usual room was the one on the ground floor, and the moving had taken "no time at all", he went in search of the Moors, though how he was going to barge in on the Ambassador to question him and his men, he didn't know.

As luck would have it, though, he didn't have to: Farras al-Awar and the boy Khalid were tidying up the hall, still bundled in layers of tunics, even inside. Both went still at the sight of Tom, faces closing in the uncertain light. They did not, it was worth noting, draw together.

"I'm sorry for your friend," Tom said in Spanish. As he'd expected, the guard translated for the frowning boy who, holding on tightly to the broom's handle, stared at him with very large, long-lashed, dark eyes.

"I'm sorry that he proved to be a thief, too," Tom insisted.

Al-Awar tilted his head. "It is sure that he was, then, *Sayyidi*?"

"When he fell from the window, he left behind a bundle of things belonging to this house. Unless… Is your master missing any of his possessions or money?"

"Not that he told me." Al-Awar translated, and Khalid raised his chin, clicking his tongue: *no*, according to Roberts. Another Arabic word earned a high-pitched answer.

"The boy thinks not. Should he ask the *Sidi*?"

"Tomorrow," said a voice in rough Spanish, coming from behind Tom.

He turned, and there stood Roberts, with Dunne at his elbow.

See how Farras al-Awar's shifted his one eye from one Englishman to the other. He was wondering, no doubt, who was in charge — Jove rain on Henry Roberts! And, because the last thing Tom wanted was for Marzuq Raìs to suspect differences between the Queen's ambassador and the Queen's Principal Secretary, he nodded at the guard.

"Yes, tomorrow will do very well."

It sounded like enough of a dismissal that the two Moors bowed themselves out, and Tom waited, counting in Latin in his head, as he always did to keep himself from speaking in anger. *Unus ... duo ... tres...* Only when the steps had faded down the passage did he round on Roberts.

"Mr. Roberts, once and for all: I'm not here to thwart your mission — but you stay out of mine!" he growled, and stalked to the room where he'd have to share a bed with the man, hoping Skeres had had at least the foresight to find a pan of embers to warm the sheets.

CHAPTER 4

What with his years of couriering, and having been on the road this past week, Tom should have known better than to hope for an early departure. It was still snowing, for one thing, and, even if it weren't, the Moors had to pray at dawn, and not before — although, how they could tell just when dawn was in the grey dimness, they alone knew. And there were the Peters sisters, whose upset consciences, fears, and scruples had greatly worsened overnight, and had to be soothed both in words and deeds.

"But these people must thank the Lord for steering the Moors their way…" Tom muttered, dropping to sit on a bench by his breakfasting servant.

Skeres snorted into his ale, glancing over the pot's rim at Beaton Peters's retreating back. "A tiger — that's what she is. Would talk a man out of 'is last penny!"

And, with a chuckle of misplaced admiration, the Minotaur pushed to his feet and announced that he'd see to the horses. On the threshold, he all but flattened the clerk — Harker, was it?

Recovering his step, the man entered the kitchen hesitantly, his cloak bundled under his arm, squinting in what light the day afforded. After spending the night coughing and wheezing — as Tom knew quite well from his own sleepless hours — he looked no better for it. In fact, the daylight revealed reddened eyes, hunched shoulders, and badly bruised cheeks — the work of yesterday's robbers — wan against the dark beard. He also looked somewhat younger than he'd seemed last night: forty, if that, but still as forlorn a sight as one could see, which made Tom uneasy about what he had to do.

"Good morning, Master Harker," he greeted, answered by a cautious nod. "Come sit and break your fast, before we part company."

There was no other word for it: the man blanched. "Part company!" he exclaimed — so hoarse, the words were hard to catch. "You leave me behind?"

"You're not in good health, and we have a hard day's travel before us." Not that Tom's conscience didn't prick him, and all the more when the fellow stumbled close, bracing himself against the table.

"The Moorish lord promised..."

"Did he?" Bless the Raìs with hot water — what had he been thinking? But then... "His Excellency isn't familiar with the roads here, and perhaps he didn't quite see how ill you are. You can't travel today, and we can't tarry."

"But I can ride, Master. I was promised... Ask the Moorish lord." No begging, no tearing of hair. Poor Harker just slumped on the stool by the fireplace, brushing a long-fingered hand down his face.

"I'm sure what His Excellency had in mind was to provide you with the means to buy or hire a mount," Tom tried — not that he was sure — only for the fellow to stare, aghast.

"And ride alone? I had horse and money, yesterday — and lost both, and nearly my life. And I must... Master, my sister's husband died. She's ill. She has no friends in London —" He stumbled to his feet on seeing Roberts come from the stables together with Mrs. Peters. "Master, in charity: I was promised. I must travel with you!"

"Ay, well..." Roberts met Tom's glare with blank-eyed perplexity.

"Surely you see that Master Harker can't travel today!" *And that we could do without a chance stranger…*

Whether in honest uncertainty or in retaliation for Tom's brusqueness, Roberts spoke most doubtfully. "I won't say he looks up to much riding — though this promise, I think His Excellency made it."

"I can ride, Masters. I won't slow you down."

It was not very encouraging that he fell to coughing again in his eagerness — and that was when Mrs. Peters, who had been studying the man with little sympathy, entered the discussion, arms crossed and chin jutting.

"This season, it could be days and days before others bound for London pass this way, my Masters. And what if he sickens worse? What would he do here alone? I say you'd better take him with you." *And well out of my hands.*

And I say he'd better stay, because we carry secrets — but how did one say so without betraying those very secrets? And besides, was it truly prudent to leave the man behind, free to give answers to anyone who asked?

Oh, well. "If His Excellency promised, then he promised. Besides, it would be unchristian to abandon a man in this predicament."

Harker's thanks were as quiet as his pleading, and Mrs. Peters had the air of one who'd had her way. When both hurried out, Tom applied himself to his ale and bread — or he would have — but Roberts sat in front of him and jerked his head towards the door where Harker had disappeared.

"I thought you wanted rid of him," he said, as disapproving as you please.

And this after bringing up the Raìs's promise! Tom swallowed his mouthful. "And so I did — not that you were much help, were you? But then it struck me that if he stays behind, who's to keep him from babbling to anyone who asks?"

"Oh." Roberts sat back, brows knitting. "About Hakim?"

"About Hakim, about the Ambassador ... because, you see, if the spy came all the way from Morocco, whether he's dead or alive now, who's to say that he had no friends waiting for him in England?"

Tom couldn't blame Roberts one whit when the man burst out, "Good Lord, but I'll be glad when we're in London, and I can be rid of all the Moors and Spaniards in this world!"

Marzuq Raìs, fresh from his prayers and clothed to ride, with his turban wound tightly around head and neck, stood just inside the stable doors, watching the falling snow. He stirred at the noise of Tom's steps, and turned with that half smile he always wore when he wasn't solemn.

"We do have snow on our mountains, but this..." He gestured towards the white street. "Such deep, untouched purity, *Señor* Ulsingam. Last night it moaned in grief with the wind. This morning, it is an immaculate veil unfurled in mercy over the errors and miseries of Mankind..."

Or at least, this was what Tom thought the man was saying — and so busy he was picking apart the flowery Spanish, it took him a moment to grasp the meaning. Why, even if he was wrong, this poetic burst was as fine an opening as he could wish for, and he seized it by observing that death seemed a harsh punishment for an error like thievery.

"*Inna Lillah!* We are in the hands of God. But..." The Ambassador stroked his pointed beard. "Do you not wonder that Hakim courted death for a few pieces of pewter, fine as they may be?"

So much for telling or not telling him… But then, the Sultan of Morocco wouldn't choose his envoy among the dunces, would he? "Some pewter and a purse of gold," Tom ventured.

"Gold that he did not steal here, that he had perhaps for a long time — and yet he never tried to run away before." *Before you arrived to join us.* "And then … he runs! He runs at night, in a storm, in a country he does not know, ignorant of the lay of the land and of the tongue. If you do not wonder, *Señor* Ulsingam, I will be much disappointed."

No, this man was nobody's fool — unless… "Have you talked to Mr. Roberts?"

There it was again, the curl of his lips, the amused glint in his black eyes. "You mean, has *Señor* Roberts talked to me — but no. There are many things that *Señor* Roberts would rather not share with me. One being…" Marzuq Raìs paused to nod at someone over Tom's shoulder. "One being, I'm sure, that Hakim was perhaps a spy of Spain."

Why Tom should be surprised to find a fuming Roberts behind him, he didn't know.

"Is this how you are careful?" the man said in English, bristling — to which Tom answered pointedly in Spanish that *Señor* Raìs had beaten them both to the notion.

It was to be hoped that Henry Roberts owned a smoother manner, and had made use of it with the Sultan of Morocco — for the way he addressed the Sultan's envoy was nothing short of curt.

"You knew, *Señor* Raìs?" he barked in Spanish, all the rougher in contrast with the amused courtesy of Marzuq Raìs.

"I did not know, but I had grave suspicions after last night, and shared them with *Señor* Ulsingam. Careful — oh, thrice careful! — as he was when I did, I am glad to see that, if thinking ill of the dead is a sin, in that sin I am not alone."

Couldn't the man see how his lofty speech baffled poor Roberts? But yes — he could and took amusement in it. It must have been eight cursedly long weeks for these two, with only half a common language and a mutual dislike!

It was a good thing that Roberts was saved from having to answer — and Tom was spared the temptation to translate for him — by Farras al-Awar. The guard approached his master, and daylight showed what both the dusk and the candles had concealed last night: from under the man's turban a dreadful scar ran down his brow, under the strip of cloth that hid his right eye, and beneath it to his chin, puckering half his face into a perpetual grimace. Some battle wound, surely…

Al-Awar started to speak in Arabic — and, with a glance at the two Englishmen, thought better of it and shifted to Spanish. "The horses are ready, *Sidi.*"

When this earned him a brisk dismissal from Roberts, the guard retreated in pointedly stolid silence.

The Ambassador raised both brows at the gruffness — and small blame to him — but Roberts? He glowered as though he'd been given offence, groused that there was no trusting such a sour, squinting fellow, and stomped away to join Dunne. Oh, Lord — was the man bent on making enemies of all these Moors? For a mercy, the Ambassador took the rudeness in his stride — but then he'd had weeks to accustom himself to it.

At length they all moved out into the street, the servants leading the horses. When Harker, who had been given Hakim's mount, bowed to Marzuq Rais before awkwardly hauling himself into the saddle, Tom couldn't help leaning close to the Ambassador to whisper, "*Monseñor*, if I can presume to give advice, it would be wise to be wary of strangers."

The Moor stopped in the act of mounting. "Giving to the needy is a pillar of my faith, *Señor*. I thought it was a great virtue in yours, too?" He leapt up into the saddle and from there smiled down at Tom. "The practice of it is as much a balm to the giver's heart as it is to the recipient's need," he declaimed and, devil pinch his poetical bent, nudged the horse into a small trot.

It was just as well, perhaps, that they had waited for full light to leave — although that meant it was past nine before they left behind Bridport. Still, as they took the road that wound northeast among the hills, and away from the coast, it soon became plain that they would not go very far that day. Not under the unrelenting snowfall, not along a road covered in sheets of ice, not even with the groom from the Boar's Head, hired as a guide for the first few miles. Because the boy kept warning of pits and ruts, and the horses gingerly felt each step, they rode at the wariest walking gait, and tightly close together.

The eager guide went first, pointing out to Tolly Dunne landmarks he alone could make out in the white whirl — as though the soldier would ever have a use for them. Then came a sullen Roberts, and Tom who kept drawing up, twisting in the saddle, squinting through the snowfall to make sure that the others followed without incident. Marzuq Rais rode with straight-backed ease, unlike his shivering page perched on a smaller nag, wrapped in a cloak too big for him, and holding onto a few bundles that were lashed to the saddle. How old could Khalid be, Tom wondered — fourteen? Fifteen? An older understanding seemed to flash at times in his velvet eyes, but that the stripling had seen little journeying on horseback would have been plain even without his master's frequent worried glances. Behind them al-Awar rode alone, better armed than the rest, stiff and vigilant.

Last came Harker, huddled and miserable, coughing often but keeping pace, and Skeres, who had liked at first the notion of bringing up the rear — until he'd found that with the rear came the Moors' two packhorses, now that Hakim was dead. Tom's assurance that he trusted none but his own man in that position had only half soothed the Minotaur, who now rode with a manner of the grimmest importance.

He cursed at the two poor beasts when Tom rode back to hasten him and Harker, as they were falling behind. "Pampered jades of Africky!" the lad groused — having also been at Marley's play. "A mite of climbing, and they grow lazy." He tugged fiercely at the leash. "Cuds-me, what are these folks carrying — a brace of cannon?"

As though two packhorses didn't make the puniest of baggage trains for a royal envoy!

"Think how much worse it'd be, but for the shipwreck!" Tom's half-hearted consolation was received with a mighty glower.

"Ay — but then they'd 'ave a score of Moors to 'aul their chattels up'ill and down'ill for them," Skeres boomed, as quiet and discreet as that imaginary brace of cannon. "I tell you, Mr. Tom: much cry and little wool — and where's the 'urry you know and I don't!"

After shushing his hopeless fool of a servant, Tom rode back up the train, wondering a little that Harker hadn't even stirred at the Minotaur's outburst. Too busy keeping pace? Too unwell? Or fearful that Tom might change his mind, and leave him behind at the first opportunity? As soon as he reached Roberts's side, he sought again the green hood at the end of the line, and caught instead something closer by: the guard's one eye studying him — or was it Roberts?

Al-Awar looked away at once, before Tom could quite tell. A sour, squinting fellow, Roberts had called him. Not that he saw much reason to mistrust him — but Tom found Farras al-Awar hard to like.

He felt even less liking for Marzuq Raìs when, not even eight slow miles out of Bridport, the man announced that he wished to stop.

Grimacing against the white glare, Tom observed their surroundings. For the first time since morning the snow had slackened, and they were trudging halfway up a steeper slope than most — and the man wanted to stop! "I was hoping to push a little past, Your Excellency. It can't be much longer to Dorchester. We're to change horses there…"

In truth, from what he remembered, it was half as far again — but he still would have liked to make Dorchester, before the snow picked up again.

"An excellent purpose, as soon as we have prayed." Shielding his eyes with a gloved hand, the Ambassador scrutinised the sky above. "It is most hard to tell the time under your sunless sky, *Señor* Ulsingam, but I judge it to be time for *Zuhr*."

Whatever *Zuhr* was — another of their prayers, no doubt, which all seemed to have a prescribed time reckoned by the sun's course. It must be either a jest or a whim, seeing as how the sun was hidden by a pall of clouds. Was this Marzuq Raìs's retribution for Roberts's gruffness or some other unknown offence?

All else apart, they were in the middle of nowhere.

"But where would you stop, *Monseñor*?" Tom gestured towards the empty road, the emptier hillside, and the whole white, rolling land that, as far as could be glimpsed in the falling snow, could have been some abandoned wilderness. "Let's at least find a house, or some shelter — or would you pray outside under the snow?"

And perhaps he would have, but for the pageboy by his side. Blue-lipped and bent almost double, poor Khalid sat on his horse with an air of the greatest discomfort, and hadn't lifted his hooded head all through the argument, like one not knowing what was worse, the cold or the fatigue of going.

Marzuq Raìs reached for the boy's shoulder — and then checked the gesture.

"Very well," he said. "Let us gain the summit of this hill of yours. If from there we can discern a shelter, we shall make for it. Otherwise, we'll stop and pray there."

Ay, where we'll be as exposed to the wind as can be, and we'll all catch our deaths. Swallowing the cross retort, Tom nodded only half respectfully and nudged his horse ahead.

As he passed Roberts, the man called to him, "What now?"

"He wants to pray."

Roberts hummed softly. "Be glad he's waited this long!"

Whether it was a matter for gladness, Tom found highly debatable — but at least, as they crested the hill, signs of a human dwelling became visible at some distance.

"There, see?" Their guide pointed down the descent, where the land folded in a shallow valley, and a little grey church sat hunched under a blanket of snow.

It wasn't quite what Tom had hoped for: they could hardly knock on a church door, seeking a place for the Moors to pray, could they? Still, because even a wall with a bolted door would offer some semblance of shelter, Tom rode back to Marzuq Raìs and pointed at the squat belfry down ahead. He couldn't blame the Ambassador for raising a brow and asking, "Will they have us?"

"They will, *Monseñor*," Tom replied, with more brisk confidence than he felt — and Marzuq Raìs, after searching the sky again, consented to try their luck at the church.

Down the road they trundled, and Roberts, it turned out, was neither upset nor overly annoyed.

"Be thankful, for we've had worse along the way," he said. He was very fond of saying it. "And we were going to make a stop, at all events."

"Ay — in Dorchester, where there are inns with good fires and hot food, and fresh horses!" Of a sudden, Tom found it hard not to fume. "What if the snow picks up again in earnest, and we're stuck in that hole all night, supperless — and all because Moors must pray when they will instead of when they can! But if the weather stays like this, they'll have to see reason, or we'll all end up —"

Henry Roberts's sudden fit of coughing cut short Tom's tirade. Under cover of reining in his skittish horse, he glanced over his shoulder, catching a flicker in the Ambassador's eyes. A flicker of what, though?

"I thought none of them had any English," he whispered, and Roberts, cured of his cough at once, exhaled through his nose.

Witness, o Lord, the fool Mr. Secretary foisted on me... "And so they don't, young Walsingham — but they ask to stop and you're none too happy, and then here you go, grousing to me like a Dutch corporal forbidden his ale. What must they think?"

What must they think indeed — and what would Sir Francis think? Half a week of riding, and scarcely a day of trying to fathom these people, and already Tom's forbearance was worn thin! The heat of a flush climbed up his neck, making the cold sting yet more on his cheeks — and there was nothing for it but spur his mount ahead, for all that the poor beast kept skidding on the snow-packed descent.

As the Fates would have it, around the church were scattered a few buildings — a cottage so heavily capped with snow it was a marvel the thatch hadn't caved in, and, more promisingly, a farm with stables, a dovecote, and a byre. The elderly farmer's alarm at first, then his mistrust of the outlandish strangers — all of it melted away at the sight of Tom's purse, and men and horses found shelter between the low narrow stables and the byre.

Still, because it was one thing to shelter a bunch of Moors for an hour, and another to suffer a heathen ceremony in one's byre, it seemed best to keep the old fellow busy in conversation when Marzuq Raìs and his pious retinue vanished under colour of minding the horses. While Skeres and Dunne gossiped with the one servant in the stables, and Harker dozed by the fire, Tom and Roberts sat at the kitchen table with their host, drinking warm cider and giving answers as vague as they were long-winded to a veritable interrogation about the heathens and their ways. It was a while before Tom could wedge in a question of his own about the road. Oh, it was but three miles to Dorchester, Goodman Colcok promised. Or three and a half, or four maybe — no more than five at any rate. But, on this he was adamant: the road was well kept and so straight they couldn't go astray. Tom wasn't sure how far he believed this, but still dismissed their guide with a good vail. A recommendation that the lad should hasten back while it was still light sent him out to the stables, and nothing could dissuade old Colcok from fetching cap and coat and accompanying him.

Twisting around in his seat beside the one window, Tom pressed his nose against the horn panes — not that he saw anything. Just how long did a *Zuhr* take?

Roberts must have been thinking the same, for he murmured, "Now pray the old fellow doesn't take it into his head to have a peep at the Moors."

But even if he did, what then? Finding himself unworried by the chance, Tom went back to his warm cider. "So let him. Perhaps we fret too much. Even if he does, how will he tell they're praying?" There being no answer beyond a low grumble, he sat back and stretched his legs under the table, wincing at the pins and needles as his toes thawed inside his boots. "And if he asks, I wish him joy of it. Does nobody have English in Morocco? The Barbary corsairs take English sailors, don't they? And there are merchants in London from Marrakesh and from Fez. I thought the Sultan would find an interpreter for his envoy."

Of a sudden, Roberts sprang to his feet. "God's bones, I've had enough: the Raìs will do better to cut his devotions short, before it starts snowing again." Fetching his coat, he went out with such abruptness as to startle Harker awake.

The man shuddered. "We leave?" he rasped, blinking his bloodshot eyes.

Would it be very unchristian to leave him to old Colcok's care? Yes, Tom reluctantly decided — even worse than having done it back in Bridport. "As soon as His Excellency is ready," he said — and still he tried: "But can you ride five more miles?"

See how the clerk sprang up from his stool, bracing himself against the fireplace. "Yes — yes, Master. I'll see to the horse."

Wrapping himself in the green-hooded cape, he limped to the door, reaching it just as it banged open, and Skeres barged in with a shout of "Oy, Master!" and a burst of chill air around him.

"They're done," the lad announced, sparing a glance for Harker as the man sidled out behind him. "Dead on 'is feet, ain't 'e?" he sniffed. "'E rides steady enough, I'll say — but must we take 'im all the way to London?"

Ask His Excellency! Tom bit down the sour retort, for Skeres had little liking for the Moors as it was, and didn't need to see them as bringers of inconvenience more than he already did. "Unless you'd dump him in the snow by the road. Where's your charity, Dolius?" he asked instead, as he donned his coat, cap, and gloves. Going, at last! He threw the door open and strode straight into Marzuq Raìs.

"Crave pardon...!" Tom stammered in English, reaching out to steady the man. "*Ruego* — no, *pido*..."

And then, Sir, there was the day when I all but flattened the Sultan's envoy in the snow and lacked the Spanish to make apology...

For a mercy, few things seemed to discompose the Raìs. But then, when he took in his courteous stride not only Roberts's manner but the death of a servant who might have been a traitor, why should he be bothered by a bit of clumsiness?

In fact, after the first startlement, there was again the one-sided curl of his lip, the amused gleam in his dark eyes, and even a pat on Tom's arm. "My fault, *Señor*, my fault. One does not stand behind a door. But I was seeking *Señor* Roberts, if he is in the house."

"He went out in search of Your Excellency," Tom replied, still flustered enough that it took him all the way to the stables to wonder, why not send al-Awar to seek Roberts? Or even young Khalid, for it took no Spanish to fetch someone, did it?

When they reached the stables to find there both Roberts and the Rais's servants, all busy leading out the horses, Tom's doubts began to take an uneasy shape — but, if the Moor was disconcerted, he hid it well.

"See, there he is!" he cheerily exclaimed, and strode to join Roberts, pausing to stroke a horse's neck, smile at Khalid, and cheer Harker.

A charming, generous fellow — and a liar with it? Could Marzuq Rais have been listening at the door, rather than stepping up to it? He claimed to have no English at all, and yet... *Careful — oh, thrice careful*, he'd said of Tom to reassure Roberts back at Bridport. But Roberts had only chided Tom in English, and if the intention had been plain, the precise words should not have been. It could be all chance, it could be that *cuidadoso* wasn't the only term for careful, it could happen for two people to walk up to the same door at once...

Sir Francis's caution echoed in Tom's mind: *a chance is but one chance, Thomas; two chances breed dubitation. Three chances, though...*

Across old Colcok's courtyard, the Ambassador laughed aloud, a hand on Roberts's shoulder. He gestured towards the thickening snow and turned to include the approaching Tom into the conversation.

"*Señor* Roberts apologises for the snow," he said. "In truth, he means it is my fault that we tarried and now it snows again — but see, *Señores*: God recompenses our discomfort with beauty! Would you not say that a thousand heavenly trees of orange and almond stand over the clouds, shedding their white petals to soften our path?"

He chuckled, likely knowing that neither Englishman would ever say aught of the sort, and, raising his hood, went to his horse.

"Soften our path, he says!" Roberts groused. "He'll find just how soft it is, by the time we stumble into Dorchester. The man's touched in his head!"

Touched in his head or something worse? Tom bit down the words. Better to make sure first, or Roberts would think him varying and fanciful in mind: Hakim first, then Harker, and now the Ambassador himself... Better to wait for that third chance first — or, if it didn't happen, to see if he could make it himself.

How many miles it was to Dorchester, Tom couldn't tell — but surely he was riding twice as much as the others, as he kept doubling back down the train. And the road might be straight enough, but it climbed up and down the side of hills and made for sluggish going. It was narrow, too, constrained by thick snowdrifts on either side — and when they ran into a cart lumbering the other way, its two big Flanders horses straining up the slope, there wasn't road enough for all at once.

Having learnt during his couriering days the obdurate nature of carters, Tom didn't even try to argue, and instead had his party of eight line up as close as they could against the road's shoulder — and if he hedged so that Marzuq Raìs was just behind his back, who was to say so, or that he noticed at all?

"How far to Dorchester, Goodman?" he called to the carter, a young fellow wrapped in a drapery's worth of layers, who scrunched up his round, red face and thought a good deal before pronouncing it two miles, three at the most, near four.

"And why I bother asking, I don't know," Tom groused, jerking on his reins as the ill-tempered sorrel tried to bite at the nearest Flanders. "But then, if he were sharp, he wouldn't be out driving in this snow, would he?"

At his side Dunne, who had been studying the sky, gave a bark of laughter. "To each the wit God gave him — but, Master, two miles or four, are you minded to ride past Dorchester today?"

Bless Bartholomew Dunne! Had the soldier meant to give Tom the way to lay a trap, he couldn't have done better — or perhaps he could, but this would do.

"I'd be very much minded, but…" Tom grimaced skywards. "By the time we've changed horses and can set out again, I'll wager you our friends will have dreamt up some other prayer. And mind, Dunne, I don't want another row with the Moors for the rooms."

The cart having at last trundled on, he nudged the sorrel ahead in what he hoped would look like ill humour. Now only let Marzuq Raìs take the bait.

CHAPTER 5

The Ship Inn, on Dorchester's High Street, was a long, rambling pile, part house, part stables, whose people made nothing of eight men and ten horses. There was the bustle of arrival, the calling voices, the grooms swarming in the yard with lanterns in the first closing of dusk, the scent of woodsmoke that promised roaring fires, the fine stables, warm with the smell of well-kept horses... How Tom had loved it all as a young courier — and, in truth, he still liked it all at nearly eight-and-twenty.

If only he could sit by one of those fires and sip warm wine. Ah, well — chances were it would be long hours before he could. To begin with, the giant of a landlord singled him out at once as the party's leader.

"You'll never be wanting the horses now, Master?" the man enquired in a reedy voice that sat ill with his ruddy sternness and large bones. "Jesu, Master, in conscience, to send you out there in this snow, this late in the day..."

"I'm not as mad as that," Tom replied softly, and, motioning for the landlord to wait, joined Marzuq Raìs where he stood shaking snow from the folds of his cloak, and drew him a few steps aside from his men.

He bowed a little. "I'd be thankful, *Monseñor*, if your prayers could wait for a couple of hours, for the day is short, and we leave as soon as the horses are ready."

And there it was: the flash of surprise, the knitting brows, the protestation barely swallowed. Barely — but not quite.

Marzuq Raìs recovered well, under a manner of restrained patience. "You seem to think, *Señor* Ulsingam, that we choose the time of our prayers — but it is not so. The Prophet dictates both the time and the timeliness of them."

Well played, Excellency — but I have you! The flare of triumph was short-lived — the triumph of Pandora, no doubt, when she broke open her box. The disaster of a Spanish spy, the treaty undermined, the Sultan either distrusting or untrustworthy, or both… It wasn't hard work at all, Tom found, to affect a frown. "The last thing I wish is to cause offence. Let me find Mr. Roberts, *Monseñor*. I'm sure we'll find a way."

It was the matter of a moment to wrench Roberts from the task of upbraiding the inn grooms over some slip or other, and to steer him, purpled-jowled and scowling, towards the stables' far end, where a small workshop stood, filled with the inn's smithing and cobbling tools.

"The fact that you're Mr. Secretary's man doesn't mean you order us all around!" Roberts started, as soon as the door was closed, flat cheeks a-quiver. "What do you mean, telling the innkeeper —"

Tom broke right in. "You say the Ambassador has no English? I think he does."

It was almost comical, the way Roberts's jaw fell open. "How…?"

But it wasn't comical at all, was it, that the Moroccans had fooled Lord Leicester's agent so well? "I don't know what he said to you, but he's lying! And if he's not a spy of Spain, the Sultan has lied to you as well!"

"I told you to be careful what you said —" Roberts's bluster halted with a grunt, and his already purple jowls coloured even more.

And at this Tom's thoughts shifted, like tiles of coloured glass making a pattern. "Yes, you told me," he said slowly.

More than once, in fact. He took an angry step towards Roberts. "You've known all the time, haven't you?" See how the man winced — this man who was a liar, and perhaps a traitor, in the pay of the Moorish king if not much worse, and to him Tom had shown his suspicions like the rawest boy. Thoughts of arrests, fights, and various disasters ground to a halt when Roberts threw up both hands and flung himself down onto the one stool.

"Sink you, lad!" he grumbled. "And sink me deeper still! A fool, that's what I am — not a traitor." And he slapped his gloves on his knee in such helpless anger that Tom was tempted to believe him.

Still... "You'll need more than that to explain why the Ambassador speaks English, and you both lied to me."

For the longest time, Roberts sat slumped, worrying at the seam of a glove's finger. Then he looked up and said, "He speaks English because he's not the Ambassador. He's ... the turciman, they call him. The interpreter."

Good Lord in Heaven and Jove in his Olympus... It was Tom's turn to gape, cold of a sudden. "He's not...?" he stammered, and then words deserted him. The treaty, Spain, the Queen, the Sultan — and, most of all, Sir Francis!

And this, Sir, is not *the Sultan's envoy.*

Of the score of questions madly whirling in his mind, Tom picked the silliest. "Then where the devil is Marzuq Raìs?"

Judging by the harrumph, Roberts found it silly too. "Dead at sea," he groused. "You never think I did him in?"

"By now, little would surprise me!" Tom couldn't help the sourness — not that he tried very hard. "But say he was drowned in the shipwreck. It still doesn't account —"

"He didn't drown." Roberts let out his breath in a great gust. "I told you we had a mast-yard broken in a storm. Well, it fell to the deck and crushed the Raìs, together with two of his soldiers. One died at once, that good-for-naught Farras was battered, and the Raìs had his skull cracked. He lasted three days, then we had more foul weather, and a storm that tossed the *Consent* all night. Like a terrier with a rat, it was. When it left us in peace, Marzuq Raìs was dead."

"And you put the turciman in his place — in sight of a shipful of sailors!" Tom paced the length of the small room, imagining dozens of angry men, stranded and out of wages, each of them eager to sell that knowledge. "What came into your head?"

"It's not as if they know," Roberts protested, and Tom halted in front of him, staring in disbelief, counting in Latin — lest he grab the man and shake him until his teeth rattled. *Unus, duo, tres...*

By *Septem* he'd reined in his temper enough to ask through gritted teeth, "Roberts, how can they not know? The Ambassador was dying, and then he was hale again — and the turciman had disappeared into thin air!"

"He hadn't!" Shy of his own outburst, the man rose to grasp Tom's sleeve and draw him close. "There was a devil of a storm that night," he whispered hoarsely, spittle flying from his mouth. "Come morning, Farras, Hakim and the boy had washed and shrouded the body — you've seen how they do it — and I said that the turciman had lost his footing and broken his neck against a beam."

Tom blinked in disbelief. "So you buried Marzuq Raìs at sea as the turciman, tucked this other fellow into his bed — and prayed no one would know?"

"Yes!" Roberts nodded eagerly, oblivious to Tom's sarcasm. "And with his wounds, it was natural that he'd keep his head well wrapped, even when the *Consent* was wrecked and we were saved. Then, when we sailed from Ireland again, the new men had never seen Marzuq Rais or Bilqasim — that's the turciman. So you see, there's not a soul that knows!"

Not a soul! Tom brushed a hand down his face and laughed bitterly. Could this man be so great a fool — this man Lord Leicester, rest his soul, had picked to deal with foreign kings?

"And what of the servants, Roberts — your own, and the Moors? And, come to that, what of the turciman himself?"

"My servant drowned at Dunmore Head. Dunne would never talk, and Bilqasim is clever, and trustworthy, for a Moor—"

"But what is there to trust him with?" Tom hit a hand against his thigh. "You can't be thinking to bring a false envoy before the Queen?" Or could he? See how the fellow gaped, cheeks washing crimson first and then pasty white ... until another thought struck Tom, which should have come to him sooner. "When you warned me to mind what I said before this fellow... You never suspect him to be the spy?"

Eyes bulging in dismay, Roberts caught Tom's sleeve again. "God blind me, no! Not in a hundred years! You think I'd have...? It's just —"

"It's just that he's not all that trustworthy, after all?"

Roberts floundered, but only for a moment. "He knows he's got nothing to gain and all to lose if he talks," he said — and look at the air of cunning he put up!

How did one answer such idiocy? "Does he? I'll hear it from him, if you don't mind."

"What? Why?" Roberts cried. "It will be worse if he thinks you've discovered him —"

Worse! But truly, this man was past belief! "Worse than what? I ask again: you never think to hide that the Ambassador is dead?" Before Roberts could find an answer, Tom strode to the door and flung it open — and checked himself, cursing: was that a man leaning against a stall half a dozen steps away?

Oh, better and better! Now they'd been overheard... But no. When the man pushed himself upright and stepped closer, a hanging lantern's light revealed Nick Skeres — and Fates be thanked.

"You need me, Mr. Tom?" the lad asked, and the offer of a trouncing was plain in the unfriendly stare he fixed on Roberts, who seethed at Tom's elbow, watching him a-slant.

Ah, well — the matter needed settling, and it could as well be settled at once. "Yes, Skeres. Fetch us the Ambassador, will you?"

"Fetch 'im, says 'e! And 'ow do I tell 'im?"

Oh, no need to worry about that! But, because there was no saying what the Minotaur would blurt out, and in whose company the impostor would be, Tom said, "You tell him this: *Vuestra Excelencia, el Señor Walsingham ruega el favor de una palabra.*"

With a sniff and a shrug, Skeres left on his errand, butchering the Spanish words to himself as he went.

And quite what he'd say to this impostor, Tom didn't know — still less what was to be done with the whole disaster.

The stables were quiet — horses huffing contentedly in their stalls, the new ones munching on their oats, and, at some distance, one of the grooms still busy brushing an animal with soft, rhythmic strokes. It must not be a bad life, that of a stable boy — naught but horses from dawn to night, and no mistakes to make that could imperil the realm. Shaking his head at his own fancies, Tom tried to muster his scattered thoughts. Who knew about the Moroccan envoy's arrival? A scatter of innkeepers between St. Ives and Bridport, perhaps — depending on how discreet Roberts had been — and inevitably Harker. None of them was likely to talk, or be believed if they did, but back in London? The whole Privy Council must know by now, and Dr. Lopes, and, of course, the Queen herself, and the Barbary merchants. Could pretend death be arranged for the Ambassador along the road? They'd have to get rid of Harker first, and then, what of the Moorish servants? Oh Lord...

Behind Tom's back, Roberts made a noise. He'd retreated inside the shop, head ducked between his shoulders, gaze fixed on the array of harness bits hanging from the wall. Could it be hoped that he was seeing the enormity of his mistake?

Having his doubts of that, it was with considerable sourness that Tom closed the door and went to sit on the stool. "But what possessed you to put up this whole masquerade, I'll never understand," he grumbled.

He hadn't quite expected an answer, but Roberts swung about, fists tight and eyes a-glower.

"No?" he asked, low and hoarse. "That's because you haven't wasted away nigh on four years out there. His Lordship, God rest him, hauled me out of Ireland. I was doing well for myself, there — but nobody said no to Lord Leicester. Not that I didn't try, mind. *What do I know of Barbary, my Lord?* asked I. *And of sweet-talking kings, and haggling with merchants?* He laughed, rest him, and clapped my shoulder. *What did you know of Ireland, before you came out here with me, Harry?* That's how he was, and I'd have gone into fire a thousand times for him, and so I went to Morocco." He wiped a glove across his sweaty brow. "You don't know how it is, out there. The heat, the flies, and none to speak God's own English — but all of that is naught. It's the weeks and months of dancing attendance on the Sultan, who sends a courtier, and then another, and then a third, all promising much and naught at once. And then they move you from one palace to the other, and then to a town, where you've a hovel of a house from the Barbary Company, and a pittance, and you must thank God that the Sultan will grant you another pittance — or how are you and yours to live? And everyone's at you — merchants and shipmasters, and the Company, and His Lordship, and the Council, and Mr. Secretary!" He snorted. "You must obtain this, Roberts, and you must protest that. Make the Sultan see this, forbid the merchants to do that … and the Sultan won't so much as sniff at you, because he thinks that, give her time enough, Spain will swallow England whole, so why bother? One audience, I had — one piddling audience in three years!" He stopped, the words drowned in a fit of coughing.

"A penance, yes — I'm sure — but still, I —"

"Still don't see, eh?" Roberts wrung the gloves between his hands. "His Lordship didn't see, either. He wrote a letter last spring, angry as a wasp. Called me a useless carpet-knight — and small blame to him, I say. But then … then good English wood, canvas and bronze sank the Armada to Hell! Ah, you should have seen it, lad: the English merchants trooping through the streets of Marrakesh, all brave with torches, their naked swords, and a painted standard, singing and cheering the Queen, and jeering at Spain. You should have seen us! Well, the Sultan, from his palace, saw it all, and it set him a-thinking. The music changed, I tell you! All of a sudden, the great and mighty Sultan was as full of sugar as an orangeado, and there was nobody he trusted better than his good friend *Sayyidi* Roberts! I only wish His Lordship had lived to know it. To know that the carpet-knight was coming home, at last, and bringing the Sultan's envoy with enough promises to make the Queen's heart dance! You see now, young Walsingham? You *see?*"

And see Tom did. He saw again his own brother sitting by the moat at Scadbury, poor Guildford, murmuring that he hadn't done too well. He saw the bitterness of failing, and the burning relief of not having failed after all. And seeing made him all the harsher.

"And what do you think Lord Leicester would have said, the moment he found the envoy was false?"

"Nobody was to find out!" Roberts growled as though it were Tom's fault.

Lord, but this man…! "Well, I have!" Springing to his feet, Tom came to stand face to face with the unspeakable dunce. "Not even a full day, and I've found out: you believe you'd have fooled the whole Council, and the Queen — and Mr. Secretary?"

One could almost be sorry for Henry Roberts as he looked away and stood with his head hung, and jaw working. And then there was a mighty knock, and the door was thrown open without a by-your-leave.

"'Ere 'e is, Master," Skeres announced, and the man who was not Marzuq Raìs walked in — calm, straight-backed, and none too pleased.

"Your servant conveyed to me your most pressing summons, *Señor* Ulsingam," he said, one brow arched in disapproval. "I trust it is not to tell me that you are set on riding on?"

The brazenness of him!

"Go and stand guard, Skeres," Tom commanded — and, the moment the door closed behind the lad, he turned to the Moor, arms crossed. "I'm sorry," he said in English. "Skeres has no head for foreign tongues — unlike yourself."

The man was quick-witted, no question of that, but Tom knew what to look for. The stiff shoulders, the twitch of the eyelids as the false ambassador kept himself from blinking —

or perhaps from glancing at Roberts. Instead he tilted back his head, challenging and haughty, and kept to his courtly Spanish. "I believe you forget, *Señor*, that I —"

"Enough, you prating jackdaw!" Roberts exploded from his corner. "He knows — you gave yourself away!"

It was like watching a snake shed its skin. The false Ambassador took a long breath and let it out slowly, and it was a different man who shrugged ruefully at Roberts. "I told you, *Sayyidi*. I told you that it would never work."

"And I told you it would, if only you'd…" Roberts swung towards Tom. "What has he done to make you see through him? What has he said?"

And this — *this* was what irked him? "What does it matter, Roberts? Be thankful that *I* did. At least we can stop this madness before reaching London." Although how they were to explain it away, Tom didn't know. "I'll send ahead my man to warn Mr. Secretary — so that he can announce that the Ambassador has died along the way." *Died before I found you*, he wanted to add, not eager in the least to have the pretend death happen under his charge. "But there are this man and the servants, who know what you tried to do —"

"So let them!" Roberts flung the gloves to the floor. "They'll go ahead with it. Why must you undo it all? Bilqasim has the Raìs's papers, the Sultan's letters. He knows what his master was to say and to do. The mission has not changed — just the man!"

Oh, the devil — and all before the impostor! Tom hit a palm on the workbench and drew the fool aside, to whisper harshly in his face, "Don't you understand what you have done? The Ambassador's death would have been nothing to the fact that you tried to hide it and put up a servant in his place!"

They stood there, nose to nose, Roberts breathing heavily until he looked away.

"Ay, and what's done is done," he muttered. "What does it help to throw it all to the wind now?"

Nothing. The thought struck Tom like lightening. It would help nothing — even if they could feign the death of Marzuq Raìs without being caught or betrayed, even if they brought to London the King's letters with no envoy to discuss the terms. All it would do was delay the treaty with Morocco at best, and wreck it altogether if word got out of Roberts's little play. And Sir Francis wanted Morocco's strength to wage war — not in another year, but now, while Spain still reeled.

Tom pinched the bridge of his nose and exhaled slowly. When he lifted his head to glare at Roberts, it was — he hoped — with the frosty authority he'd learnt from his cousin.

"Only until we reach London, and Mr. Secretary — and he alone, mind — can make a decision. Until then..." Ignoring Roberts's long, hitching sigh, he addressed the impostor in Spanish. "*Monseñor*, I concede to your wish: we stop here for the night."

The man, who had been waiting in stony silence, looked startled — and whatever flickered in the black eyes, it was not relief. His nod was deeper than any the Raìs had ever offered, almost a bow. "*Señor*, I bear the name of Ahmad Bilqasim, but will forget it until London and speak the words of another, if this is your wish."

So poetical long-windedness was something else that man and mask shared. "More than my wish, it is my command," Tom said — and didn't they sound like Marley's parlaying Moors and Hungarians at the Cross Keys! That Marzuq Raìs would still have to die at some point after he'd discharged his mission and before Bilqasim could return to Marrakesh ...

well, this he could keep to himself for the moment. "Now, *Monseñor*, we've kept you too long from your prayers."

Bilqasim's mouth quivered at the corner as he acknowledged the dismissal. It was almost a grimace, Tom observed as they filed out of the shop and into the dim stables. Had the man hoped to be rid of the rigmarole? Small blame to him, if he had — but he still held fast to his part.

"I think it best to have a room to myself to pray with my servants," he said. "But since I have no English, it must be arranged for me."

And must Roberts retort in English? "Ay, ay, Excellency. I'll see to it, if Dunne hasn't. As if we haven't done it ever since Ireland!"

Thinking unkind thoughts, Tom watched the man steer the Moor out to the yard, just as Skeres emerged from the shadow of an empty stall, sleepy and baffled in equal measure.

He gaped at the door, and then at Tom.

"'E 'as English!" he mouthed, still pointing at the door.

There — so much for secrecy! But then, Roberts trusted his servant. He'd had no reason to keep such a thing from Dunne who, of course, had known all the time! Skeres, on the other hand... The lad's tongue-wagging back at Richmond played itself again in Tom's mind — and the unrepentant pout at being told off.

"He understands a little," was what Tom settled for, "and thought it clever to conceal it." All of it true enough, after all.

And see how the Minotaur chuckled to himself — tickled, of all things!

"Cuds-me, and you nosed 'im out?" A shake of the head. "Just as well, though, eh? Makes me a mite less ginger of 'im."

It took a moment for this curious utterance, and its pleased colour, to make their way through Tom's tangled thoughts — but when they did, he stared at the lad.

"Shouldn't that be a mite *more*?" he asked.

"Why, no! It plagues me less if 'e speaks God's own English."

"And that he was lying about it, and would still be, if I hadn't nosed him out — doesn't that plague you at all?"

It did a little, judging by how the lad sucked his teeth, tilting his head this way and that. After a while, though, he gave a most Minotaurish shrug. "Say what you will, I'll trust a man sooner for speaking English than for babbling in Spanish."

This drew a huff of laughter from Tom — and yet... There was some unease in trusting where one had to speak in what was supposed to be the common foe's tongue. How many more would think so, on learning of this alliance with the Spanish-speaking heathens? Behold, the Minotaur subtle!

But, because Nick Skeres's subtlety couldn't be counted upon to extend to his actions, Tom thought it best to issue orders. "Ay, well, at any rate, see that you don't talk to Marzuq Rais in English. Better still, pretend you know nothing of this."

The lad pouted in the way that meant he charitably refrained from taking offence. "What do you take me for, Mr. Tom? Would I blather to the inn folks?"

"Nor to anyone else — not even Harker."

The notion earned a bark of laughter. "Why, that poor wheezing rat!"

"That poor rat knows that Marzuq Rais is the Sultan's envoy. Do you want him to wheeze to all who'll listen about how the envoy has been lying to the Queen's men?"

Having been scolded for his loose tongue more than he liked these past days, Skeres looked down, rubbing the point of his shoe on the packed-dirt ground. "Silent as the grave," he rumbled. "That's what I'll be."

Which Tom would have liked to believe — and instead now he'd have to watch his tongue around his own servant, at least until they reached London. When he shivered hard, Skeres eyed him and sniffed.

"You want a fire, Master. And warm ale, and a good night's sleep — that's what you want."

And to reach London, and decent weather, please the Lord, and that you, and Roberts, and the Moors hold your tongues, since I can't have this whole tangle undone. "And so do you, I'll wager," Tom said. Clapping the Minotaur's burly shoulder, he dashed out under the snow, with still two things to do before he could sit by the fire.

They still had to share rooms — but at least the Ship had goodly ones. Although the one he shared with Roberts possessed no fireplace, it shared a wall with one that did.

"The Moors nabbed that one," Dunne informed Tom when he repaired there, to find the soldier busy warming the bed, and the soldier's captain pacing. At the sight of Tom, Roberts stopped short and flung himself to sit on the bed, for all the world like a sulking child.

Would it be prudent to send Dunne away? But no, what was the point? He'd been there when the true Raìs had died; let this be a caution to him as well as his master.

Coming to loom cross-armed over Roberts, Tom took his sternest mien.

"You say that the Ambassador has the Sultan's papers," he said. "I'll take that to mean that you have them?"

Whatever Roberts had been expecting, it wasn't this. "Why, I … yes!" he spluttered. "Why do you…?"

"Then I'll have them, Mr. Roberts."

"Not on your soul!" The man sprang to his feet, a vein throbbing large at his temple. "The Sultan entrusted them to me —"

"The Sultan entrusted them to Marzuq Raìs, who died while in your charge —"

"Ay, so now the papers are for me to —"

"To play your own games? I think not." Tom held out a hand, palm up, and waited.

Facing each other nose to nose for the second time in less than an hour — this was becoming ludicrous. Out of the corner of his eye, Tom could see Dunne approaching, ready to defend his master, no doubt — and a good thing it was that Skeres wasn't there to start a row.

A most useless row it would have been; it only took a few heartbeats before Roberts harrumphed and wheeled away to sit gracelessly back on the bed.

"Fetch me the box, Dunne!" he growled.

The soldier must have had his own notions on the matter, for he was slow in retrieving the box — a small oaken chest — and he handed it to his master most reluctantly.

"Oh, let him have the cursed papers, and wish him joy of them!" Roberts seethed as he fumbled inside his doublet. He produced a small key, hanging from a piece of silken cord that had perhaps been red before much fingering blackened it. Fingers made clumsy by fury, he turned the key in the box's lock and rummaged inside until he fished out a leather case — which he all but flung at Tom.

It was a handsome affair, the leather dyed the deepest black, tooled with gold, and fastened with silken cord and seals that bore, instead of pictures, patterns of stars and symbols.

"Is this all?" Tom asked.

"And thank God that we saved it!" Roberts went back to rummaging. "Bilqasim did when the Raìs's trunk was smashed in the wreck. Most of the finery was lost, and another box with the gifts for the Queen. Jewels, mostly. Stones and pearls — all lost."

There was a hum from Dunne. "I'll say, Capt'n —"

"Ay, ay! You've said it often enough, Tolly." Roberts turned to Tom. "He thinks someone from the *Consent* helped himself in all the ado — and I won't say he's wrong. All that remains is this."

He unwrapped a piece of water-stained green silk to show a gold medallion as large as Tom's palm, shaped like a star with eight points, marvellously worked, and encrusted with emeralds that glittered in the candlelight. Three of the points ended in small empty rings.

"It hung from a carcanet of pearls, and there was an emerald this big." Roberts showed the tip of his forefinger. "All gone by the time the pageboy found it — or so he says. All gone but this. Maybe it will do as a brooch for the Queen." Again, he scowled up at Tom, mouth twisting sourly. "You'll have it too, Mr. Walsingham?"

The spiteful, mean-minded idiot! Tom held up the leather case. "Believe it or not, Mr. Roberts, my one concern is the treaty. I'm not out to steal your glory — or the Sultan's baubles."

Wrapping up the medallion, he dropped it on the bed — and, while Roberts's hand shot out for it, the man had, at least, the grace to flush. "We go ahead with it, then? You're not giving me away?"

Trust the fellow to only think of that! "I told you: it's not mine to decide," Tom said. "Tomorrow I'll send word to Mr. Secretary. Until I hear from him, we go ahead."

And, having a most interesting letter to write, he went in search of ink and paper.

CHAPTER 6

One of Tom's prayers, at least, was granted: in the morning the snow had all but stopped, dancing in small, light flakes in a breeze that now and then tore apart the clouds above, to show slivers of pale sky — and even, at one point, a beam of sunlight.

It was something of a relief — as was sending Skeres ahead with the ciphered letter for Sir Francis sewn in the lining of his doublet. For once and for a wonder, the Minotaur didn't even try to protest. Whether he felt himself still on sufferance after the chiding, or was content to go by himself because of it, he trotted away at first light, without so much as a grumble.

To the rest, in spite of the landlord's moans about the unchanciness of weather, Tom imposed an early start. Surely, the sky could hold this half-smile for a handful of hours, all the way to Cranborne? A little less than twenty miles were not too much to ask for.

It lifted Tom's heart that by noon they had ridden twelve miles of these twenty and reached the bridge over the Stour. From there, for a penny, a young lad led them for the last half mile across a stretch of steaming, sucking marshland. There was — or at least there had been — a sort of gravel causeway, but it was half washed away, and what remained was drowned in the half-frozen mud. They had to dismount, and not just follow the whistling boy, but carefully watch the ground for each step they took. It seemed a long, slow way before a row of houses and a church's tower emerged from the haze — and Blandford was there to enter.

A pity that the snow had been thickening again for the last hour or so, heavier and wetter. So the long-faced fellow in Dorchester had been right with his woeful prophecies. Tom's charges must be wishing he'd minded the man, he thought, as they dismounted in the yard of the Red Lion. Well, they could be satisfied that he was just as drenched to the bone and chilled as they all were. He'd made a stop here on his way down, and it warmed him a little when the young and pretty landlady bustled to welcome him like an old friend, until she offered the same greetings not only to Dunne — who had passed this way twice in less than a week — but to Harker the clerk, who certainly hadn't. Likely she would greet Roberts and Bilqasim in the same way and, Tom supposed, every soul who crossed her door. Still, in spite of two parties having just coming in from Cranborne way, she settled them at their own table in the taproom, where the light from a great fire gleamed merrily off a wealth of polished copper hanging from the wall.

And there, who must be sitting hunched on a bench by the hearth, clutching a blanket around himself and feigning the gloomiest preoccupation with the flames? Perhaps he thought, like small cats do, that if he didn't see, he'd be invisible. Look how he didn't move until Tom stood looming right over him, and then only to hitch the blanket a little higher around his ears.

"What are you doing here, Skeres?" Tom wanted to know, and the lad emerged from his cover, looking forlorn. Forlorn and wet as a drowned rat, bootless, coatless, and doublet-less under the blanket. Jove — what of the letter? Would the spy have had time to arrange for Skeres to be set upon? But wait! Wait and see how the lad squirmed and picked at his thumbnail... Hardly the honest outrage of the Minotaur set upon, was it? "What the devil happened to you?"

There was some more squirming before Skeres threw up both hands — gathering up the blanket in haste when it fell open — and exclaimed, "'Orse dunked me in the plaguey bog, that's what 'appened to me! Took me till Doomsday to catch it again. 'Twas so frisky by then, I 'ad to leg it all the way 'ere!" And, having found his step, Skeres was working himself into the outrage he hadn't mustered at first. But still…

"What of your guide?" Tom asked. "Didn't he help?" And was that more squirming? "You did hire a guide, didn't you?"

There was no surer sign of guilt with Nick Skeres than the way he had of colouring in patches. "What for, a guide?" he protested. "An 'alf-mile of straight road? Prigging brats wanted a penny!"

"And to save a penny —" Tom checked himself and bit his lip. *Unus … duo … tres…* "You lackwit, where's…?" He followed the lad's guilty squint to a little heap that lay on the hearth, not ten inches from the fire. He snatched it up — it had been paper; now it was a fistful of mud-stained pulp that came undone between his fingers.

"Let it dry, and I ride," said Skeres — the dunce!

"And much good it will do!" Tom flung the quondam letter in the flames — where it hissed and smoked — and strode away to join the others at the table.

Someone — most likely Roberts — must have ordered a hearty meal, for the friendly landlady had served beef stew, pork pies, and rather fine ale. Once the first hot spoonfuls of stew had thawed him, though, Tom found he had no stomach for dinner. By the time Bilqasim joined them after his prayers, he'd given up in favour of sitting back against the wainscoting to observe his table fellows. Had anyone in the taproom been watching — which nobody was, after some curiosity for the Moor — they must have made a glum company. Having ensconced himself in the corner, Roberts was working grimly through his second bowl of stew, while Skeres sat perched on a stool not quite at the table, nibbling at a piece of bread with unusual restraint. Dunne, on the other hand, had been demolishing pies with the lust of a clear conscience — and, as soon as he was finished, brushed the crumbs off his doublet and disappeared towards the stables. Harker, his bruises fading to green and yellow, never looked up from his trencher, eating at the Ambassador's expense, supposedly — but since Bridport, the Ambassador's travelling expenses had somehow merged into the accounts Tom settled with Sir Francis's money. Did Harker know that Mr. Secretary himself was funding his travels? No, the man likely thought himself indebted to the late Marzuq Raìs. Tom sipped his ale, musing to himself until Bilqasim asked what sort of meat was in the pies.

"Pork, I believe. But the stew is..." Tom was raking his memory for the Spanish for beef when a sudden, shrill gibbering sounded from the kitchen, along with a clang of metal and stone.

What now — what else? Tom sprang up, upsetting his beaker in his haste, and dove for the curtained door, only to find himself shoved into the wall as Bilqasim charged past. Cursing in all the tongues he knew, he followed, with Skeres on his heels, and Roberts demanding to know what the devil it was all about. When they all spilt into the kitchen, where their cloaks and coats were spread to dry by the fire, they stumbled into a most curious scene. A fiery-eyed Khalid crouched before the row of hanging garments, clutching a bundle to his chest and chattering like a magpie. He straightened at the sight of his master and pointed an angry forefinger at Farras al-Awar. The guard stood stiffly, feet planted wide, and glowered at the boy.

At the long table's end, the landlady huddled together with a young girl and a middle-aged servant. One of them must have dropped the copper pan that lay on the flagstones at their feet amidst a steaming puddle. Had these three never seen men argue?

They scurried away when Tom waved them off — for, whatever this was, he very much doubted he wanted the inn-folk to witness it. Little as they would understand, the guard's intent was plain when he spat a few Arabic words that sent young Khalid into another passion.

"Dunne?" Tom called, and the soldier appeared at his elbow.

"The boy caught Farras rifling among the cloaks, if you believe him," he said — which was a curious way to put it.

"And you don't?" asked Tom.

Dunne raised one shoulder. "Farras says he was seeking his own things."

Bilqasim seemed to nurse no such qualms, judging by how he had moved to Khalid's side, a hand on the boy's quivering shoulder. When he addressed a tilt-headed Farras al-Awar in Arabic, Tom stopped him.

"In Spanish, if you please, *Monseñor*."

"The boy only has Arabic…"

"Then please translate for him."

Which was a great irony, considering, and also a most unseemly manner in which to order about a royal envoy. It was a good thing that none of the customers who were crowding in the passage could have any Spanish, and much less Arabic. Still…

"Skeres, see these good people back to the taproom, will you?"

Before the Minotaur could, Harker pushed his way into the kitchen.

"I would have my cloak, Master," he rasped thickly. "If there's a thief here…"

One never cries "thief" without making a stir. Al-Awar's one eye flared, and the customers began to clamour in the passage, heedless of Skeres's bellows. All they lacked now… Tom snatched from the line the cape with the green hood, and flung it at Harker, who caught it clumsily.

"Now, Harker, go and help my man with these people," Tom commanded. *Because, in truth, I don't trust you very far…*

Whatever he thought of it, the clerk hurried out and closed the door, muffling Skeres's shouts for order. Now Fates just keep the lad from starting a brawl…

And perhaps Roberts thought that Tom had taken enough upon himself for the day, because he stomped to the centre, arms akimbo, and growled, "So now let's hear it."

He growled it in English, which was of little use but obtained silence. Khalid stood at his master's side, young face ablaze and hands balled into fists — a hawkling ready to strike. Even when Tom turned to al-Awar first — the guard being the one he could question in Spanish — the boy did no worse than glower with a fierceness that aged him.

"Your master will know better what to do with you, Farras al-Awar. But I ask this: what does the pageboy accuse you of?"

Another flare, hard to read in the guard's misshapen visage. "The child lies, *Sayyidi.*" He said "child" with such careless disdain, it was a good thing Khalid couldn't understand him. Or could he? It would be no great marvel, after all.

"And what is it he lies about?" Tom insisted.

Al-Awar's scar twitched. "He says that I was stealing." The disdain again — and then the guard drew tall, his ruined face a mask of sternness. "But, *Sayyidi,* it is not true — as it is not that I have a master here."

Was this where Farras al-Awar denounced Bilqasim's imposture? Not that it mattered, since all that were in the kitchen knew. Tom himself might have been the one in ignorance. Hadn't Bilqasim told his men…?

"I am a soldier, *Sayyidi*, not a servant. I was given the order to watch over Marzuq Raìs by al-Sultan al-Mansur, Commander of the Faithful." Having said this most proudly, al-Awar glared at Khalid, his scar twitching as his jaw worked. "By the Sultan's will I act and see," he said. "And, *Billahi*, I am no thief."

"That means *by God*, *Señor* Ulsingam," Bilqasim translated. "He swears by God that he's no thief."

And, also by God, he made it known to all where his loyalty lay. "And you trust him?" Tom asked — and he didn't just mean about the thieving.

It was answer enough that Bilqasim hesitated. The guard's brow darkened — as any man's would in that predicament, innocent or otherwise.

And now for young Khalid.

"Ask the boy why he made all that racket," Tom ordered Dunne, and it was no great wonder that the soldier sought his master's eye first. After his first outburst, Roberts had retreated aside, glumly surveying the ado, glaring now and then at al-Awar, but letting Tom do as he pleased. Now he just nodded at his man, who spoke to Khalid in broken Arabic. And it occurred then to Tom, as the boy answered with great sullenness, how easy it would be for them all to lie in concert. Because Dunne was Roberts's man, and Roberts had bribed or browbeaten the Moors in this imposture, and who was to tell what Dunne was saying to Khalid, and Khalid to Dunne?

"Boy says he came in here and found al-Awar stealing," the soldier announced — and Fates send that he wasn't lying.

"And what did he steal?"

When the question was translated, Khalid only lifted a shoulder.

"He doesn't know," Dunne offered.

"Yes, Dunne — I'd gathered that. Then he didn't see Farras do the stealing?"

At first the boy just gaped, and then, when Dunne asked again in different words, he tilted back his head with a click of the tongue — the Moors' strange way of saying *No*. It took a nudge from Bilqasim for a remark to be added, which made al-Awar take a step forward.

"He only saw Farras mess with the cloaks," translated Dunne.

At the same time, the guard exclaimed, "Yes, seeking my own!" He stood, towering over the boy, who held his ground, tight-lipped and stiff.

And Roberts... After watching for a while in silence, Roberts chose that moment to explode in Spanish, "And what the devil did he want with his cloak, eh? It seems a thief's excuse, to me!"

Which it could well be — but then... "A thief of what, though?" Tom asked. "Never of cloaks: what else was there to steal?" He nodded to Dunne. "Ask the boy."

Again, young Khalid lifted one thin shoulder, stealing a glance at Tom from under his long lashes. If he felt al-Awar's bitter gaze on him, he made no sign of it.

But truly, not two days yet, and Tom had had enough of Moors to last him for the rest of his life! Then again, would it have been any easier with English soldiers and pageboys?

"So, have your men eaten, *Monseñor*?" he asked Bilqasim.

For a mercy, the turciman was quick-witted, and prompt in dismissing al-Awar and a sulking Khalid — and Roberts caught on at once and sent Dunne to keep an eye on them. And, as the landlady reappeared with her husband in tow, Tom cut short their protestations by assuring them that no harm was done, and demanding the kitchen parlour for their use.

"What a fine retinue for an ambassador!" Tom snapped, the moment they were alone and the door was shut. "Thieves, and spies, and liars…"

"And pretenders," Bilqasim finished unsteadily, hand to his brow and shoulders shaking.

Why, the man was never crying…?

Roberts harrumphed, in a way that said: *What will you have?* And it took Tom a bewildered moment to see that the Moor was laughing. When he lifted his head, he showed a large, rueful grin and eyes that danced.

"I do not expect that you have formed a very good opinion of the people of Morocco," he said — and Tom found himself half wanting to laugh back, half fuming.

The fuming won. "What I have formed, *Monseñor* — and it goes for you too, Roberts — is a question: if Farras al-Awar is so very staunchly the Sultan's man, how are you reckoning that he won't make his report the hour he's back in Fez? That he won't tell his lord what happened? When I agreed to go along with this disgraceful pretence of yours, I thought —"

"You thought, you thought!" Roberts slammed a palm on the table — hard enough to make an earthen jug totter. "Thinking isn't the same as knowing. You'd think that one-eyed scoundrel is the Sultan's own bosom friend, eh? Well, he's not. For one thing, he never was all that great of a captain, and for another, he's disgraced. One of his men, back on the *Consent*, told me that he was sent with Marzuq Raìs as punishment for something or other. If he goes back saying that he guarded the Raìs so well he died, what welcome do you think he'll have, eh?"

Smug fool! "Didn't it cross your mind, Roberts, that even if they behead him, it will be because they believe his story?" And yet it must have, for Roberts to always be so distrustful of al-Awar — as though it weren't far too late!

And see if Bilqasim didn't come between the squabbling Englishmen! "What we reckon, I think," he said, all placid reason, "is that Farras will not take the chance."

Or wouldn't he? The proud turbaned head thrown back... *By the Sultan's will I act and see.*

They'd made a seat of the one window's sill, and Tom went to lean against it, arms crossed behind his back. "Wouldn't he try to win back the Sultan's favour by uncovering the machinations of the English? I think I would, in his place — but you know him best."

The turciman considered a good while, head tilted and fingertips joined before his lips, heedless of Roberts's mutterings. Only when Roberts called the guard a poltroon did Bilqasim look up, frowning.

"Poltroon means *cobarde*? I do not believe that al-Awar is that," he said. "He threw himself under the falling yard to shield the Raìs and was injured for it."

"Much good it did!" Roberts grumbled.

Bilqasim spread his arms. "*Inna Lillah.* We are in the hands of God — and it was God's will that the Raìs should die, and not Farras."

Was it unchristian to grow impatient of Mussulman piety? "Yes — so Farras is favoured by God," Tom groused. "What else do you know of him?"

"You call him favoured? The Raìs knew him for a soldier of many battles, and yet all they had to call him was al-Awar: the

One-Eyed! He fought at al-Qasr al-Kabir — you'll know it as Alcácer Quibir — when the young King of Portugal led his knights to water the desert with their blood, and many Faithfuls found their glory. But Farras? He lost his eye and, it seems, found precious little."

"So what?" Roberts growled.

Bilqasim stroked his beard, unperturbed. "So, I say, if a soldier has even only one feat of valour to boast, you name him after it, not after a misfortune. And now another misfortune must have come to him, that he is in disgrace. I think that he is not favoured at all — not by God, and not by the Sultan."

Thinking of the man's bitter ways, Tom couldn't find it in his heart to disagree.

"You know how we floundered from storm to storm?" Roberts held up a forefinger. "The sailors kept saying that we had a Jonah. Maybe it was our Farras!"

This must have eluded Bilqasim's English. "A Jonah?"

"A man who'll bring ill luck to the ship," Tom said. "It's only a tale, but even if it weren't, a life of misfortune won't make your guard trustworthy."

"Or innocent of stealing," Roberts grumbled.

As though a theft were the worst they had to fear! And besides… "Nothing was stolen, was it? And the boy had little to say for his accusations…" Tom raised a brow at the turciman, who shrugged.

"Do I trust young Khalid, you do not ask? I do," he said. "Could he have mistaken what he saw? He could — for he is afraid, and fear will see ill intent where there is none. Do I believe Farras al-Awar a thief? In truth, it would surprise me very much. Do I trust him not to betray us to the Sultan? *Allahu a'lam* — God knows best. And yet I will say this: Farras al-Awar strikes me as a man who does not expect to be believed. It is a great weight to bear, bound to crush a man's soul."

Oh, Lord, more poetry! Tom met this grave-voiced utterance with a huff — and yet... It was true that, but for the flare of pride as he rejected the page's charges, Farras al-Awar had the bleakest manner. Always keeping to himself, always watching the English, always hovering at the edge.

"To crush his soul — or else to sour his loyalty."

Bilqasim only lifted a brow at this, but Roberts harrumphed and said, "Is there anyone, lad, you don't think a Spanish spy?"

That Roberts had better cultivate some wariness of his own, Tom refrained from pointing out, which was quite charitable of him. Instead, he exercised patience and explained, "Since there was naught he could steal, I can only think of two reasons why al-Awar would be rifling through the cloaks: either to find his own, as he said, or to feel for papers sewn into the linings — as a spy would."

"Why..." Having started to scoff at the notion, Roberts thought better of it. "Why, yes — and he speaks Spanish, doesn't he?"

There was a shrug from Bilqasim. "It would be strange if he didn't, for Farras al-Awar is a *muwallad*." He smiled thinly. "Christian-born, and then converted to the Faith. "You would call him a *renegado*."

"Converted?" Tom wished he hadn't sounded so disbelieving. Even if Roberts hadn't told the story already, to his mind one converted to the Christian faith, but could only renounce it under the cruellest constraint. Wasn't a Moor bound to see it otherwise, though? "I didn't mean..."

Bilqasim's smile widened, if a little askew. "Yes, you did. But then, we do not look very kindly on how the Faithful are turned into Christians."

But in England we force no one... A sudden thought of Dr. Lopes, who had been born a Jew, stifled the retort in Tom's mouth. Lopes, his large family and his friends — had they not converted, what place would there be for them in England? Not that Bilqasim would care for the plight of Jews, would he? Then again, a new Christian was a saved soul...

It was a good thing that Roberts lost his patience then. "Ay, ay — but this is neither here nor there," he said, waving like a housewife shooing away a chicken. "What of your al-Awar?"

If he knew aught of the guard's conversion, Bilqasim didn't say. "He was born in Spain. If he was old enough when he was taken captive, then he *would* remember the tongue."

"As if that made him innocent!" Roberts scoffed. "A Spaniard taken captive, whipped into conversion — and for all reward some puny soldiering, and now he's in disgrace... Why shouldn't he spy for Spain?"

Why, indeed — but Tom was only half listening. *If he was old enough when he was taken captive*, Bilqasim had said. Bilqasim, who spoke such good Spanish. Tom narrowed his eyes at the man.

"And you're Spanish too," he said. "Another ... how did you say? A *muwallad*."

The thought of lying flashed in Bilqasim's eyes, plain as daylight, and then he sighed. "Most turcimans are *muwallad*," he said. "Men of two tongues."

"I should have known," Roberts exclaimed in disgust. "Morocco is aswarm with them. Soldiers, merchants, turcimans, eunuchs in the Sultan's court... At times I thought he liked to flaunt them in my face: see how many Christians

I've turned! I should have known he'd beset us with Spaniards!"

Bilqasim gave a mirthless chuckle. "It's been a long time since I was a Spaniard, *Señor* Roberts," he said. "He seems like someone else now, that *Andalùs* lad, bound for a seminary and priesthood, whether he liked it or not. I was thirteen when the corsairs captured me, and for a long time I prayed that I would be ransomed. My prayers were not answered, and every hope died — but, you see, I was still alive. So I embraced the Faith and now I'm of Morocco: Spain means nothing to me. It hasn't for a long time."

"And you like it?" barked Roberts.

Bilqasim considered for only the briefest while. "As a Christian, I would never have become a Royal envoy."

"You aren't one as a Moor, either," Tom reminded him, and only then observed that it wasn't snowing. Fates be thanked — they might still make Cranborne, as long as they left at once.

CHAPTER 7

It was, of course, Skeres's notion that, after Tom paid for the whole dinner, they should pack up what remained of it. So he wrapped in a piece of cloth a wedge of cheese, half a loaf of cheat bread, and two pork pies, tied the bundle together, and brought it to the stables. It was perhaps equally expected that he should fuss with the bags on the packhorse, much against young Khalid's liking. Both the boy and the Minotaur were still vexed, each over his own misadventure, and the two fell a-bickering without understanding each other at all, until the bundle came undone, and Skeres's hoard lay ruined on the ground.

The dethroned kings of Persia didn't bemoan their lost crowns as the Minotaur wailed at the greasy mess of meat and broken crust, at the gravy soaking the straw. Still, must Khalid recoil from it as from a plague-corpse?

"There!" Skeres bellowed. "See what you've done, you little 'eathen! Now, you clean it up!" He bent to salvage what he could, brushing the bread on his sleeve, and shaking the gravy off the cheese — and only then observed the boy backing away, mouth twisted and hands behind his back.

"You clean it up, I say!" Skeres mimed sweeping, shouting still louder — as though noise must make the Moor understand. "Clean … it … up!"

When young Khalid backed further away, Skeres stepped over the mess, advancing on the boy. "You want trouncing, you brat —"

Oh, Jove rain on the Minotaur! "Skeres!" Tom strode to stand between the two, much to the lad's indignation.

"But see 'im, Master!" He pointed a baleful forefinger. "Too fine to clean the mess 'e made, is 'e? Ah, but I'll teach 'im…" He lunged for the boy around Tom, who grabbed him by the arm.

"Enough, you fool! Leave him be."

It was a belated order, as Khalid had leapt away already, and sought his approaching master's protection.

Whatever it was that Bilqasim said, it quietened the boy — and then the turciman explained very gravely, "It is the pork meat. Our faith forbids that we should eat it."

But never let it be said that Nick Skeres could be quelled. "Eat it!" he groused when Tom translated. "Nobody's going to eat it now. I told 'im to clean it up, is all."

They had gathered an audience by now — not only Roberts and Harker, but the grooms, a maid, a few guests from the taproom, and half the folks in Dorchester — and before them all Bilqasim answered Skeres's English outburst!

At least he had the sense to do so in Spanish. "Pork meat is forbidden because it is impure. Many of us are as loath to touch it as we are to eat it —"

"What's that?" Skeres cut through the explanation in that booming growl he called a whisper. "What is it 'e called me?"

And that was what discomposed him! "Go and fetch my horse," Tom hissed, and shoved the lad towards the door.

Oh, the betrayed pout as Skeres obeyed — and truly, what Tom had done to be saddled with such a dunce, he didn't know.

And then there was Bilqasim, stern as one of Marley's royal Moors.

"I beg Your Excellency's pardon. My man…" *My man is an ignorant blockhead, and I was told about pork meat, but it never crossed my mind that it would be my business what you will eat or won't.* Tom

100

didn't know whether to be thankful or annoyed when Bilqasim broke into his flustered pause.

"Your man will not allow for what he does not know or understand, *Señor*. It is a common fault."

There had been moments in Tom's life when he had appreciated a touch of magnanimous philosophy. Right then, in the midst of a keen little crowd hoping for a brawl, he didn't appreciate it in the least.

"I'm sure it is," he said, as evenly as he could. "On every shore of all the seas. I'll see that we have no more incidents like this. Now, if we could make ready to leave…" And without waiting for an answer, he strode away.

He found a sullen Skeres leading both their mounts. With barely a glance for his own — a huge black gelding — Tom snatched up the reins and threw them to the nearest groom. That done, he dragged Skeres away from the doors.

The lad must have been waiting for a dressing down, perhaps even rehearsing doles in his head. As soon as they were out of hearing inside an empty stall, he wanted to know, "What's it that 'e said? What's that 'e called me?"

"In his place I'd call you a disrespectful boar," Tom seethed. "Being a better man than I, he only said that touching pork meat offends their faith."

It was no great marvel that this was met with a snort. "Ay? I like that one, for when I've no mind to do something: it offends me faith!"

Another might have read the signs of a gathering storm — but Nick Skeres? See the smug, slow nod that said, *Be gulled if you like — I'm not!*

It was a proof of great patience, Tom thought, that instead of boxing his servant's ears, he gritted his teeth and counted in Latin: *Unus … duo … tres…* "You know nothing of these people, and that's not your fault — but have at least the wit to remember that their master is the Queen's own guest."

A harrumph. "Ay, and what 'ave I done, I'd like to know. 'Ave you ever seen a Christian make a row over a scrap of meat on a fish day? Even Puritans only say no and go the other way!"

"Their faith doesn't work like that." And not knowing quite in what way this was true made Tom all the angrier.

Skeres failed to take warning, judging by how mutinously he cried, "And 'ow was I to know?"

"Yes, Skeres, you didn't know — and ignorance should always tread carefully —" Tom caught himself on the brink of shouting. "If they balk at something, leave them be. Better still, don't order them about, don't argue with them, don't..." He raked a hand through his hair. "Just stay out of the Moors' way!"

Was that a flash of hurt before the lad looked away? "Ay, ay," he mumbled. "I'm a lack-Latin, a niddycock and a mope. Don't even know that Moors go to 'Ell for touching pork pies!"

"It shouldn't take Latin to know to tread carefully where —" And then Tom stopped, for someone was approaching.

"Walsingham?" a man's cheery voice called — one Tom wasn't sure he knew.

Stepping out of the stall, he saw a tall figure, black against the open door, rubbing at his arms.

"Thomas Walsingham, is that you?"

"Who's there?" Tom asked, as the fellow advanced in the dim light of a lantern. He knew that loose gait, surely? The broad shoulders and the tiny moustache that did little to adorn the square face?

The man gave a crooked smile. "Rolston, remember? It was the devil's own work to find you!"

And this set Tom's teeth on edge at once. "It can't have been too hard," he answered. "We're on the one road there was to take."

Anthony Rolston, sometime one of Sir Francis's tame Catholics, was the sort of man to throw his head back when he laughed. "Bless you — so you are! 'Tis just that I expected to find you a good deal nearer to London."

I wish you'd tried it — snowstorms, thefts, burials, prayers, pork pies and all. Tom bit down the sour retort by a whisker, and mostly because he caught Skeres crimson-cheeked and fuming to explode.

"See that all is ready to leave, Skeres," he ordered — and, when the lad would have protested, he snapped, "Now!" Then he rounded on Rolston, not much more amicably. "And why were you in such a hurry to find me?"

Having winced at the Minotaur's sulky retreat, the man half grinned again — for he had fine white teeth and knew it. "It was rather premature, I see now — but I was sent to warn you that the Barbary Company is giving the Ambassador a grand welcome at Ludgate."

Well, now... Tom frowned. Surely there must be more — there must be worse, for Mr. Secretary to send out a messenger like this? "And...?" he prodded.

The man shrugged, as careless as you please. "And, when you get there, you must stop at the Dolphin Inn by Temple Bar. You know the place?"

"And that's all?"

That devil-may-care shrug again. "Some of us carry great weighty secrets all the time, and some others aren't Mr. Secretary's nephew —"

"Cousin! My father was Mr. Secretary's —" Tom cut himself short, hearing the pettiness of it. "No matter. Have you no letter for me?"

"For that much of a message? I was just to warn you, for the Barbary fellows are all agog to make an impression — which is just as well, isn't it?" Rolston peered past the half-open door to the Moors waiting in the yard. "Lord above, what a bunch of beggars! Where are the rest?"

Ah, well, now Tom understood Roberts's cheerless laugh at the same question two days earlier. "The rest died in the shipwreck," he said — and confusion flitted across Rolston's countenance. Hadn't he been trusted even with that much knowledge? Then Tom wasn't inclined to enlighten him further — aside from what was plain to see. He needed no more, after all, to carry back a letter. "I'll give you a letter for Mr. Secretary tonight in Cranborne, so tomorrow you can ride back ahead of us."

For the first time, Rolston seemed put out. "Tonight in Cranborne!" he cried. "I just arrived from there — and had the devil of a time of it!"

"The road's never closed, is it? People have been coming in, and said naught of it."

"No...!" Rolston huffed like one not knowing whether to laugh or growl. "It's just the infernal snow — snow and more snow all morning, thick as feathers, so you can hardly see your way."

"All the more reason to catch what daylight remains now it's stopped — otherwise I'd write now."

"And I have no orders to ride ahead at all! I was to find and join you."

"And now that you have, I'm in charge — and I say we're for Cranborne at once." It was most annoying that Tom had to

104

tilt his head back to stare down his nose at the man. "Of course, if you're too spent after your devil of a time, you can rest here this night and follow tomorrow as best you can."

How Rolston coloured, how his nostrils flared! "I told you," he said through gritted teeth, "that I'm to travel back with you. What if you get hitched again?"

Hitched — the pompous, useless idiot! "I've managed well enough without you so far, Mr. Rolston."

Fates send nobody burst in on them — Mr. Secretary's men trying to out-glare each other like two roosters. But the Fates must have been otherwise concerned that day, for they were still at it when Roberts came calling.

"Walsingham, lad, have you changed your mind?" he asked. "It's chill out there, and the horses grow frisky."

"We're leaving at once!" Tom hadn't reached the doors when Rolston called to him. The grin was back in place, if a little strained.

"Well then, since you're in charge... Let me find a fresh horse, and I'll be ready."

Even more than the annoyance at another delay, it was the mocking glint in the man's eyes that made Tom retort, "We're not waiting. Have a warm ale while they saddle you a horse: I'm sure you'll be able to catch up with us on the way."

As Rolston saluted jauntily and strode off in search of a groom, Roberts watched him over his shoulder.

"Friend of yours, eh?" he asked, not bothering to wait for the man to be out of earshot.

One of those who think I've naught but my name to my credit. Was Tom letting his dislike colour his judgment? And yet... "Tony Rolston never liked it that he's one of Mr. Secretary's lesser servants. And because of that, there's no need to tell him much."

For the first time in their acquaintance, Henry Roberts favoured Tom with a chuckle of unmitigated amusement. It was a marvel how it changed him, carving a web of lines on brow and cheeks that made him older and jollier at once. "No need to tell him aught, you mean, eh, lad? Well, well, you may be right. For one thing, I don't like that puny moustache of his — not one bit."

Well, Fates be thanked for small mercies, since with the larger ones they would not bother. Clapping Roberts's shoulder, Tom hurried outside into the milky light. The sooner they left, the better.

They hadn't gone three quarters of a mile before Rolston caught up with them. By then Tom had had time to explain his misgivings to Bilqasim — not quite trusting Roberts to do so, and finding instead that he had. It was with a measure of relief that he took up again his work of riding up and down his little train, all the more eagerly because he meant to keep Rolston well away from the false Ambassador, if nothing else.

It was harder work now, because, for all their zeal, the folks at the Red Lion had done them no favour with the horses. Several were but well-groomed nags, and Tom's own gelding had no liking for the snow at all, riding all stiff and flat-eared, shying at every snowdrift, and startling at the crunch of ice underfoot. All went well enough as long as they kept to the bottom of the Frome Valley, wide almost to flatness among its gentle hills — but soon the road began to climb uphill. Slight as the slope was, the pack-beasts trudged with heads hanging in misery, and twice Bilqasim's mare slipped on a patch of ice. As the road dipped again — just steep enough to make the going uneven — they ran into snow again.

Tom quenched the temptation to question his own wisdom. The snow fell so thin and feathery, he told himself — it was nothing that need stop them. He spurred the gelding to join Dunne, and the soldier pointed at a clutch of houses further down, where a river curved across the whiteness and half a dozen curiously round hillocks dotted the land.

"Don't know what it's called," Dunne said. "It's the place with no bridge."

Oh yes, Tom recalled the hamlet, and fervently wished they could have horses of a steadier temper for the fording. There being nothing for it, he ordered "Let's push past, before the Moors decide it's a fine place to pray."

With a snort that made a white cloud in the air, Dunne nudged on his narrow-buttocked jade, leading the way at as good a pace at they could keep, until they reached the cottages and a small church, all of them half-smothered under the snow. A little way past, the river made a sluggish curve, where the half-frozen water swirled black and oily as a snake's back against the snowy banks. On either side, by the frost-powdered willow trees that marked the passage, other riders had trampled the snow. Two sets of deep cart-ruts showed in the mire, filled with muddy water.

Rolston reined in at Tom's side. "You see those marks?" he asked, as cheerful as you please, and loud enough that all would hear him. "A wagon all but overturned there this morning."

"It's a good thing we have no wagons, then," said Tom — although, in truth... Was it good sense or stubbornness to keep going with these people? See the blue-lipped Moors, the clerk hunched almost double in the saddle, Roberts scowling to himself — and at least six more miles to go... Ah, well, it was too late to change his mind now.

"We cross," Tom commanded, in English and then in Spanish. "You must be careful, but the water isn't deep." Or at least, it hadn't been five days earlier. Had it reached this high over the willow's roots, though? He turned to Rolston, who had come this way in the morning.

"Knee-high or so," the man said.

Which was deeper than Tom remembered it — but then, plenty of snow had fallen these past days. Pushing his horse to the trampled brink of the water, he reckoned the distance: at least the river — the Tarrant, wasn't it? — hadn't swollen wider.

"Rolston, Dunne — you know the crossing best," he called. "You go first, sound the way. Next the pack-beasts, then the rest."

Off they went, Dunne leading, slow and watchful, and Rolston sketching a mock salute as he followed, which Tom ignored in favour of translating for the Moors. The two crossed safely, if slowly — Dunne's bay shying only once. The soldier threw a caution over his shoulder to his companion, and, as soon as they had both climbed up the other bank, he wheeled the beast around and stood in his stirrups.

"There's a mite of ice halfway!" he bellowed, a hand cupped around his mouth. "Mind that, and aim for the willow. The rest is easy enough."

Once more Tom translated, and had young Khalid and Skeres led forward the two packhorses.

Skeres went first, dragging at the unhappy pack-beast. He wasn't yet halfway across when, well behind him, Khalid's nag balked, dancing sideways and raising great plumes of icy water on each side. The packhorse didn't like to be drenched. It yanked at the lead-rope, and, finding that ice of Dunne's, stumbled and tore the rope from the struggling boy.

"Let go!" yelled Dunne from the other side, just as Bilqasim shouted in Arabic from the near bank — but no! See if the young fool, instead of obeying, didn't leap out of his saddle with a great splash, snatching for the packhorse's harness! With a neigh shrill enough to awake the dead, the beast stumbled again in the treacherous black current, and would have toppled, but for Khalid planting his feet and holding tight.

Lord watch out for little fools! Tom jumped right into the hip-high, freezing water, wading in clumsy strides until he managed to grab the lead-rope with one hand, and Khalid by the collar with the other. For a moment he thought they'd all tumble in that churning chill, but then he threw back his whole weight against the current, and the boy did the same, strong for all his smallness. Al-Awar was there to steady them, while Harker waddled past after the frightened packhorse, whose harness had come undone. Hanging on to the guard's saddle, Tom dragged himself and Khalid towards the bank, thrust the sodden boy at Bilqasim, who had walked knee-deep into the water, and scrambled in the frozen mud until Roberts and Skeres hauled him up onto dry ground.

"Cuds me, Mr. Tom!" Skeres shouldered Roberts away. "What were you thinking? Sit you down, now."

"I'll catch my death if I sit down here, Dolius." Finding that he was after all down on his knees, Tom clambered up, stumbling on feet he couldn't feel. "Where's the boy? What have you done with the horse?"

"The 'orse!" Skeres groused, steadying Tom by the elbow. "A miracle 'e ain't drowned, and 'e thinks of the plaguey 'orse! It's not like we're riding on today, is it? Moors won't choke dead if they're on the road another day…"

Villagers were emerging from the nearest cottages, running to see what the matter was, pointing at the trembling and white-eyed beasts — not just the packhorse but also young Khalid's mount, for Dunne had crossed back and recovered it.

Amidst the gathering little crowd, Tom made a quick tally of men and beasts. Bilqasim was scolding in Arabic as he wrapped his own cloak around the shuddering page, and there came Harker, carrying a sodden saddlebag and Roberts's box — and Rolston crossing back, his roan picking its way as gingerly as a pattened lady in a London street. At least he hadn't lost anyone, Tom thought between shivers. Lord, but he was cold. He must have swayed, for someone gripped him roughly, and Roberts was peering at him, thin-mouthed and worried.

"A fine ado, eh?" he grumbled. "My box is half-smashed, and one bag lost."

"The box…" And just yesterday Tom had taken the Sultan's papers from it! He ran a hand down his face, soft-kneed with relief. "What of the medallion?"

"About the only thing that didn't go downstream," harrumphed Roberts. "As though I weren't beggared enough! Well, we aren't riding on today, that's for certain."

Hades and Hell — half a day lost! Tom's shoulders fell. He might as well have kept them all back in Blandford and spared himself a plunge in the Tarrant — to say nothing of Rolston's mocking grin. But truly, the snow was thickening again, and he, Harker and the boy were going to need a fire. It would be late by the time they were dried and warmed enough to ride on, and look at the packhorses, spooked and winded…

"No, we're not," Tom ground out through rattling teeth — though where they would find room in that dismal little clutch of cottages, Heaven knew!

The whole population of the hamlet, it seemed, had run to watch the trouble at the ford, so that, by the time they'd dragged themselves out of the water, they had an audience of men and boys and one magpie of a woman — all gawping at the Moors, and offering wisdom about the crossing that might have been of use half an hour earlier.

The matter of putting up nine men and a dozen horses for the night unleashed a flurry of broad Dorset speech, whose gist was that the beasts could be spread among a number of sheds; as for the travellers, only the magpie-ish woman, a Goodwife Payne by name, was bold enough to take a bunch of Moors — *Moors*, Lor' guard them all! — under her roof.

Her roof, it turned out, was that of a cider-house, a cottage of two rooms, with stairs that promised some loft or attic up under the thatch.

What a comfort it was to step into the dim warmth, with the smell of woodsmoke and sour apples, and the crackling fire. Another consolation was that whatever objections Goodman Payne was inclined to raise to this invasion were silenced without ceremony by his bustling wife. Tom was very thankful, once he was ensconced by the fire and relieved of his sodden boots, that he wouldn't have to go outside. How they were all going to fit into the cramped cottage was another matter — one, he decided as poor Payne grudgingly pressed into his hands a pot of cider, whose sorting could wait a little while.

The cider was blessedly warm but sour. Were the Paynes getting rid of last year's dregs? Across the earth, young Khalid sat cross-legged on the floor, bundled in blankets, sniffing at his pot with a scowl to scare small children. *They drink no wine, no ale, no spirits*, Dunne had warned with a sneer. But, bless the boy, how did he think he'd warm himself? Tom sat forward, pointing.

"If I were you…" he began in Spanish, which was no good, so he turned to the hovering Bilqasim.

"Perhaps, *Monseñor*, he could be allowed a breach, just this once?" he asked. "As a medicine of sorts, to warm him a little."

So this was what it took to thaw Ahmad Bilqasim? Fishing his page out of the freezing Tarrant earned, instead of the usual curl of the mouth, a true, warm smile.

"He has my leave, *Señor*," he said, an arm around Khalid's shoulder. "I would thank you for it, but that you have a far greater right to my gratitude. When this reckless child jumped into danger, you rescued him without hesitation. I thank you from the depths of my heart, Tomàs Ulsingam, and I call you my friend." He bowed, touching the tips of his fingers to his heart, lips, and forehead.

Such an extravagant compliment! Tom blinked at the turciman. "It was no more than my Christian duty, *Monseñor*." Would it be ungracious to point out that Khalid had never been at risk of worse than a coldment? But perhaps it wasn't quite true, not in such freezing water, not if he couldn't swim and was wrapped up as he always was. So Tom nodded back, once deeply at Bilqasim, and once at the boy, who, at his master's urging, said something in Arabic — more thankful hyperboles, no doubt, for all that Khalid didn't seem poetically minded. The cold had pinched his cheeks, making him gaunter and older. Just how old was Khalid, with that grave, distrustful manner, and hands that had clung so strongly to the maddened horse?

And yes — the horses. Tom sat up straight and surveyed the small, rough-walled room. Roberts sat at the trestle table together with their host, while Harker tried to make himself small in a warm corner, and Goodwife Payne fussed about, spreading garments and boots to dry by the fire. And was that a dish of milk — some offering to whatever strange folks they believed in hereabouts?

She caught his look and straightened at once, mouth flattened to a distrustful line. What she held was a small bowl of milk and barley bread.

"For the Shades, Master," she said, and her narrow-eyed glower dissolved only when Tom smiled. After all, as his old nurse had used to ask, what was the ill?

"I've seen it done back at home in Kent," he said, "for the Hobs."

Reassured that she wasn't going to be ridiculed or scolded, Goodwife Payne went back to her business, and Tom to his head-counting. He seemed to be doing little else, these days.

Could it be hoped that the absence of Dunne, al-Awar and Skeres meant that the horses were being tended to? Of Rolston, too, there was neither hide nor hair to be seen. Right as Tom pushed himself up from the stool to go and seek the rest of his party, a door he hadn't observed before was flung open, and the Minotaur clattered in, wearing a pair of pattens tied to his stocking feet. With him was Rolston, who, on entering, clamoured for two pots of cider. And, rain on all witless dolts, see how Skeres beamed and licked his lips!

There was some truth to the saying that an angry man never goes cold. "Skeres!" Tom barked, all the chill gone from his bones of a sudden. "What have you done with the horses?"

The grin wavered and then fell, as the lad motioned behind his back. "I've stabled them, that's what —" He stopped short, slapped his forehead, and clunked out again.

Following him, Tom found himself in what the Paynes called their stable — a rickety, badly thatched wattle-and-daub affair, where three horses were crowded together with the house's placid jade. The creatures' great dark eyes gleamed in the light of the lantern that hung from a low beam. Wishing he'd spared the time to pull on his boots, Tom leant with his back against the door, crossed his arms, and glared at his servant.

"I can't let you out my sight, can I? What did Rolston want with you?"

The way Skeres never looked up from the bag he was busy unbuckling from the saddle was most unpromising. Nor was the one-shouldered shrug reassuring, nor the answer when it came: "What must 'e want? 'E 'ad me mind 'is 'orse."

"And he kept you company while you did?"

Another shrug — and those buckles must have been most stubborn.

"What did he have to say?" Tom insisted. "Or to ask?"

The lad's hands stilled on the bag, and he shot Tom a sideways glance, face knotted in calculation. "Did you say *Nick Skeres, keep away from Mr. Rolston?*" he grumbled.

Which was no answer at all: the Minotaur dilatory — never a good sign. "What have you told him?"

"What was there to tell? 'E called the Moors a pack of ragamuffins — which is the Lord's own truth — and 'ad a good laugh about it, for 'e's a jolly gentleman, Mr. Rolston is." *Unlike some bugbears I know*, went unsaid.

Besides, *Mr. Rolston* again! There was one thing alone that would make the Minotaur so ceremonious over a stranger. "And over that, he buys you a drink?"

"No." Skeres yanked the bag away from the saddle with Tamburlaine's own vigour. "That was for me troubles as I took with 'is 'orse, 'e said. Not that I had a whiff of it, mind you."

Even in the dim yellow glow, the red blotches stood out on the lad's neck and jaw.

"So, for your troubles, a pot of cider and what else? A penny, say?"

And see how the blotches were drowned in a crimson tide! "Ay! Maybe 'e likes me work. Maybe 'e wants to 'ire me!" Skeres shoved the bag at Tom the way he would a ram.

"God help him, if he knows no better! Until he does, though, stay away from Rolston."

"Ay, ay!" With a formidable harrumph, Skeres went to busy himself with his own bag. "If you say so, Master, and you'll know why — though I swear I don't. Such a jolly gentleman, 'e is — and ain't it 'Is 'Onour as sent 'im?"

Indeed, wasn't Rolston sent by Sir Francis? And yet...

There are a few reasons, Thomas, why a man would make friends with another's servants — not all of them innocent. Tom moved Sir Francis's piece of wisdom in his mind. What about the innocence of one's servant, though? "That's as may be," he said. "But tomorrow at dawn you ride ahead — and this time, you get to London."

And, having dismissed any thought of trusting Rolston with even a scrap of writing, he stalked away in search of ink, paper, and solitude to write his letter again.

CHAPTER 8

In the morning — a blue-grey, hazy morning, with a spiteful little wind that bit through cloaks and clothes — every soul in the hamlet of Monkton was there to see the Moors on their way. Whether this was on the assumption that the foreigners could not be trusted to cross the ford alone, or out of eagerness to see the last of them, Tom neither knew nor cared. He'd spent a wretched night on a bare pallet, with a thin blanket for all comfort — and had risen well before dawn to find that his wet boots had all but frozen stiff. If he escaped a coldment this time, it would be a miracle.

For a blessing, Skeres left early, with a young lad as a guide, and an air of silent and thankless obedience that was best ignored — but that seemed to have dried up the well of blessings for the day.

It took an eternity to have the horses saddled, and the pack harness had been so strained in the accident that it had to be patched up with a length of rope and a dozen knots the devil alone would know how to undo, come night. Also, one and all were full of dire warnings about the unchanciness of the chalk land ahead, where pits gaped, sometimes unfenced — so travellers must keep to the road or perish. It was full light by the time all were ready, and the Moors emerged from their prayers, and the party could at long last take to the road again — with a score of villagers escorting them to the ford, like Tamburlaine's first ragged hordes.

Once past the ford, only their hired guide remained — a freckled, yellow-haired lad of thirteen or so, brother to the one who'd ridden off with Skeres.

"Ye've done zummat to dander the Shades, Master," the youngster said, when it became plain that the night's snow had all but concealed the road.

Those same Shades that Goodwife Payne had meant — and seemingly failed — to appease with milk and bread. Tom couldn't help the huff of laughter. "What's that?" he asked. "Ghosts? The fairy-folk? I'd never angered either before."

The lad didn't laugh back. "You'd better be afeared, Master — for all that…" He peered over his shoulder at one of those curious mounds that dotted the snow-smothered fields, and then back at Tom. "That be where the Shades hide, see? My grammer, she says the Shades don't like the Moors — but who knows? They be all heathens, after all."

Although no ghosts came to either help or hinder, it proved a good thing to have hired the young philosopher, for they'd gone a good quarter of a mile before they found a set of cartwheel marks, deep enough to show where the road lay — and even then it was hard going. The wind grew sharper as they climbed towards the bare, bleak chalk downs, making the snow, fine and dry as ground glass, dance and pile in deep drifts that concealed landmarks and accidents of the road alike. Once their guide lost his bearings, and then only Tolly Dunne's keen eye saved them from going a-wander.

And, because the uncertainty, the biting wind and frozen boots weren't enough, at one point, Rolston nudged his horse abreast with Tom's to shout over the wind's hiss.

"A good thing that blasted ford stopped us yesterday," he called, as loud as he could, "before we found ourselves lost up here by sundown! What you were thinking, truly I don't know!"

Bootless, malicious, smug-minded, viperous nithing — never mind that he was right enough. With Herculean effort Tom bit his tongue and didn't point out that the wind hadn't been half as bad yesterday. He counted in Latin in his head, instead, and hunched lower in the saddle, and endured. By the time it pleased the Fates that they reached Cranborne, he'd mastered a great wish to strangle Anthony Rolston.

"Is there a Mr. Walsingham among you?" asked the landlord. "For there's a man wanting to see him."

Again. Stomach queasy of a sudden, Tom lowered his knife and cheese. What could have happened that another courier must follow on the heels of Rolston? Ignoring Roberts's frown and Rolston's lifted brows alike, he followed the landlord upstairs to a long, sparsely furnished room with an oaken floor and two thickly glazed windows.

"There was a duel was fought in here, once," the man cheerfully recounted. "Some thirty years ago, when the Fleur-de-Lys was newly built. This Frenchman — cousin to a great noble — came to my father and said..."

Before the tale could grow long, a man spun away from the furthest window, calling, "Mr. Walsingham!"

He was still little more than a black shadow against the window's milk-coloured light — but the voice was one Tom knew.

"Yes?" he asked.

The shadow moved into the yellow halo of the landlord's branch of candles, taking the shape of a big young man with a keen, olive-complexioned face. And Tom wondered, *What now?* For this was Lopes's scrivener — what was he called? Galvam? — bedraggled and all agog.

"Mr. Walsingham, I thought I'd never —"

Waving for quiet, Tom dismissed the landlord who'd been hovering, all ears. What had Lopes taught this youth? Not much, judging by how he shifted his weight from foot to foot while the landlord bowed himself out, with many assurances that, for whatever they needed, the gentlemen only had to call.

The moment the latch clicked, Galvam sprang forward. "I'm Lucas Galvam, Master — Dr. Rodrigo's scrivener." The youth pronounced his master's name in what had to be the Portuguese way. "I thought I'd never find you, what with this cursed snow…" He thrust at Tom a tightly folded packet. "From Dr. Rodrigo. Most urgent."

The thing bore no superscription. Moving to the window, Tom broke the commonplace seal and unfolded a single sheet that only bore half a dozen neatly inked lines.

Mr. W, the physician wrote in Italian. *Samuel Xavier has learnt of the matter at hand.*

Tom cursed at the codename: SX. All they lacked now — *all they lacked* was young Essex pushing his eager and unskilled nose into this confounded matter.

I have my suspicions about how it happened.

And so did Tom, for young Essex had been raised under Lord Burleigh's roof and wing, and the Lord Treasurer didn't always see the need to curb his fosterling's misplaced ambitions. A good thing that Dr. Lopes had ears everywhere.

I wouldn't put past our friend to have sent a man, to try and glean what he can. I'm advising your kinsman, who isn't back in London yet — and at the same time I send Lucas Galvam to you, so that you can be warned.

Good man — and he didn't know half of what there was to keep from Essex! Whether and how much to tell the physician was for Sir Francis to decide, but for now…

Tom folded the letter and turned to Galvam, who hovered at his elbow. "You know what it says?"

The youth nodded eagerly, eyes shining with intent. "Dr. Rodrigo had me write it. He said I should look out for a man…" He peered around and dropped his voice. "A man of Xavier's."

"And you found none, I take it?"

"I don't rightly know." Galvam's brows drew together in one thick bar. "I kept asking wherever I stopped — not that it was easy, not knowing what sort of man I was seeking. This morning in Salisbury I heard of one, riding a day or so ahead of me, who'd fallen ill in Andover. I didn't know what to do: ride back and check, or find you. Now I think I was a fool…" He stopped, looking away with a click of his tongue.

How old could this lad be? Sixteen, seventeen perhaps? Tom remembered himself at that age, new to the game, ever eager to please Sir Francis, ever fearful of making a mistake. "No, you did well," he said — and meant it, because a notion had already formed in his head. "I'll wager good money that your sick man in Andover is innocent — unless you tell me that Mr. Secretary sent someone else before you?"

Galvam, it seemed, did nothing by halves, and when he thought, he did so with tilt-headed intentness. "Not that I know, Master," he said at last.

"And there was no talk of the Barbary Company giving the Ambassador a welcome?"

"Why, yes!" The boy stared at this seeming piece of omniscience. "Mr. Cardenas said to tell you: you'll be met at the Dolphin, by Temple Bar."

And that settled the matter. Tom whistled low between his teeth: the Barbary Company had been Leicester's own venture, and young Essex had succeeded his stepfather in more than just the Queen's favour. If he didn't have his finger in that particular pie, he might well be looking to it: what would be more natural than a merchant or three seeking preferment with a dead patron's stepson? And therefore…

"Perhaps we've been maligning my Lord Burleigh in our minds, your master and I," he told a startled Galvam. But there was someone else he hadn't maligned at all, even if it was just out of mistrust and unreasoned dislike. And if the satisfaction of it was petty, Tom cared very little.

"What are you to do, now that you've found me?" he asked Galvam.

Had young Galvam possessed a tail, he would have been wagging it. "Dr. Rodrigo says I'm yours to command, Master. To ride with you, or to carry a message, or…"

Was this pup so eager to ride with Mr. Secretary's kinsman? Or just to obey any order that was given? Well, Tom remembered that, too.

"Go to the kitchen," he said. "Have some dinner and warm yourself by the fire — for we leave soon, if I can manage it. The kitchen, mind — not the taproom — and, while you go, tell the landlord to fetch Mr. Rolston for me, and to show him here."

When the lad was gone, Tom placed himself by the window to wait — now having, besides a pretend ambassador and the chance of a Spanish spy, Essex's man to add to his list of worries.

Rolston arrived at once, Solicitous Concern in person. In he strode, brushing aside the landlord and slamming the door shut in the man's face.

"What is it?" he enquired, joining Tom by the window. "Have you heard from London?"

It afforded Tom some satisfaction to glare at the lying scoundrel and tell him, "Oh, yes. I've heard that you've a new master."

Only for the shortest moment did the man stiffen, vexation creasing his brow — and then he had the gall to laugh.

"Ah, well!" He dropped to sit in the corner of the windowsill, long legs crossed at the ankle. "I'd hoped to have a little more time, but…"

And to hear him, wouldn't one think he'd lost a match at tennis? "Time for what, you bare-faced liar—"

"Oh, come now!" Rolston drawled. "You're not thinking straight. Did I let you think I was sent by Mr. Secretary? Yes — and much good it did me, for you're a close-lipped dog. I say it makes us even."

"Even!" Tom choked.

"I tried to trick you, and you found me out. Now that's out of the way, why can't we work together?"

It wasn't often that Tom Walsingham found himself speechless — but this…! It took some work, and still he wasn't sure he managed the amused disbelief he was aiming for. "You take Essex's money behind Mr. Secretary's back, come here under false colours — and now you want to work together!"

"But yes!" Rolston sat forward, elbows on his knees. "Why not? You must see that his lordship is no enemy of your uncle."

Cousin. "Why, no: he's so great a friend that he sent a spy!"

And wouldn't one think Rolston in earnest, with his rueful grimace? "He's young, he's a tad eager — but can you truly blame him? He didn't even know of this embassy, like a boy kept in the corner while the grown men talk. It's little wonder that he chomps at the bit."

"The Queen, you'll notice, made him her favourite, not a Privy Councillor."

"Until he proves himself to her — but how can he do so, if he's not trusted with certain matters?"

"By going to Lord Burleigh, and asking for his chance?"

At this, Rolston tossed his head and laughed. "Come now, don't play the dunce. Burleigh has sons of his own: what room is there for his lordship? Mr. Secretary, on the other hand, has no heir, now that Philip Sidney's dead."

Yes — and poor, widowed Frances, bemoaning over and over that she'd given her father no grandson... "You know, taking up Mr. Secretary's work isn't just a matter of wanting!"

Too much earnestness! Tom could have bitten his tongue when Rolston's grin sharpened.

"Nor just a matter of blood, eh?" the scoundrel sneered. "Your uncle chose Sidney, gave him his daughter in marriage, was teaching him his ways... Not that his lordship ever said so, mind — but why couldn't it be the same with him?"

His daughter in marriage... His stomach clenching, his fists so tight his nails dug into his palms, Tom groped for a retort. "Because, for one thing, Sidney would never have bribed Mr. Secretary's men into betraying him."

"I didn't —" Rolston bit off the rest, drawing up his smirk the way he would a heavy mask. "Betraying him, now! It's just that Mr. Secretary grows no younger, and his ship won't stay afloat forever —"

"Ay — and at the first whiff of uncertainty, rats abandon ships."

Under the little moustache, Rolston's mouth worked for a moment, before he threw back his head to laugh. It was a sour laugh. "Your uncle's loyal little hound! Where would you be without Mr. Secretary? Where are you *with him*, come to that?" He leant forward, eyes a-glint with malice. "And where will you be, when his lordship weds the daughter and becomes the heir?"

Frances. Frances married to yet another man who only saw in her a token of her father's friendship — and this one the Queen's young lover... Surely Rolston was making this up, out of spite? Tom struggled for indifferent evenness.

"We'll see," he said. "Meanwhile, it's a matter of where *you* are, I'd say — and that's out in the open. In your place, I'd hope your new master likes a blunderer."

"If I'm found out, then I'll put the choice to the Ambassador himself. I'm sure he'd like to make friends with the man who has the Queen's ear..."

Which Tom rather doubted, considering Bilqasim's position — but what of Roberts, who had been Leicester's man, and had a good hold on the Moor? It would have been wise to concoct some way to stump Rolston's attempt more thoroughly before confronting him — and see if the scoundrel didn't know it!

"Yes, little Walsingham," he drawled, stroking his clean-shaven chin. "that's what I'll do."

But then, all Tom had to do was to warn Bilqasim and Roberts, wasn't it? Buy himself some time... "Will you? Well, not for a while, I think — for we're leaving this minute, and you have no fresh horse." He affected to squint through the window behind Rolston's back, and the man twisted around to clear a circle of glass with his cuff.

"What in blazes do you mean?"

"Before I sent for you, and you ran here so eagerly, I told the landlord that he could dispose of your beast, as you're staying behind." Tom smirked when the man swung around, gaping. "Oh, he was greatly relieved, for a courier had just come in, clamouring for a fresh horse, and there was none..."

A fine notion — if only it were true. But it was enough to send Rolston springing to his feet, all jolliness gone.

124

"You meddling rascal! You never…! That idiot wouldn't…"

"No?" Tom shrugged. "You'll find that Mr. Secretary's name still holds some sway — whatever you and your master like to think."

And off Anthony Rolston stalked in a fuming hurry. And, before the man found out he'd been cheated, Tom went in search of Roberts in some haste of his own.

As luck would have it, Tom ran into Roberts and Dunne at the foot of the stairs. "Fetch us the Ambassador, Dunne," he commanded.

With a glance at his master, the soldier disappeared whence he'd come, and Tom led the way upstairs and into the empty room. Roberts wasn't in a mellow spirit, and started grousing at once. "Make marvellous free with other men's servants, do you, lad?"

But they had no time for this, and Tom cut right through. "Rolston is Lord Essex's man. What have you told him?"

For the shortest moment Roberts stared, cheeks quivering and purpling. "He's never!" he protested. "You said he was sent by Mr. Secretary!"

"I said nothing of the sort. He did — and it was a lie."

Roberts chewed his underlip, brow darkening more and more, until he asked, of all things, "But why? Why would Lord Essex…?"

Oh Jove! Roberts perhaps had been clever at storming Irish fortresses — which made it a great pity he hadn't been allowed to continue in it. "Lord Essex is bent on learning by mischief what the Council and the Queen won't have him know," Tom explained with what patience he could muster — and it wasn't much. "Not yet, at least — so I'm asking again: what have you told Rolston?"

"I haven't told him a word — for you said..." Rocking back on his heels, Roberts wagged a forefinger at Tom. "You had your doubts before, hadn't you? *Before* this message came..."

And, before Tom had to admit that only plain dislike had kept him wary of the man, there was a knock on the door, and Bilqasim entered.

"I have been summoned?" he asked, one brow arched in a manner of haughty enquiry that wouldn't have disgraced the Sultan himself.

Just in case someone had a mind to listen in, Tom shifted to Spanish. "Anthony Rolston has been lying," he said. "He isn't what he claims to be."

Had Roberts never heard of such tricks before, that he should shake his head like a stunned ox? "Lying..." he repeated.

"What do you call claiming to be Mr. Secretary's man when he's not?" Tom turned to Bilqasim. "The man's master, Excellency, is the Earl of Essex, a young courtier of more ambition than sense."

Roberts, devil pinch him, still had to hum and haw. "He's Lord Leicester's stepson, though," he said. "They say he has the Queen's ear."

And who *they* were Tom would have liked to know. "He enjoys her favour, yes — but he's no member of her Council."

"Unlike Mr. Secretary, your kinsman?" asked Bilqasim.

"Unlike Mr. Secretary, my kinsman." Had the man truly been the Ambassador, Tom would have sighed in relief — but it was Roberts who had to be convinced.

"You've been away for a long time, Roberts. Essex isn't another Leicester, and the Queen is at pains to never let him forget it. Any great enterprise he were to back, she'd likely regard as a wild game, and all the more if there were to be some risk to it, some irregularity. To be plain, if this masquerade of yours is to work, it will take a wiser and steadier head than that of Lord Essex to convince the Queen."

Now Roberts was well and truly thrown. "Ah, this is marvellous!" He cried, pacing this way and that. "And what do I tell Rolston when he comes speaking for his master, eh? Do I lack trouble, to make an enemy of Lord Essex?"

That Secretary Walsingham was an even worse enemy to make, Tom didn't bother to point out. "But perhaps he won't come to you at all," he said instead. "He'll go to Marzuq Raìs, if he has any wits."

"And Marzuq Raìs..." The Moor tapped a forefinger to his lips. "Yes: Marzuq Raìs has little liking for a man who approaches him with lies and subterfuge. Little liking and even less trust — although he will not say it so crudely. It is the Queen's friendship that al-Sultan wants, and Marzuq Raìs would be a poor envoy to put that friendship at risk."

This made Roberts bark with bitter laughter and shake his head at Tom. "Let's have it your way then, young Walsingham," he said. "If Rolston's a lying rogue, he's best kept at arm's length. Still, when little Essex sets out to ruin me, mind, it's you I'll blame."

Lord — did the fellow truly think himself so important that Essex would take notice? At least he didn't seem inclined to trust Rolston for now — and Fates be thanked for this one little victory, for all that it had cost them time and daylight.

"We'd better be on our way now," Tom said — and, when he went to open the door, he all but walked into Dunne, who stood scowling down the passage.

"That fellow Harker was asking after the Capt'n," the soldier said. "Like it's his business to say the horses are ready, and that Rolston is making a row."

*

A row indeed, which rang across the whole stables, and made the bewildered landlord appeal for Tom to witness that he'd never given away the gentleman's horse — never had the thought crossed his mind — although he would have, had His Honour asked — not that His Honour had, or not of him, at least... Could it be that His Honour had asked someone else in the stables? And all with such wringing of hands!

Ah, but the fellow wasn't cut out to run an inn! Taking pity, Tom assured him that it was of no moment and all was well, since there were horses for all, weren't there? Again the poor landlord stole an anxious glance Rolston's way — and lo! Rolston's bluster had cooled to a sulk that was directed wholly at Tom.

"You think yourself cunning, do you?" the man hissed — a piece of childishness Tom didn't bother to answer, other than by not paying for the churl's fresh horse.

And then, having hired a pockmarked groom for a guide, he hurried along their departure as much as he could. If Essex's spy was so eager to ride with them, he could go without dinner!

A petty thought and a worse action. Later, as they laboured up the windswept sides of Cranborne chase, as they had to dismount again and again to lead the horses, as the merciless gusts drove the snow into their faces like handfuls of needles, Tom's conscience stung at the thought of the empty-stomached Rolston. He could see in his mind that little frown Frances had for him when he confessed such things to her. This time he wouldn't tell her, he thought, brushing the rapier's hilt, and knowing all too well that he would. He must be the most foolish of lovers, wishing for his love to think well of him as much as the next man, and yet he couldn't bear to have her think him better than he was! Sidney — a fine poet among his many perfections — would have made a sonnet out of it. If he'd ever been petty in his life. If he'd ever loved his wife enough to care what she thought of him…

And how far lost he'd been in these contemplations, Tom didn't know until Dunne's call startled him out of them. All were dismounting for another stretch of dreary trudging, leading the horses — and, most alarmingly, Anthony Rolston had managed to sneak his way to the Ambassador's side.

Lord smite all traitorous snakes — and all lovelorn dunces who let their minds wander! Jerking his horse's head around, Tom cantered back to join the two, so briskly that the dismounted al-Awar stepped in his way.

"What do you think you're doing, you fool?" Tom snapped, throwing the reins at the guard as he swung himself out of the saddle. He all but landed on Rolston's toes, and called in urgent Spanish, "Excellency! As I said, this man —"

And see the lordly way the gloved palm was held up… Who would have thought the fellow a plain turciman?

"This man, as you said…" Bilqasim pushed back his pointed hood just enough to stare at Rolston down his nose. "This man has tried to impress on me the importance of his master. A master who is *not*, I gather, the very excellent and most wise *Señor* Secretary Ulsingam. I have listened to *Señor* Rolston, as courtesy dictates — but both the Sultan's instructions and my own notion of honourable conduct —" a gracious nod at Tom — "dictate with greater strictness that my trust must rest with Mr. Secretary — and his kinsman."

Such an onslaught of flowery disdain! With each word of it, Rolston paled a shade. In the end he bowed to the man he believed to be Marzuq Raìs — and a very stiff bow it was.

"I should have known that Mr. Secretary's kinsman would poison Your Excellency's mind against my master," he ground out.

The stern lifting of Bilqasim's chin could have frozen all the deserts of Arabia. "I have never heard of your master, for good or ill — nor has, I believe, al-Sultan Ahmad al-Mansur, Commander of the Faithful, Shadow of God upon Earth. Your own doings, though, have poisoned my mind against yourself."

And here was another unedifying little tale for Frances — though she would laugh to hear how Rolston stomped away in a stiff-backed sulk. A pity that she couldn't also hear of the mischief glinting in Bilqasim's eyes as he raised his hood back in place.

"Ah, you were right, *Señor* Ulsingam," the Moor said. "Your Rolston has the charm of..." He sketched a gesture, as if snatching something out of the air. "I don't know what it is called in Spanish: a little serpent of our deserts, pretty in its many-coloured scales, and somewhat poisonous in its bite. It is not deadly, although I am sure it would like to be — only a traitorous, unpleasant nuisance."

A huff of laughter escaped Tom's lips together with a cloud of vapour. "Is this what Marzuq Raìs sounded like?" he asked.

"Being a bold and blunt sea captain, he sounded more like our much-esteemed *Señor* Roberts," the Moor whispered. "This is what *I* would sound like, if I truly were the Sultan's envoy. But then, my friend, I am a poet."

It was hard not to like this man — and see how well he'd dealt with Essex's spy. With a slightly lighter heart Tom went back to the head of the train — to find that, instead of yet another climb, it was a descent that they were facing, down towards a wide, flat land that he remembered. How metaphorical, in its way, of that lighter heart Tom felt in his breast.

"Is that the Avon Valley?" he asked of their guide.

The stable lad rubbed his pockmarked chin, like one thinking hard. It took a good deal of rubbing before he pointed into the grey-white, hazy distance. "Down yonder, see? That's Salisbury."

Much as he squinted down yonder, Tom could see nothing like a city — and was ready to wager that Dunne couldn't, either, even with his battlefield eyes. The soldier seemed convinced enough, though: when he lifted a brow at Tom, it was to seek permission, not to raise a doubt. Ah, well, what else was there to do?

They began their descent on foot, leading the horses.

Bilqasim stopped a moment to contemplate the plain below. "Is your London close now?" he asked. "Down in this valley?"

"We still have three days to go, I'd say." *If all goes well and the snow takes pity*, Tom didn't add.

The turciman's profile was hidden by the hood, from which his words emerged muffled — and yet... Was that worry in the tilt of his head, in his thinned mouth? Well, what man in his right mind wouldn't fret at the thought of bearing another's name to meet the Queen of England? And yet the next question wasn't that of a fretful impostor.

"Three more nights that we must spend in hovels?"

As though they were doing it on purpose! Did the fellow think he was the Sultan himself? "Salisbury is a fair city." Tom gave the smallest, stiffest bow. "I'm sure the inns there will afford enough comfort to please Your Excellency."

When the Moor gave a small smile, Tom couldn't quite read it: was it rueful? Repentant? Mocking? Nor was the remark that went with it much plainer: "Very well, *Señor* Ulsingam. I trust that, God willing, it will be easier now."

What was to be easier? If Bilqasim meant the road, he was soon disproved. It was true, as they climbed down into the valley, that the wind gentled, and the snow thinned to almost nothing, and if the cold didn't ease, at least it stopped to finger its way inside cloaks and hoods and clothes. The road itself, though! Little as the horses had liked the climb up, the climb down they hated with a passion — and Tom found it hard to blame them. Over the last few days, the old snow must have melted and then frozen again, so that the new white layer concealed patches of the hardest ice, moulded in holes, and ruts, and slippery sheets, and crests with edges like battle swords. No, there was no blaming the poor beasts as they skidded, stumbled, and shied with flattened ears and trembling muscles. What the Moors chuntered to themselves there was no saying, but the Englishmen all cursed thick and loud — save for the ever-quiet Harker. It would be a great mercy if they reached Salisbury without laming man nor beast.

There was a fellow in the stables at Sir Francis's country place in Barnes, an aging groom, as stout and gnarled as an old oak, always grumbling that one shouldn't even think such thoughts. And, as if to prove him right, the memory hadn't quite formed in Tom's mind when a frightened neigh pierced the air, and Harker's nag stumbled into Tom's mare, one hind leg flailing on the edge of a sudden chasm.

Just by a clumsy whisker Tom skidded away before being flattened between the two brutes, but Harker, yanking at the reins, lost his footing and fell into the snow, under his horse's lashing hooves. He would have rolled down in the pit, but Tom dove to haul him away from the brink, joining him in the snow before he managed to drag them both out of harm's way

— and Fates be thanked that al-Awar and Roberts ran up to catch one horse each.

A little winded, Tom clambered to his feet. He held down a hand to Harker, and the clerk caught it to brace himself upright, a tad unsteady on his feet. Side by side, they peered down the steep fall they'd both narrowly avoided: six or eight feet of rough chalk wall, down to more ice-crusted chalk — fit to break a horse's back, or a man's neck.

And only then their guide made his way to them, gawping and breathless. "God's lid, Master!" he exclaimed. "'Tis a chalkpit!"

"You don't say! Don't I pay you to warn us of those?" Tom turned from the flustered fellow to Harker. "Are you hale?" he asked, and was rewarded with a tight nod and a fit of coughing.

Then the clerk bent to pick up Tom's hat from the ground, and brushed the snow from it with his sleeve, before holding it out.

"I'm sorry, Master," he rasped between coughs. "You help me, and get a hat full of snow for it!"

A hat and a cloak, and a collar, come to that. "A broken neck would have been worse." Another utterance that Sir Francis's groom would have disapproved of, Tom thought, as Harker ducked his head, either in agreement or more thanks. Raising his green hood again, the clerk then hurried to recover his horse.

Always so eager to stay out of the way, this fellow. Was he still afraid to be left behind? Not that Tom hadn't thought of it, now that they approached Salisbury — for all that the man made himself as small and quiet as a mouse. With a mournful shake of the velvet rag that had been his hat, Tom took from al-Awar his still fidgety mare.

"You feel ill-used, eh, poor girl?" He patted the horse's long nose — and, as he did, he could have sworn that the guard was watching him.

If nothing else, the snow had stopped meanwhile, and the descent grew milder as the hills receded, like white-clad ladies curtsying low. It was a pleasure to mount again after the long walk: the Avon Valley stretched before them, windless and placid, with the river winding closer, tranquil and fringed with frost-silvered trees. They could even proceed at a small trot, at intervals, on the large and well-marked road, for it had snowed a good deal less here. At length, at the head of the train, Lucas Galvam gave a shout.

"There!" he called, pointing forward — and, when Tom joined him, there it stood, grey in the distance like a ghostly arm raised in blessing, a sight to thaw a man's heart: the great spire of Salisbury Cathedral, at last.

CHAPTER 9

Oh, what a fine inn was the George in Salisbury! How bright the light of the wax candles, glowing clear through the glazed windows. The grey afternoon was closing in with shadows when they entered the spacious yard, and the whole house shone like a great lantern, beckoning to the travellers.

Or perhaps it didn't. It must be all workaday enough to those who lived there, day after day — but to Tom, as he at last warmed himself by the fire in the wainscoted parlour he'd secured, the George felt like a great prize. And if his hands and feet were full of pins and needles, if his nose was clogged with the beginnings of a coldment, there was the beaker of buttered beer the apple-cheeked daughter of the house had brought for him: warm, thick, and spicy with nutmeg and ginger — fit, as the young woman had said, to melt a winter's worth of chill!

So that was how Tom sat — drowsily fixing the flames, with all the day's fatigue and aches descending on him like a fog — and only half listened to an anxious Galvam. He should have been attending more closely, perhaps — and a few times his tired mind provided Sir Francis's disapproving hum — but then, the lad's conversation circled round and round.

"What if Rolston tries something? Without your servant, you and I make two against one. But what of the Moors? And Roberts? I spoke with Dunne a little, and he has little liking for Rolston, but —"

"You spoke…" Sitting up, awake at once, Tom checked himself and lowered his voice. "Lucas, tell me: just what were your orders?"

The boy coloured. "I... Dr. Rodrigo said ... I was to bring the letter and then stay with you, but..."

"And that you've done. Did Dr. Rodrigo also tell you to question people?"

"I didn't *question* him! I was careful..." Catching Tom's raised brow, the boy broke off his protestations. "It's just ... when you and Rolston had that row earlier, Dunne called the man a snivelling ferret, and I said I disliked him, and he said it goes to show I'm a bright lad — not that he meant it — and that's all there was to it, I swear!" He clapped a hand to his breast, eyes ablaze like a painted saint in a French church.

Tom swallowed a sigh. "Then I'll need no oaths — but let that be that, will you? See that you don't not-question anybody else — for you are under my orders while you ride with me."

"Yes, Master." Contrition showed briefly, soon burnt away like mist by a new dawn of eagerness. "But, Master, what would Roberts do, if it came to you or Rolston? And what of that other fellow of his?"

"What do you think Rolston will do — black murder?" And then Tom's sluggish mind caught up with what the boy had said. "What other fellow? Roberts only has... Oh, you mean Harker?"

"I don't know what he's called: the old man with the green hood!"

Old man — poor Harker! The ale at the George must have been strong, for Tom found himself wanting to laugh. But then, his own eight-and-twenty must have seemed like slow-witted dotage to this lad. "No, that's a stray the Ambassador picked up out of charity — so you can leave him out of that pitched battle of Good and Evil you're painting in your head."

One wouldn't credit the hurt and anger that chased each other, pinching the suddenly sallow face. How did Lopes put up with this mercurial whelp day after day?

"I only want to help, Master," the whelp murmured, head lowered to hide the storm.

"Good — then you'll help best by doing as I say." Not the brightest of notions, Tom saw at once, because now Galvam expected to be told what to do. They'd had a spaniel pup like that, as children at Scadbury — trailing after the girls all day long, tail in perpetual motion, soulful brown eyes begging for some small way to please. It had jumped into the duck pond one day in its eagerness and drowned. "For now you can find out where Rolston is, and what he's doing — but mind —"

"Don't worry, Master — I'll be careful." And with that, Galvam vanished. Careful — ay!

Ah, well — there was little harm he could do, for Rolston knew himself to be distrusted on all sides. Tom sank deeper into the chair, hardly raising his head when the door opened again and Roberts came to join him. He was grey with tiredness, poor fellow, with a red and swollen nose, and he lowered himself into the other good chair with such ginger, moaning stiffness, one could nearly hear his joints creak. But then, he must be nearly twice Tom's age — truly almost old.

"Ah, but Morocco ruined me, young Walsingham," he rumbled. "Ruined me fit for an early grave…"

Tom held up his beaker. "Have one of these made, then," he said lazily. Roberts grunted and sat back, spreading his legs before him. Did he expect Tom to go and fetch drinks for him? He wasn't *that* old, after all — Morocco or no. "To think they say that Morocco is warm, and dry, and pleasant…"

Another, deeper, mightier grunt. "Ay — dry's the word. The cursed air's so hot and dry, it bakes your lungs like Lenten figs, until they can't take good English air no more — so when you come home … bah!" A twist of the lips, a shake of the head, and Henry Roberts fell silent, double chin lowered to his breast, the very picture of ill-used virtue.

What did one say to that? Nothing, Tom decided — and for a little while there was only the crackling of the fire, the scent of nutmeg and woodsmoke, and that delicious warmth. A most pleasant state of things, conducive to empty-headed rest…

Until the cursed door opened again — by the width of a hand. Tom could have moaned aloud when a curly head appeared in the gap: the Moorish pageboy, Khalid.

Oh, what the devil now? Tom opened his mouth to ask, only to close it again when the boy put a finger to his lips. He glanced at Roberts, who had dozed off, and then back at Tom, beckoning. When Tom beckoned in turn, the boy tilted back his head. *No.*

All pleasant warmth and languor drained out of Tom as his innards clenched. He climbed stiffly to his feet, checked the snoring Roberts, and padded out to join the young Moor. After sitting by the hearth, the damp chill in the passage set him a-shiver, and he blinked in the gloom. There the boy stood in tense silence, eyes glinting in the beam of the firelight that filtered through the half-closed door. How they were to talk to each other, Tom didn't know.

"What is it? Where's your master?" he asked in slow Spanish, and, just as he'd expected, the boy's brow knotted in incomprehension. Still, his thin hands clasped Tom's sleeve.

"*Excelencia,*" Khalid stuttered, butchering the Spanish title, though not quite past recognition. "Marzuq Raìs. *Ven!*"

Come where? Is he ill? Is he in trouble? Is this a trap? The useless questions crowded on Tom's tongue for no longer than a heartbeat, and yet the boy's face contorted in anguish.

"*Ven*!" he repeated, urgent fingers digging into Tom's arm.

He was wearing, Tom noticed, his cloak — so, whatever this was, it had happened outside. In his mind he saw again the innyard in Bridport, Hakim's body sprawled in the snow... Fates forbid! "Wait," he ordered, and made to go back to the parlour, but the boy clung to him with that surprising strength of his and blurted one liquid Arabic syllable of unmistakable meaning.

"Wait," Tom repeated, and, tugging free, sneaked into the parlour for his cloak, sword and dagger. He cursed as the buckles tinkled, and Roberts half-awoke.

"What is it?" he muttered, words thick with sleep.

"Nothing to worry you," Tom said — and, for a mercy, Roberts settled down again.

Back in the passage, there was no one. Had he dreamt it all? But no: Khalid slid out of the shadows, where he'd hidden, no doubt, in case Tom had summoned Roberts after all.

Why don't you want Roberts? "Al-Awar?" Tom asked instead, only half surprised when the boy scowled. Well, Tom didn't trust the guard as far as he could throw him — but shouldn't it be different for this boy? All such preoccupations would have to wait. *Supposing I'll be alive to hear the answers...* Chiding himself for fancifulness, Tom wrapped himself in his cloak and donned his cap, tugging it as low as it would go, and followed the boy along the passage to a side door, and out into the shadowed, empty street. Shivering, he gripped the rapier's hilt under his cloak. Fanciful or not, he was glad of Frances's fine gift strapped at his side.

Carrying a small lantern, furtive and urgent, Khalid led the way from the High Street to another large street at straight angles, both sporting these overlarge runnels Salisbury liked so much, and then into alleys that stank of guts and fish even in the frosty night. Crossing another larger and runnelled street, they dove into a passage as black as sin, and this led them to a narrow yard. On the right side of it, Khalid's lantern shone unsteadily on a rickety, half-timbered house. Meagre light glowed through grimy horn windows, heaps of ordure lay on each side of a weatherbeaten door, and the stench of piss filled the bitter air.

Oh Lord... With a sinking heart, Tom paused on the threshold. "What the devil is he doing here?" he asked — the most doltish of questions, asked of a boy who couldn't understand it, and besides, what did one do in such a place? Never bothering with the slow-witted Englishman's qualms, Khalid shoved the door open with a small grunt.

Inside it was even worse. The draught from the door made the halos of a few rushlights blink through a fug of soot and grease and unwashed bodies — and, in the sudden silence, a number of unpleasant gazes were directed towards the newcomers. None of those gazes belonged to Ahmad Bilqasim — but that would have been too easy, surely? Instead, eight or ten rascals stared askance, like stray dogs studying easy prey... Oh, for the Minotaur's menacing presence — and that of al-Awar, come to that! But there was naught for it: Tom drew himself up, letting his coat fall open enough to show his hilt, and strode ahead as loftily as he could. It worked to the extent that a greasy, bald-headed fellow came forward, a rag between his hands, and asked, "Can I serve you, Master?"

Yes — by producing at once the Sultan of Morocco's envoy, whole and hale... "This boy —" Tom pushed Khalid forward a step — "this boy came here earlier this night, with a companion. I've come to fetch the man."

See how the taverner's wet eyes slid sideways, see how he kneaded the rag. "What sort of man, Master? We've all sorts, here…"

"This boy's companion," Tom repeated, his voice a tad frostier. "I'm sure that you remember."

Now Fates send that these hard-faced scarecrows all around took no notions into their heads. But no: the taverner's manner changed at once. Smile falling, he bowed almost double.

"Ay, Your Honour — ay: the boy's companion. I mind him now." Slinging the rag over his shoulder, he moved crabwise, motioning to the room's shadowy depths. "This way, please, Your Honour."

That it pleased him very much, Tom couldn't say, but…

Once inside a nest of vipers, Thomas, there is nothing for it but forge ahead, and never show hesitation.

Let Sir Francis be right, Tom thought as he followed the taverner, one hand on Khalid's shoulder, the other on the hilt — and all the time he felt each scarecrow's stare pricking his back like so many needles.

One good thing to say for this hovel: as far as could be observed in the gloom, it had no great complications of build, no nooks and crannies to make ambush easy. At the room's far end, a curtained door led to another. It was largish and well-lit, and in a better sort of house, it might have been called a parlour, with a sideboard and a square table where six men sat — four of them playing a game of what looked like One-and-Thirty. They all looked startled at the intrusion, all clearly vexed but for one who broke into the brightest grin that ever failed to touch a pair of wretched eyes.

"Ah, my friend!" the idiot turciman exclaimed, affecting an accent that was of no known land. "You have come seeking your poor Ahmad!"

Yes — to wring my poor Ahmad's neck for him! But perhaps — *perhaps!* — Bilqasim had had the wit to keep the Ambassador out of this disaster? "I've come to fetch you," Tom said, gruff with relief. "You're wanted — so, if you'll make your excuses…"

"Ah…" Bilqasim winced. "The truth of it is that…"

Of course. Tom's heart sank — and then sank a little lower when one of the other players pushed back his stool and rose cumbersomely, for he was large and fleshy, with a boar's small and shrewd eyes.

"The truth of it is, my master," he announced thickly, "that his excuses ain't enough."

The other men all shook their heads and shifted on stools and benches, and something on the table caught the light — a knife, its naked blade resting among the cards.

Oh, marvellous! Tom resisted the urge to close his eyes. "How much?" he asked.

And didn't the Moor have the gall to grin again? "A pittance, truly, that I am trying to win back —"

"Ay," the boar-faced giant growled, eyes all but disappearing into the folds of his scowl. "Trying mighty hard, he was…"

It seemed that a thought was sluggishly stirring inside the man's skull — and not a pleasing one. Now see how Bilqasim stood gaping like Perplexed Innocence itself… He'd never been reckless enough to cheat, had he?

"Well, he won't have to, now," Tom hastened to assure the men. "How much are you owed, good people?"

"Four-and-twenty shillings, six pence," another player squawked, licking his teeth like a fox. "And that's to me alone."

More than a pound — Hades take the man! Under Tom's glare, Bilqasim raised a shoulder and a palm. *We're in God's hands,* the gesture said.

"And eight shillings to me. Eight and tuppence." This from the Boar.

The fourth player, a young fellow with lank, gingery hair, was silent — which would have been encouraging, but for Bilqasim's forlorn grimace.

"What about you?" Tom asked.

"Me you needn't worry about, Master," he said, half smug and half insolent. He reached into his sleeve. "I'm paid already." Something glittered in his palm. Gold, and green…

Behind Tom's back, Khalid gasped, as well he might, for his nitwit of a master had gambled away the medallion — all that remained of the Sultan's gifts! It was a good thing that all words deserted Tom.

And the turciman? Oh, he grimaced ruefully. "That was meant for your cousin's good lady, I know — but…"

But, indeed, and just to make things better, the players and watchers alike were growing restless, eyeing the medallion and Tom, elbowing each other, leering at the Moor, at each other, at the landlord fidgeting in the corner, at the blade on the table.

"*How much?*" Tom asked for the third time. "For how much did you lose it, *Ahmad?*" And pray the dolt hadn't sung the plaguey jewel's praises too high…

The man with the red wisps must either have a knowledge of gold or a mistress to woo, though, for he jutted out his chin and closed his fingers around the medallion. "Now, look you, Master —"

"No, my good man, *you* look." Tom squared his shoulders, taking a half step back — and nearly stepping on Khalid as he did — so that he could at once loom over the fellow and glare sternly at the whole company. "I'm sure none of you set out to take advantage of a poor, guileless foreigner." This was met with thoughtful silence. "So sure I am, that I will pay you all that he owes, all of it — and that means also the value of this trinket." *Supposing that I can...* He reached inside his sleeve for the purse — and lo! One of the silent watchers groped for the knife on the table, and at once three more nasty knives glinted in the dancing light. Hades and hell — must Bilqasim have chosen the most criminous den in the whole of Salisbury?

In one move Tom stepped back, pushed the boy behind him and slipped out his rapier by half — only to be elbowed aside as the landlord came between.

"Friends, friends!" he cried, hands waving and pink head a-gleam. "And Your Honour, please! There ain't no need for this! Put away those blades!" This advice he enforced by cuffing the Fox's shoulder, hard enough to make him stumble. "You want the Watch at my door, Gib Foster? Batty, lad?" This being one of the silent watchers, a younger, nastier likeness of the Boar. "His Honour's paying — ain't you, Your Honour? — so what's the ado?"

Yes, Tom was paying. He half-wondered, as he counted the coins out of his purse, how often did this fellow break up brawls like that, and just how tightly he held the reins of these squint-eyed villains.

In the end, it was the fox-like man who grunted in assent. "As long as we get our winnings," he mumbled. "And besides..."

Besides, we've fleeced the Moor for all he's worth?

Quite likely, because there were hums and wary nods all around; only the Judas-headed youth dug in his heels, devil pinch him, clinging to the plaguey medallion. Tom could have cheered when the landlord cuffed the idiot.

"You'll buy another with the money! Tell His Honour, and be done with it!"

At last the fool shook himself like a wet dog. "Rot you all!" he griped. "'Tis sixty-two shillings, three and a half!"

Tom's jaw dropped open. Sixty-two... Three pounds and odds! Surely, *surely* he had it wrong? "What did you say?"

"You heard that, my fine Master!" The man came toe to toe with Tom, breath stinking of onion and bad teeth. "Sixty-two, three 'n a half. Unless you say your friend lied on this trinket's worth!"

He tossed it in the air and caught it, the emeralds sparkling in the bilious light. Behind his back, the two boar-like brothers had grabbed their knives again.

And then, Sir, the false ambassador was murdered under my nose in the lowest tavern in all Salisbury, having gambled with, lied to, and perhaps cheated, a gaggle of cut-throats...

"Sixty-two shillings, three pence and a half," Tom repeated slowly — and counted himself lucky that it was not even near the medallion's true value.

That was the moment Bilqasim choose to point out in Spanish, "I believe that one of these sons of mangy dogs must have cheated."

Serves you right, Tom would have said — had he known the Spanish for it, and it was just as well that he didn't, for the foreign tongue made the villains stiffen.

"What was that?" yapped the Fox. "What did he say?"

"He wishes he'd never touched the shadow of a deck of cards!" Tom said in English, as repressively as he knew how — and began counting more coins. More than five pounds in all — how had Bilqasim managed to lose so much at One-and-Thirty, in a couple of hours? Ah, well — easily enough, as Tom knew only too well from his disastrous gambling days back in France, but such ruinous stakes in such a place...? And, as he mused, he must have slackened his counting, because the junior boar — Batty, was it? — stepped forward.

"You're never out of silver, eh, Master?" he enquired, uncrossing his arms most unpleasantly amidst a ring of unfriendly stares.

Even the taverner leaned back on his heels, shaking his head with an air of great reproach. "Fair's fair, Your Honour. You said you'd pay…"

"And what do you think I'm doing, plague take you?" Tom shook a few more coins out of the purse — and wished he hadn't: see how the jingling — and the glimpse of gold — lit the rogues' eyes… "There, five pounds, five shillings." He set the coins in a pile on the table.

"An' a half!" This from young Judas, of course.

"Oh, yes, forgive me — *and a half!*" Fishing for a smaller coin, Tom only found pennies, and, reckoning the benefits of a swift retreat, dropped one by the pile. "Drink the rest to my friend's health!" he groused. Five pounds five — Lord! How would he pay their way to London on what was left?

But this was a worry that could wait. The money was counted, the medallion was returned, and they were suffered to leave without further incident — and Fates be thanked!

Once back in the yard, Tom fumed as he strode through the frozen filth, an arm threaded none too gently through that of Bilqasim, with Khalid lighting the way. Only after they'd gained the larger street did he round on the turciman.

"What the devil were you thinking?" he asked in an angry whisper. "Sneaking away to gamble in a place like that! To gamble at all! To gamble with the Queen's gift!"

Stopping right in the middle of the boards that crossed the runnel, the Moor tugged free and, of all things, bowed — not very deep, but ludicrously solemn in the yellow light of Khalid's vacillating lantern. "I'm sorry, *Señor* Ulsingam. Sorry that I misjudged those men, and my own skill at cards."

As though an apology made it better! "And to lose such a sum so quickly... How on earth did you find a place to play for such stakes?"

"I asked at the inn. Here, as in Fez, stable grooms know more than is good about gambling." Bilqasim sobered. "But I was reckless, and those men... Can we not go to the *alguaziles* — the Watch? I truly believe that someone was cheating."

Lord — how Tom wished he could shake the man until his teeth rattled! "You, for one — don't even try to deny it! And when I call the constables, they'll want to know who I am, and who this Moorish gentleman is that I'm escorting... Good Lord, man! Have you no sense at all? It would be bad enough if you truly —"

And then something — a noise he couldn't name, stifled the rebuke in his throat, and raised the small hairs on his neck. Steps...?

"What is it?" Bilqasim looked about, an arm tight around Khalid.

"I'm not sure. We'd better go." But where? Was that their alley, yawning just across the street? Tom thought he recalled it, and the heap of dirty frozen snow at the corner. He pointed. "There?"

When Khalid nodded, they hastened into the black maw, the boy leading the way barely a step ahead, lantern held high, eyes gleaming whenever he peered back over his shoulder. Tom loosened the rapier in its scabbard — and, on a cautious whim, moved the medallion to his boot, the way Nick Skeres swore was safe. It was hard to hear anything over three men's steps, but he didn't like to stop again.

"You *are* armed, aren't you?" he enquired of Bilqasim — although what help a translator would be in a fight, he didn't want to wonder.

The Moor opened his cloak — not his own, but one of English cut, with a round hood — to show a heavy, flower-shaped hilt. "Why? You never think…?"

"I think that perhaps we were a tad too eager to buy back the medallion, and they liked the sound of my purse a tad too well —"

The rest Tom bit down with a hiss — for there *were* steps behind them. Spinning around, he elbowed his cloak out of the way and drew. "Run!" he called in Spanish, then set his back to a wall, rapier and dagger ready in a *guardia seconda*…

As though street robbers cared for Italian swordplay! They came running — three of them, armed with cudgels and long knives. The Boar with his brother Batty, Tom would have wagered. As for the third…

"You truly like that trinket, do you, knave?" he called. "Enough to pay for it in blood?"

When the man stomped forward, his ginger hair showed in the lantern's glow, proof enough that the third malefactor was the Judas-headed youth.

The lantern, yes — because the Moors hadn't run, after all. Bilqasim had come to stand by Tom's side, and if his stance was not that of a swordsman, he still wielded a wickedly curved blade — the sort Sultans wore in Marley's play. Behind them, Khalid was pressed against the wall, lantern held high — bright boy! — to light the villains, and, with any luck, to blind them a little.

"I told you to go," Tom hissed, though in truth, he was glad of the madly grinning turciman's company.

But whatever impression this closing of ranks had made, it was short-lived, and, at a muffled cry of "Quick, quick!" from Judas, the rascals fell to it with cudgels and knives.

The alley wasn't so narrow that Tom could defend its width alone, and at once he found himself confronting two assailants, while the third crowded Bilqasim. In truth, Tom's longer blade — and nicely wielded, if he said so himself — made the miscreants a little shy at first, but there was the difficulty of always keeping an eye on the Moors. It wasn't long before Bilqasim stumbled into Tom.

"Are you hit?" Tom asked, lunging across the turciman's body to make the Boar lurch away, and wasn't much reassured when the answer came.

"Just clumsy!" the reckless fool cried, waving about his curved poniard in a manner that made Tom's hair stand on end. How long before one lucky thrust or a well-aimed blow pierced the man's unpractised guard? Why, he didn't even truly stand on guard... And it was plain the three rogues had noticed as well. See how they closed in, panting and low on their haunches, like hounds at the quarry...

And then it happened, as it was bound to: just as Tom thrust at Judas's face, there were cries in Arabic, and a clatter of metal. Bilqasim stood unarmed and stunned, clutching at his right wrist. Hades and Hell! Tom leapt in front of the man, pushing him back against the wall, and at the same time lunged at the Boar, half slipping in a puddle of sludge. *There — we're done for.* Only by a whisker did he catch himself against the advancing Judas, and they grappled together, tottering and unbalanced. *Too far, too far...* Tom disengaged his dagger arm, and it would have been the end of Judas, hadn't a cudgel crashed down, catching Tom's forearm. It was a glancing blow, but hard enough to numb all under the elbow, and the dagger flew to clang on the ground.

Shouting a curse, Tom managed to shove Judas away into Batty, and backed towards Bilqasim, point held high, bent in a half crouch as he clumsily groped for the dagger in the trampled snow. Just as his aching fingers closed around the thick Moorish hilt, a screech made him jump — and swing around just in time to receive another cudgel blow on the forte of the curved blade. It held well, but it felt strange and unbalanced, and the rapier was little use at such close quarters. All Tom could manage was a sawing cut that would have made his fencing master cringe, but still made the Boar jump away with a yelp.

Judas surged in his place, teeth bared and knife held high ... only to receive the heavy lantern right on the nose. Let it not be said that young Khalid didn't aim true: down went the rascal, howling in the sudden darkness, as the boy screeched again like a hunting owl — and it was little marvel that a window should slam open overhead, and then another, with shouts of *thieves*, and *murderers*, and *Watch*! There came more crying in Arabic, and enough candlelight flooded down from one open window to show a cloak-less Khalid struggling and kicking in the grasp of the Boar. And look at Bilqasim, rushing to the rescue without an inch of steel on him! Running past the fool, Tom sprang at the Boar and — as the man stumbled back, growling savage curses — flung his dagger arm around the boy's waist to swing him out of harm's way...

And for the second time that night, his jaw fell.

For what he had grasped was not a stripling boy's form, but the soft curves of a woman.

It was a heartbeat's time, as Tom gaped, cries rose all around, and torchlight limned Khalid's face, which wasn't boyish at all as he … as *she* scolded in shrill Arabic. How Tom could have ever thought this fine-boned shrew a lad, he didn't know; but if she was calling him an idiot, she was right — for the little street was alive now, and people in heavy coats and nightcaps had gathered around the mewling, recumbent Judas. The boars, it was worth noting, had disappeared, leaving their friend behind — but not Tom's fine dagger.

Nor, Tartarus take it, his purse! The front of Tom's doublet hung open — from when he and Judas had grappled, likely, and one of his purses was gone.

Jove fulminate all thieves! Tom hissed through his teeth, uncertain. Should he go back, and try to recover the money? Too many meddlers, too much calling for the Watch — the last thing they wanted! He thrust the woman into Bilqasim's arms. "Away with us," he ordered. "Don't run."

They slunk away, unremarked upon for a mercy, around the corner and into the next murky alley, stopping in the shade of a jetty to find their bearings… And Tom at once saw that, to his great annoyance, he could not. Gripping the arm of the one who was not Khalid, he drew her towards where a little light spilt from the aftermath of their brawl. She was wrapped in Bilqasim's borrowed cloak, who hovered close with knitted brows, and would have spoken if Tom hadn't done it first.

"Where?" he asked.

"My lady has no English," said Bilqasim, "nor Spanish."

"Doesn't she?" Tom couldn't help the bitterness. "There's little that would surprise me, at this point."

If Bilqasim cringed, the woman made no such sign of unease, much less of contrition. When the question was translated for her, she peered around, nose scrunched up like a vixen scenting the air. Then she pointed with a single word that could only mean, *There*.

"Let's hope your lady makes a better guide than she does a servant," Tom growled at the turciman and, having checked to make sure nobody was following, motioned for the woman to lead the way. So they went, quietly and as fast as they could without a light, past a sort of round porch first, then into the shadow of a church spire, then across a street, splashing across the runnel, and never mind the crossing boards. Part of Tom's mind was busy hoping they wouldn't stumble into a watchman as they were, lightless and disordered from the fight, with a woman in man's clothes — for it seemed to him now that Khalid's true nature must be plain to all who looked. But hope and reason were waning fast as, with each stride, anger swelled in their stead. A turciman pretending to be his master, a woman in boy's disguise, a servant who had been a thief and perhaps a spy, and a disgraced guard behaving like a robber at the play... If all Moors were like this, small blame to Roberts for wanting to have seen the last of their Barbary lands!

At least the woman did know the way: soon they reached the High Street, and there were the spotless door of the George, the sign with the painted saint skewering a dragon, and the glazed windows blazing. Tom had them enter by the stable yard's postern, where a sleepy young groom stood guard, though not so sleepy that he didn't gawp at the three scarecrows.

"You're covering yourself like a woman, *Señora*," Tom hissed.

The turciman translated, and she rearranged herself into the boy Khalid with a consummated player's art, just as the taproom door opened, spilling into the passage a stream of ruddy light — and who must stand there, with his hand on the latch, but Harker! The clerk blinked at the sight of them — and why shouldn't he? Oh, let him! Ignoring the man, Tom shepherded the two Moors past to their little secluded parlour.

Before the door the woman stopped in her tracks, hissing to Bilqasim — who, with the mad fire of the fight gone, shivered hard, and seemed more than a little lost.

He gripped Tom's arm. "Is Roberts there?" he asked unsteadily. "You must not tell him —"

"What — that you are a thief with all the rest? That your boy is no boy at all?" Very much out of charity, Tom yanked free. "You'll have to take what comes, for I want to know what else —"

"He doesn't know!" In the storm of his mind, the turciman stopped short — far too late, if anyone was lurking in the quiet passage, dim enough to conceal a whole host of eavesdroppers! Couldn't the dolt see? And look at the woman, clinging to Bilqasim's arm, black eyes blazing as though she were ready to murder the high-handed Englishman.

Without pausing to knock, Tom swung the door open and shoved both Moors into the parlour. It was deserted, thank the Fates, and lit by the ruddy glow from the remnants of the fire. As soon as the woman followed inside, Tom closed the door and at once came Bilqasim's urgent whisper: "*Señor* Ulsingam, my friend —"

"I think that Mr. Roberts found his bed early, *Monseñor*," Tom broke in ruthlessly, and went to stir the fire, so that he could read miens. "And now Your Excellency will have the goodness to confide in me."

"But —"

"But it is the best course, after all. The Barbary Company has its own interest in mind..." In one sudden movement, Tom threw the door open and leant out into the passage, checking this way and that.

Nothing. No darker shadows lurking, no hushed steps, no rustle of cloth.

Good.

Closing the door again, Tom leant his back against it and narrowed his eyes at the two Moors.

"Is there one — even just *one* of you who isn't lying?" he asked harshly. "And what the devil do you mean, that Roberts doesn't know? You'll have me believe he's had no part in —" he waved at the false boy — "in this, too?"

"He has not — and, if you hold a shred of pity in your heart, he must never know. This…" He held out a hand, and the woman slowly put her own in it, although her gaze never left Tom. "This is the Lady Khalida bint al-Muqaddam, daughter of captains, jewel of her house, the Rose of Fez —"

And this was when, with a sharp little sigh, the Lady Khalida herself took a step forward and pointed at herself.

"Khalida bint Yusuf," she said, chin held high and eyes steady, so sober and so queenly at once, that Tom found himself bowing low.

"*Señora*," he murmured, before he remembered that this queenly, sober lady was a liar, and he was as furious with her as he was with Bilqasim. And, because the turciman was the one he could berate and be understood, it was on him that he rounded. "Not that this even begins to explain this other disgraceful masquerade," he griped. It was half a lie, for there was no mistaking the light in Bilqasim's eyes when they fell on the woman. "Is it too much to hope that the lady is your wife?"

Of course it was: look how the man winced!

"She would be, I swear to you!" he cried. "She would be my wife a thousand times over if only I weren't a penniless *muwallad* poet, with nothing but a glib tongue to his name! But my lady's father is nobly born, if poor. A captain in the Sultan's army, like his father before him, and his father's father — all of them wise and pious and honourable, although none of them as honourable and pious and wise as my lady's father, Yusuf al-Muqaddam."

"Which," Tom pointed out, sour after three days of the man's high-sounding ways, "didn't keep you from taking his daughter from under his roof."

"Not his roof!" he cried. "Never, for Yusuf al-Muqaddam was always good to me. But, in his penury, he married his only daughter, the pearl of his heart and mine, to a fat, old dog of a merchant."

This startled a laugh out of Tom — a very mirthless one. "Ah, well — not her father's roof, her husband's. This makes it all right, then!"

"Don't mock, *Señor*," rebuked Bilqasim. "That dog beat her because she could not bear him a child. He used her as no better than a servant to his two other wives — when he wasn't…" He bit off the rest and turned away, teeth gritted and fists tight.

Oh, Lord… And see how the Lady Khalida touched his arm. She must have picked up some Spanish during this time? And even if she hadn't, she was no fool, that she shouldn't guess the gist of her lover's distraction. Now that he knew, Tom called himself all kinds of dolt for not seeing it before: not a boy, but a young woman, no older than twenty, fine-boned and clever-eyed, and slender. To think of a greasy old lewdster using her so roughly! Were Frances in such a plight…

Would I have the courage? "And then you had to leave." Tom's voice gentled of its own accord.

Bilqasim hung his head. "There are not many turcimans who have both Spanish and English, and when the Sultan's order came…" He looked up. "I wanted to refuse, even if they whipped me for it — until the princess of my heart saw what I did not: a way to leave Fez, a ship to bring us across the sea. It was a gift from God in his mercy!"

This, unless the Moors' God smiled upon adultery, Tom rather doubted. "And so you hid her in the Ambassador's retinue."

"Marzuq Raìs was seeking servants, and I told him of my cousin's son, who was a well brought-up, clever lad." A small smile. "Very clever — about this I did not lie, for my rose found a way to sell certain of her jewels, so we would have gold, once in this land of England."

A thought stirred in Tom's mind, like a piece of coloured glass. "So that's where Hakim's pilfered hoard came from!"

Bilqasim made to protest, and stopped when the Lady Khalida questioned him in impatient Arabic: those who wrote of Moorish women being veiled and silent creatures must have missed something. There was a brief, inscrutable exchange, which the woman ended with a sharp little gesture Tom-wards — some command that Bilqasim took with a sigh.

"My lady's purse was lost in the shipwreck, or stolen — we do not know," he said. "And it never held coins of Venice. The one Hakim had, we had never seen before."

Supposing it was true — but if it wasn't, why hadn't these two run before? Waiting to be lost in the London crowds, perhaps? "Still, you have it now, and it's a fat little hoard. Weren't all those gold ducats enough, that you should take such a foolish risk?"

And, of all things, Ahmad Bilqasim pouted. "If I had that purse, I would have never gambled. Our faith forbids gambling on chance. It is a sin." He stole a glance at the Lady Khalida. "My rose did not want me to, but what was I to do? When Hakim died, *Señor* Roberts took away the purse the moment you turned your back."

And these two! Gambling was a sin, and still Bilqasim knew his cards well enough to cheat; and his mistress disapproved of cards, but had no compunctions when it came to adultery, scandal or lying. As for Roberts… "Well, he wasn't wrong, was he? God knows where you would be by now, had you had the purse. The marvel is he left the medallion where you could find it!"

But no — of course he hadn't. See how the turciman squirmed… Impostor, gambler, cheat, abductor of (willing) wives, liar — and thief! *And* meant to meet the Queen in a few days — oh Lord! Tom firmly quenched a laugh. "Any other secret that you're keeping, Bilqasim?" he inquired instead. "You may as well tell me."

The man's reproachful look almost made him regret the flippancy, and he waited while the lovers consulted with each other in hasty and mysterious Arabic.

"If you're of a mind to murder me and run," he warned, "let me tell you: it's a most witless notion."

Also, it must have been a notion that amused Moroccan minds, for Bilqasim chuckled bitterly before translating it for the Lady Khalida, and she huffed.

Still, the turciman sobered at once to the most earnest sadness. "*Señor* Ulsingam, understand this: we can never go back to Fez. It would be the death of us." He took his mistress's hand. "My rose they would stone in the streets — my rose who trusted you and came to fetch you so that you could save my life, at the cost of the lie that protected her! If a spark of mercy burns in your heart…"

Ay, what then? What did they expect, standing there, holding hands, watching him so hopefully? That he'd throw to the wolves his master's trust, and the good of England? *You must think that, having been a fool twice, I can well be a fool again.* But Tom swallowed the retort. What cause had he to be angry? "You're right," he said — and could have laughed when two pairs of eyes narrowed at once. "And you're also wrong. It may be death for you both back in Fez — but it's death here, too, if I denounce your imposture."

It was a good thing that Tom had kept hold of Bilqasim's curved poniard, because what must the man do, but reach for the hilt he wasn't wearing? He stopped at a sharp syllable from the Lady Khalida, frozen with his hand in mid-air and rather wild-eyed. "You would not! What of Roberts? Why, you yourself —"

"Whatever happens to Roberts, he'll have brought it on himself by trying to pass you off as Marzuq Raìs. As for myself, I only just found out. How would I be to blame, if I denounce you all the moment we enter London? Or long before that, if you ever try to run. And then, think: a hue and cry all over the kingdom, the Queen's men chasing you — two Moors alone and penniless. You've seen it: England is not kind to foreigners. But…" Tom held up a hand as the turciman's face twisted, half in anguish, half in rage. "But it may still be that my master has some use for you, so listen well: keep up the pretence, meet Mr. Secretary, and do what he says. After that, I'll do everything I can to ensure that you have freedom and the means to enjoy it. You have my word." He spoke for both. "Tell your lady, Bilqasim. I'm sure she'll see the wisdom of agreeing."

The turciman held Tom's gaze as he translated — and soon Khalida joined him in his scrutiny. There was a spell of silence when Bilqasim was done, broken only by the clicking of the low fire, and the strains of a drunken song from somewhere in the inn. Then came the woman's whisper, and Bilqasim's shoulders rose and fell.

"My lady says, God send she was not wrong in trusting you. But you must not tell Roberts of this night's doings. He does not trust me; he never did."

Not that Tom saw what difference it would make at this point. "Small blame to him, I'd say. It's also a good thing that he has Hakim's purse, for he'll have to pay for what I can't, now that you've had me fleeced and robbed! Oh — and there's the matter of returning the medallion."

And see if Bilqasim didn't hold out his palm. "I'll put it back where it was," he said — and one would believe him the most honest fellow on both sides of the sea!

"Lord, but you are shameless!" Tom laughed, earning a rueful smile. "I think I'll find a way."

CHAPTER 10

There were, after all, several ways Tom had to find — first of all to talk Roberts out of some six or seven pounds, which he thought would make for a sleepless night. It didn't, because he was too tired from the day's riding and the evening's brawl, but nonetheless he awoke stiff, and full of bruises and aches — and with only one notion in mind that would explain not only his suddenly reduced means, but also the lost dagger and the bruises on his arm and jaw. It was a poor one, and rather awkward, but how else was he to persuade Roberts without telling more than he was minded to? So at dawn, after making sure that the Moors were busy at their prayers, he went to find Roberts and told him he'd been robbed.

"Most of the money I had on me," he grimly said. "They set at me when I went out. Two of them, I think." He would have liked to say four, or at least three, but he'd be showing worse than a few bruises after a bout of one to four.

Or perhaps he shouldn't have worried, because Roberts, sitting in bed only half-awake, gawped and scratched at his unshaved chin. "You went out?" he repeated.

"You remember when I left last evening?"

"You said there was nothing to worry about..."

"Well, I was wrong. I'd glimpsed someone through the window, a man in the street — watching the inn."

All sleep clearing at once from his face, Roberts sat up straight to ask, "And you went out *alone*?"

"Alone, yes!" Tom didn't have to feign his irritation, for who likes to admit such a mistake? The rawest boy would have known better. "Whoever it was fled, and like a fool I followed into an alley. They threw a cloak over my head, and cudgelled me as I struggled to draw my dagger..." He rubbed unfeignedly at arm and wrist. "Then someone opened a window and shouted, and the rogues ran — with one of my purses."

"Thank God you weren't hurt worse!" Roberts exclaimed. "What did the Watch have to say?"

"Ha — the Watch!" Tom snorted, sure that, watches being what they were all over the kingdom, he could wave the matter away in favour of the true aim of his Canterbury tale. "The trouble is, though, that I'm left empty-handed, for they filched most of my travelling money and all of my own. I don't have half enough left to see us to London."

"Sweet Jesu, that's trouble for sure!" Roberts grumbled. "Can't you..." He waved vaguely at Tom. "What of those papers of yours? Can't you get horses with them?"

Did the man think Tom wouldn't have thought of it, if it were so simple? But then, he'd just admitted to walking alone into the arms of armed robbers... "For myself, yes, and perhaps another — but a dozen beasts? And then there are lodgings, and meals, and tolls, and everything... You'll have to help me out, Roberts. We'll keep note, and you'll be refunded to the last farthing —"

And that was all he managed, for Roberts broke in with a harrumph. "But Lord keep you, lad, who d'you think paid for the passage from Ireland, and all the rest, all the way from St. Ives? I'm owed a pretty penny already, be it from the Company, or your Mr. Secretary, or the Queen herself, I neither know nor care — and I'll call myself lucky if I ever see the half of it!"

Purblind, thick-headed, tub-minded fellow! *Unus ... duo ... tres...* "But I'm telling you: Mr. Secretary will see to it that you're paid — provided we reach London, and we won't unless you put in a few pounds —"

"Capt'n?" Dunne's voice called as the door opened, and the soldier stepped inside with a basin of steaming water, and the scowl of one who found his master being harrowed.

Roberts irritably waved his man inside. "Come in, Dunne — and close that door. It's just that Mr. Walsingham was set upon last night."

With a low whistle, Dunne entered and kicked the door shut behind him. "'Sblood, Master. Here at the inn?" he asked, looking around as though he expected the thieves to be still lurking in a corner. "I'd ask that Farras, if I were you. Damn Moor, always slinking about, watching with that devil's eye... Why, even last night I caught him padding up the stairs like a cat, two steps at a time in the dark —"

"Well, then he wasn't out in the streets, assaulting passersby, was he?" And, having silenced his man, Roberts spread his hands in dejected appeal. "I'm not saying you're wrong, lad — but truth is, if I've five shillings left, it's all I can call mine. I swear, if we hadn't met you when we did..." A shake of the head.

Which led straight where Tom had been aiming from the start. "Well then, it will have to be Hakim's purse. Does Bilqasim still have it?"

Perhaps, in seizing Hakim's hoard, Roberts had set his heart on it: see how his jowls fell as he asked, "The purse?"

"I've about three pounds left; add Hakim's purse, and we should make it to London..." A thought occurred to Tom that made him chuckle. "Why, if it's Spanish gold, what a fine irony to employ it for the confusion of Spain's plans!"

But it was plain that Roberts didn't care a straw for irony. In fact, as he pushed away the covers, he stared at Tom as he would at a bedlamite. "Didn't you listen, lad? I'm sure I told you: my box was smashed at the ford the other day, false bottom and all — and most of what was in it, the Tarrant swallowed."

Yes, he'd said so — now Tom recalled. Only, he hadn't thought... "The purse, too?"

"The purse, the dagger with the silver hilt that the Sultan gave me, all of my papers... A good thing that you took the Rais's case." Roberts rose heavily from the bed. "Four years out in that cursed wilderness, and all I've left fits in two saddlebags!" He stomped barefoot across the room where the two bags sat on a trunk.

For a moment Tom thought he'd hold them up in demonstration — *witness, o Lord, the extent of my misfortunes* — but the man only cast one aside and rummaged in the other, until he extracted a fine ivory comb inlaid with silver. "Would you believe this is the finest thing I own now? The way things are going, I'd better have it sewn into my clothes, like the medallion — eh, Tolly?"

Oh, yes — the medallion. Because there was that, also, and just how was Tom going to put back the plaguey thing, if it was supposed to be sewn inside ... what? "You carry it sewn about you?" he asked in a lukewarm show of disbelief.

"The very last of the Sultan's gifts? Sink me if I let it out of my sight!" Throwing down the comb, Roberts went to recover his doublet, where Dunne had spread it to dry last night, and patted the front. "Now there's no losing or filching it. Tolly's notion, I'll say — and if only he'd thought of it a bit sooner, I'd be richer a purse of —" He stopped short, scowling as he fingered the lining.

"What is it, Capt'n?" Dunne inquired, only to be briskly asked for his knife.

Because the lining had, who would believe it, a loose corner — and, when Roberts cut to enlarge the hole, something peeked out of the sliced seams — a piece of crumpled, frayed and water-stained green silk.

Clever enough to make it seem like an accident, were it discovered before the lovers could flee. Clever, yes — and, Tom would have wagered, the Lady Khalida's doing. He brushed a hand down his face to hide an urge to laugh.

See how he stared, poor Roberts, eyes large in the pasty visage. How he wailed, "I lost it!"

But Dunne took the doublet and observed it by the candle's light. "'Sblood, Capt'n!" Dunne exclaimed. "It's cut, not frayed. I think you're robbed, too!"

"Robbed!" Roberts looked up, flat jowls a-quiver — half incensed and half hopeful. "Then I didn't...?"

"The knaves who tussled with Mr. Walsingham!" Dunne turned to Tom. "The one you saw watching from outside, Master? Playing sentry for his burglar cronies, that's what he was doing."

Well, at least this made Tom's own supposed mishap a whit more plausible. It would also make it possible to sell the cursed medallion underhandedly — no matter how he'd chided Bilqasim — for how else was he to pay their way to London now?

It was a short-lived temptation.

More than Virtue, more than Roberts's crestfallen manner, it was the thought of Sir Francis, eager to salvage this ill-fated embassy, that sent Tom striding to the door to go down on one knee, making a pretence of observing the latch and bolt.

"Did you lock this last night, when you came downstairs?" he asked — all the while casting around. And there was a sideboard pushed against the wall, covered with an old tapestry: his back to the room, Tom took the medallion and slipped it under the falling tapestry, letting it just peek out. "Did they take aught else?" And, just to make sure, as he rose, he contrived to touch his boot to the jewel, making it tinkle. "Why, what's —"

He never went further, shoved aside as Roberts threw himself on his knees by the board, feeling beneath it.

"God's bones!" he hiccupped, emerging with the plaguey medallion.

"They dropped it when they ran, for Mr. Walsingham scared away their watchdog." Dunne decided, eyeing Tom with something akin to new respect. And, if it was unlikely that the burglars had gone to the trouble for one jewel, and then lost it, Roberts failed to notice in his relief. He sat on the bed, breathing on the medallion and burnishing it with his shirt's sleeve. It was a little while before it occurred him to ask, "But how shall you do for money, lad?"

How, indeed! There was only one way, and it had already sunk Tom's heart while those two were exclaiming over the recovered treasure.

"I'll be back in an hour," he said. "Sooner if I can. Be ready to go, by then, and see that no one hears of this — Rolston most of all..." But then, wasn't he all kinds of fool? "Oh, what does it matter! We were all robbed, weren't we? There's no great secret to keep."

And off he strode, heedless of Roberts's calls.

"A fine toy enough, I'll say..."

The squat, well-fed swordsmith handled Tom's rapier with the placid care of one assured in his craft — and only a little interested. "Thirty ounces or so, I'd reckon..." He turned the blade this way and that to make the maker's mark catch the light. "Never London-made, is it?"

"Italian," said Tom through gritted teeth. Oh, to have Skeres to deal with this! "And let me tell you at once: I paid ten pounds seven for it — and I'll have no haggling."

A guess in truth, for this was Frances's gift — and a foolish thing to say.

In any negotiation, Thomas, never show what it is that you truly want. Always ask for more than reason suggests, and then allow your opponent to draw you where you wish.

Let Sir Francis never know how his kinsman and pupil had given himself away from the very start to a tradesman in the provinces — and all for the love of the cousin he should not love!

The swordsmith, for his part, having grasped at once his visitor's ill humour, hummed and hawed a good deal.

"Ten seven, Master? Eh, that's when it had a dagger to go with it, I'd think. Let me call my son, Master. He has a good eye for these modern things."

He called hoarsely into the part of the shop that held the forge — a firelit cavern full of the ringing of hammers and the panting of bellows — and the son emerged, a stocky young Vulcan with the blackest beard and his sleeves rolled up. He wiped a forearm over his sweaty face and took the rapier from his father.

"Italian," the old man said, lifting one shoulder as if to say: *what will you have?* Vulcan pulled a face. To see them, one would think them surfeited with fine Italian rapiers! Did they even do rapier-and-dagger in this place — a middling cathedral town in the middle of nowhere? Hard to tell by the jumble of blades, long and short and most of them broad, that hung from the walls and lay arrayed on the counter.

"Now, goodman," Tom began, "I told your father —"

"Seven pounds," Vulcan blurted. "Eh, Father? Seven four, if you're large."

"Seven…!" The shameless cock lorel… Tom's own fault, for showing his haste, and his disfavour — but truly what was worse, selling Frances's rapier for a song, or haggling over it? Having no answer, and in spite of the money he needed, he held out a hand. "Very well, then," he said, as wintry as he knew how. "I'm sure even in a place like this I'll find some honest craftsman."

Which, in his mood, he much doubted — in Salisbury or in any other place they'd pass through — but look: Vulcan and his sire taken aback! They must have expected him to make a market.

The father was the first to give signs of yielding. "The gentleman says ten seven…"

"Ten seven — never!" Vulcan observed Tom askance. "That's seven ten that you mean, Father?"

Which would have been enough, in truth — and yet Tom held the man's eye.

"Seven twelve?" The old man was growing plaintive. "You want to see me ruined, Your Honour."

Vulcan leant over the counter to observe Tom's unarmed state. "Seven twelve, Master, and m'father will throw in an old sword — for you can't go about without some iron on you."

Seven pounds twelve shillings. Enough to see them all to London, Fates willing, and some sort of sword with it, and no more time squandered. His task against Frances's gift, Frances's gift against his task… "Make it a sword and a parrying dagger, and it will do."

Father and son seemed satisfied enough, after all — which likely meant they would have yielded more, if pushed — and the blades were the paltriest bits of iron that ever came out of a forge, unmatched and awkward, but they would do. Latching them onto his girdle, Tom stepped out into the cold street seven pounds the richer, telling himself that, if there was a woman on God's earth who could understand him selling away her gift, that was Sir Francis Walsingham's daughter.

No snow, for once and for a wonder, and money enough to travel... When he entered the George's stable yard and saw the clutch of men and saddled horses in a corner, Tom added a third blessing to his count: Roberts had all ready to ride.

Unless, that was, there was cause for alarm in the grim manner of Galvam, detaching himself from the group at a half run.

"They're all there," the youth announced as soon as he was within hearing. "His Excellency, guard, and boy."

Which Tom could see for himself. "And they've gone nowhere?" he asked. He would have liked to question Bilqasim before running out on his errand — but, the Moors being at their endless prayers, he'd set young Galvam to keep an eye on them.

Disappointed at having missed last night's doings, Galvam had jumped to the task with the greatest eagerness, and now was brimming with his tidings. "Nowhere at all, Master." He shook his head, curls bouncing. "They prayed in their room, and then broke their fast by themselves, and came out here. That Farras came and went with the bags and the box, but was never out of sight long enough for mischief." He leant close, dropping his voice. "You think they're up to something? Mr. Roberts was robbed too, last night, wasn't he? Perhaps they had something to do with it?"

Had they! If only this far too keen lad knew… "The Sultan's ambassador and his people? You're growing fanciful. Now, if we're ready…"

As Galvam went from eager to crestfallen, Tom mounted the horse he'd been given: a big-boned, white-faced bay with the looks and the amble of a draw-horse — yet another irritation, as he led the way out into Salisbury's busy High Street.

The road wound its way around the foot of a cone-shaped mound their guide called Old Sarum, and it was a marvel how even the palest beam of sunlight turned the land friendlier. It made the frost glitter on fields and bare trees, and painted the snowy waves of chalk the most dazzling white under the pale sky. The cloudless night had hardened the snow, making it easier for the horses, if a little slippery at times, and even the chill wind tearing at cloaks and hood as they climbed up the next large hill didn't much mar the easiest — and the fastest — going they'd had in days.

Riding at the train's head with Dunne and the guide, Tom found that he enjoyed the view, and the clear air that scoured his lungs clean with each breath. By the time they stopped halfway up the chalky slopes of Haradon Hill, his humour was as restored as it could be, all things considered.

"There it is, Master." The guide pointed to the place where a solitary pile of stones stood half buried in the snow. "That's the crossroads, see? And that-a-way's Andover. We've gone as high as you need to, for today."

For once and for a wonder, the descent proved gentler than the ascent had been. Why, it all went so well that it was little past noon by the time they reached Andover, and the day was still so light that Tom dared to hope: could it be that, even with the prayers in between, they'd still make the six more miles to Whitchurch?

He was discussing this with the guide in the stables when he caught sight of Bilqasim and his pretend pageboy. Oh, he'd had those two very much on his mind since last night — and, interrupting the guide in the middle of a long-winded explanation, he made haste to join them.

"*Señor* Ulsingam," the turciman greeted — smile pinched at the corners. "*Señor* Roberts went to find a room for our prayers."

"Good of him." Tom lowered his voice. "Did he tell you that he was almost robbed last night, but found the medallion again? Hakim's purse, on the other hand, was lost back at the ford."

Bilqasim tossed his head with impatience. "Do you not think that, if I had that money, we would have gone long since? I give you my word..." Bilqasim stopped short when Tom huffed in disbelief.

"You give me your word, and in the same breath tell me you'd have fled but for lack of money? You make it hard work to believe you, Excellency."

Such a bitter curl of the lips from the man, and such a scowl from the Lady Khalida — now all boy again... Fates send that the whole exchange had looked like strained courtesies in Spanish.

As the two Moors stalked away, there was a gasp from behind Tom's back — and there stood Lucas Galvam, a saddlebag slung over his arm, gaping like a startled hare. Not at the Moors, though: whatever made young Galvam look away in haste, it was in the stalls, where most of the others were busying themselves with horses and baggage. Rolston was there, and Tolly Dunne rolling his shoulders, and Farras al-

Awar, and Harker, shaking his green-hooded cape. For a heartbeat, they all froze in place in the sunlight that streamed through the wide-open doors — and then, ducking his head between his shoulders, Galvam all but ran out to the yard like one pursued by the Furies.

"So, what is it now?" Tom fumed, having caught up with the boy under the timbered archway. "Were you thinking to run away?" He rubbed at his arms under the coat. It was bitter out in the yard, and a nipping wind was picking up.

Perhaps it was not the cold, though, that made Galvam tremble like a leaf as he stood stiff and wide-legged, arms tight around the bag and his gaze averted.

"What is it?" Tom insisted.

All he earned was a shake of the head and a reply of: "Nothing."

"A pretty nothing, to make you run like a startled coney!"

The blush was expected, and the set mouth, too. "It's just … I saw…" Whatever else he was, Galvam was no quick liar. His jaw worked as he cast about for a fib and found none.

"We know what Rolston is, so I'll rule him out. Was it something Dunne did? Or the Moors? Al-Awar?" Perhaps the guard had betrayed an understanding of English? It would be no great marvel at this point. "Was it Harker?"

And there it was — the smallest of jolts.

Harker, then — the hapless clerk… "What has he done?"

"Nothing!" the boy exclaimed, a tad too earnestly.

Oh, Lord give patience! "What has he said, then? Play no games with me, Galvam!"

It was the wrong thing to say — or perhaps not: when the youth recoiled, it was not just in anger. "Games!" he spat.

"Games, yes." Tom gripped a sturdy shoulder. "Only, I don't know yet how childish — or how dangerous."

With a strangled laugh, Galvam jerked free. An unease at lying? A prickling conscience? Great weaknesses, if Lopes meant him for more than a scrivener — easily taken advantage of.

"Dr. Lopes put you under my orders. What will he say if you keep what you know from me?" Check! See how the boy squirmed... "Unless, of course, it's something your master wants to keep from mine, and then —"

"No!"

"Tell me, you goose-cap! I expect foes to keep secrets, not friends."

It was almost too easy. Young Galvam stamped a foot, child that he was, angry tears welling. "Dr. Rodrigo is loyal to Mr. Secretary, you know that!"

"Do I? Then you'd better show loyalty to me, Lucas. What's with Harker?"

And checkmate! For the shortest while the boy stood stiff, teeth worrying at his underlip, and then looked away. "His name's not Harker," he murmured, so softly that Tom had to bend to hear. "He's *Senhor* Manuel d'Andrada. He's the King's man!"

And yet another liar, was Tom's first, rather inane thought — and the first question that came to his lips was hardly better: "The King?"

"King Antonio!" Galvam huffed in his impatience. "*Senhor* d'Andrada is his man."

And why he should be astonished, Tom truly didn't know. It was very much like Dom Antonio, a distrustful intriguer if ever there was one, king mostly in his own head, and in the hopes of a handful of Portuguese exiles — one of them, Manuel d'Andrada. Tom had heard the name before, though he'd never met the man. This boy, in Lopes's household, certainly had — and yet...

"Are you sure?" Tom asked. "It took you a full day to know him."

It all came out in a torrent: "I hadn't seen him well before, not in daylight. Always with that hood down to his chin, and what with the beard, and the bruises ... but now I've had a good look, Master. I'm not mistaken: it's Manuel d'Andrada!"

The hood, yes, and the hoarse rasping to disguise an accent, and that manner of keeping out of the way — eager to follow, loath to be left behind, but not for the reason he claimed. "And yet you wouldn't tell me."

It was like watching one lost in a maze, seeking his way out word by slow word, gaining speed as he thought he'd found it. "Back at Richmond, Dr. Rodrigo said that you should sound the Moors about the King, and then here was the King's man..." Galvam ground to a halt, colouring at having given himself away.

"Sharp-eared, are you?" Tom couldn't help the sourness. "Then you also heard we didn't want the King to have truck with the Moors — yet. Didn't you think that I should know it may well have already happened?"

Under Tom's narrowed gaze, young Galvam's face crumpled. "I didn't know..." he blurted out. "I didn't want..." He took a sharp breath. "And now I've given it away! Now he knows he's discovered. If he saw me startle..." Had he let a Spanish *tercio* inside the walls of London, he couldn't have looked more guilty — but, truly, what had he thought?

"We all saw you startle, Lucas, and half the inn-folk. It couldn't have been plainer. Besides, if you know him, it's as likely as not he'll know you."

This the boy waved away, lips twisting. "Know a scrivener — ha!"

"Well, he can't have missed that you saw him — but that's not a bad thing of necessity. If he knows himself discovered, there's little that he can do." The matter being, of course, what he'd done before. Here was another who must never learn that Marzuq Raìs was not Marzuq Raìs — supposing he hadn't already. Precautions had been taken to that end, but a Portuguese agent must have Spanish, and could well see through what might have deceived a plain English clerk. "What do you know of him?"

The lad knew a good deal about Manuel d'Andrada. A Portuguese nobleman of very old blood, he'd tied his fate to that of Dom Antonio and been loyal ever since. He was brave. He was devoted. He was honourable. He'd hazarded his life again and again. He'd sheltered the King's sons and almost snatched his daughter from the claws of Spain. He'd paid dearly for all this, with his blood and his estates. "They say the Spanish offered him a pardon, and he refused it to follow his king in exile," was the grim conclusion. "Poor as a church mouse, and always loyal."

It was the sort of story that should have inflamed such a boy's heart with passion. It would have inflamed Tom's at sixteen — and he hadn't been half as fervent. And yet...

"If he's such a knight of old, Lucas, why don't your eyes shine in the telling of his deeds?"

There seemed to be very little that didn't bring a tide of blood to Galvam's cheeks. He shrugged. "These are only things they say." He clutched the saddlebag to his chest. "But if he's so faithful to the King, and if Dr. Rodrigo is faithful to Mr. Secretary, why does *Senhor* d'Andrada work for Dr. Rodrigo sometimes?"

Because in this way, most likely, Dom Antonio had learnt of the Moroccan ambassador, and of Tom going to meet him. A slip on Lopes's part that Sir Francis wasn't going to like — bad enough if the Ambassador had been the Ambassador. As things stood...

"Master..." Young Galvam shifted his weight from foot to foot. "You never think that Dr. Rodrigo told the King, do you?"

Did he? No, Tom decided. Not willingly, at least — but this he wasn't going to share with the boy. "No - nor that he told Lord Essex," he said instead. "What will you have, with so many people knowing? The whole Council, the Barbary Company... I'd say it was just a matter of time."

The youth didn't seem soothed. "And now?" he asked.

"Now..." Tom watched the vapour of his sigh disperse in the icy air and clapped Galvam's tense shoulder. "Do you play chess, Lucas? You've just checkmated your first spy."

This earned yet another blush and a small, uncertain smile. Such a child — but that didn't make him trustworthy, or even honest: the fact remained that he had recognised Andrada and tried to keep it to himself.

In spite of everything, it was still early enough, once the prayers were done and the fresh horses ready, that Tom decreed they should go on. There was some grumbling from Roberts — dropped the moment Tom told him just who Harker was — and more from Rolston, who had much to say about the rising wind, the cold, the chance of more snow...

And, it had to be said, the weather didn't prove Rolston wrong. The wind had been a chilly annoyance in Andover; as they ascended the gentle white slopes of the downs, it grew in bitterness and in strength, whipping the snow in clouds that glittered around the horses' legs, higher and higher. But the road was good, and the first miles easy enough, until they gained a descending slope, and Dunne called back that there was ice on the road. Then all dismounted to lead the horses, and Tom contrived to walk abreast with Dom Antonio's spy — much as they had the day before on their way to Salisbury, before nearly falling down a chalkpit. The difference was, of course, that now Tom knew who Harker truly was.

"Is your cough better today, *Senhor* d'Andrada?" he asked softly.

There was the faintest exhalation, and the man pushed back his hood. He had a mellow smile, this Portuguese spy, and an even mellower voice, now that he wasn't feigning a rasp, half-singing with the lilt of his own tongue — if a little short in the wind.

"I was waiting for you to ask," he murmured. "That lad of yours wasn't subtle. How does he know me?"

And, in spite of that warm smile, Tom found himself unwilling to give Galvam away. "He saw you once with King Antonio…"

This was like playing chess — not Galvam startling for all to see. It was Andrada's thinned mouth, and the calculating eyes.

"You will understand that His Grace is nervous of this diplomatic mission. With his own son all but a hostage in Fez, with things never advancing… But you know all that: can you truly blame His Grace for wishing to know how things stand?"

"No. I can blame you for all the mummery, though. Joining the Ambassador's party under a pretence!"

"Ah, Mr. Valsingam: had your master been a little more forthcoming with the King, I would have gladly spared myself this … mummery." Andrada tugged his collar closer, shuddering in the rising wind. "I went to much trouble to find your ambassador, and more trouble came to me when my horse threw me." He touched the fading bruises on his cheek. "By the time I found His Excellency, I truly was horseless, penniless, and half-frozen. The robbers were a pretence, but the *resfriado*… How do you say? The coldment was not."

That much was plain from the flushed cheeks and the trembling — and Tom had fallen for it. Or not quite, for all the time he'd known not to trust this mouselike stranger, and yet had let him continue with them because he *was* injured and ill. Then again, he'd expected the Spanish to spy on them, not one who should have been an ally.

"This will hardly make Mr. Secretary trust your master, you know," he groused.

"Will you believe that I meant to tell you?" Andrada studied Tom a little, and what he saw made him smile. "Oh, but it's true! It was on my mind, and then that Rolston arrived. Two men of Mr. Secretary Valsingam — and there was no love lost between you, and still less trust. It set me wondering: you bear Mr. Secretary's name, but the other was sent after you… I didn't know what to think — and, when I don't know, I keep things to myself." He gave a rueful tilt of his head. "Not well enough, though."

All of it very plausible, for Dom Antonio wasn't always kept abreast of things – so it was fair enough that he — and his man — should be none too trusting in return. Of course, there was the matter of Rolston. Could it be hoped that Andrada truly didn't know Rolston for Essex's man? And yet, if he didn't, could he be left to believe Rolston safe?

No, he could not, Tom decided — nor could he be allowed to talk freely to Bilqasim. "I'd keep things to myself a little longer, if I were you. With the Ambassador, because neither he nor his Sultan will like this ploy of yours — and with Rolston."

"Rolston?" The sudden frown made the man look like Harker again. "I thought him one of your men."

"Yes, well — the matter is…" Lord — but to confide in this man! "Anthony Rolston only pretends to be Mr. Secretary's man. He used to be, but now he works for the Earl of Essex."

Andrada raised both brows. "*Entendo —*"

"No, you don't understand at all." Tom broke in in a harsh whisper. "In your place, I'd consider well how young and unexperienced the earl is. He's also ambitious, true — but if the Queen had wanted him to meddle with matters of the State, she would have made him a Privy Councillor. She won't thank your master if he tries to draw the earl into what she wants to be no concern of his. Nor will it help your master's cause if Lord Essex thinks there's mistrust between him and the Council."

It seemed to Tom that he did little but explain this again and again to one and to the other.

For a while Andrada just walked in silence, nodding to himself, like one lost in thought — and how Tom had taken that haughty countenance for that of a common clerk, he didn't know. "*Entendo,*" he repeated at length. "I must tell my master of the earl's interest in this matter. Together with it, though, I'll tell what you just said: I'm sure my master knows where his best interest lies." He seemed amused, of all things. "For now be sure, *Senhor* Valsingam: as far as this Rolston is concerned, I remain poor, sick, penniless Harker — who has been pestering you, yet again, not to leave him behind." And with this he bowed again — the hapless clerk's listing, hunching bow.

A clever fellow, and no mistake. How far he should be trusted was another matter. Should he be warned against the Spanish spy? The spy who might have died at sea, in Ireland, or

178

in Bridport, or perhaps was still travelling with the party. And yet... Young Galvam's grim recounting of Andrada's many perfections echoed in Tom's mind. If he was an agent worth his salt, surely the man must have his own suspicions of Spanish ears, and yet he hadn't even hinted at anything of the sort. Neither had Tom, to be sure — but...

Trust must be earned, Thomas, or, at least, bartered. No more of it than is needed, and on the fairest conditions for both parts — which is not to say fair at all. At the moment Tom had little to barter with Manuel d'Andrada, and much to keep from him when it came to the Ambassador — until Sir Francis decided what Dom Antonio must know of Roberts's charade. Meanwhile Bilqasim must be warned, and the matter of the Spanish spy could wait.

When Dunne bellowed that they could all mount again, Tom curtly dismissed the false clerk, glad to climb back in the saddle. As he did, he caught a flutter of movement out of the corner of his eye — and there he was: Farras al-Awar, studiously holding the stirrup for his false master, his scarred face turned away. And yet, Tom could have sworn the guard had been watching him — again. Watching him as he spoke to Andrada, as likely as not. Well, then: the Moor had been watching one time too many.

CHAPTER 11

When Bilqasim said they were to stop for prayers, at first Tom wasn't half as displeased as he might have been, for this was a chance to corner the guard at last — if only there had been the least trace of a shelter on the windswept slopes.

"Can't it wait a little longer, *Monseñor*?" He motioned towards the white expanse, at the clouds of snow blown this way and that, enough by now to obscure sight. "Whitchurch won't be much farther."

There went that tightening that only two things brought to the turciman's jaw — his mistress and his prayers. "Not much farther is too far, my friend," he said, every inch Roberts's gentleman and captain, and he pointed to a tree stump at the road's side. "See how the shadow is longer than the stump itself? That means it's time for us to say *Asr*."

"And for us all to freeze to death while you do!" Tom retorted. "How does this go with your great virtue of charity?" For truly, hadn't they shown great respect and indulgence to these people's faith?

The Moor's mouth twitched at the corner. "In truth, our faith prescribes to give to the needy —"

"While freezing them to death is no great sin?"

Taken aback, Bilqasim gaped and then burst out laughing. "*Ya Allah*!" he exclaimed, eyes dancing. "There is little in our Holy Books about ice and snow — but you are not wrong. We'll do as we did the other day: we shall pray under the first roof we find."

Ah, well. There went that steely smile again, a sure sign that the Moor wouldn't concede more. What could one do, but hope that Whitchurch lay just over the next hillside?

It did not, but, for a small mercy, a farm did, a little distance off the road: a few enclosed fields surrounded a farmhouse, half-hidden by an unkempt coppice of hazel and ash, and one towering oak. There was some grumbling when Tom ordered the party there — most of all from Rolston.

"Can't you tell them to pray inside their heads?" he groused, drawing abreast with Tom. Even the big bay was struggling on the uneven ground and in the knee-high snowdrifts, and Rolston's bow-legged mare had it much worse — never mind the pack-ponies.

Then, being the first to round the coppice, Dunne halted in his tracks. "'Sblood, Capt'n!" he bellowed. "If it's a roof you want, we're out of luck!"

Because what the trees had concealed was that the house was a roofless ruin — its windows gaping empty, its doorway only closed by brambles, its soot-black beams and broken wattle sticking out from the crumbling daub.

"Burnt down some time ago," Roberts said — as though Tom might have missed the fact — just as Rolston threw back his head and let out a bitter laugh.

"What a fine shelter, Walsingham!" he drawled. "You'll be glad we didn't stay back in Andover…"

Jove rain on the blathering peacock, and on all the others, who stood around gaping, like so many innocents led astray. Hear Lucas Galvam even asking: were they staying here the night?

"We'll be in Whitchurch soon," Tom snapped, loud enough that all should hear. "We leave as soon as His Excellency is done with his devotions." And if he sounded impatient or irreverent, he didn't care a straw.

He nudged his horse ahead to what had been the farm's little court. What a desolate place! Of the house proper, with what had been perhaps an outer kitchen, there only remained scraps of blackened wall and wooden frames, where the roof's big beams had crushed everything in their fall. Perpendicular to the house, rows of charred stumps made a long square. It might have been a timbered barn once, reckoning by shape and size. Now in place of the walls grew blackthorns, with sloe berries still clinging to the branches. Hard by it, a roofless, sooty dovecote gaped skywards. Across the yard, though, a largish building stood still intact. It had walls of some whitish, wood-framed stone, with darker cornerstones and lintel, and a roof only sagging under the double weight of neglect and snow.

"There." Tom pointed. "That will do." *Do as shelter, stables and chapel at once*, he didn't say, just in case Moors didn't have chapels, and took offence at being offered one.

The place seemed sound enough, when they walked in — if dim and stinking of mould, soot, and long-gone cows. It had a small loft at one end, a floor of packed earth, and half a dozen stalls, some of them broken, a couple encumbered with old wheels and a half-burnt barrow. More wrecks lay around, piled at sixes and sevens under the loft; the sudden invasion sent a dozen rats scurrying for cover under it, and under the rotting straw heaped in the corners. In spite of it all, and of the cobwebs hanging everywhere like a funereal draping, the byre wasn't going to crumble down around their ears. While Dunne and young Galvam busied themselves at once with the horses, disagreeing on where the beasts should be put up, Bilqasim stood in the middle, where grey light slanted through the open door, looking around with disfavour.

Good Lord give patience, for Tom was all out of it! *Unus …
duo … tres…* It was not until *octo* that he trusted himself to
approach the Moor.

"Your Excellency said any roof would do — and this is a
roof."

But of course Bilqasim found cause to complain. "*Señor,* I
can hardly ask you all to keep silent while we pray, and much
less to wait outside in the snow." He held up a placating hand.
"No, do not mistake me: what I say is that we will pray in the
granero."

By the time Tom had recognised the Spanish word for a
barn, Bilqasim was striding out, with page and guard on his
heels — Tamburlaine himself in rags! Ignoring the others,
Tom gave chase across the yard.

"There is no barn left, *Monseñor,*" he called — and could have
told the doorjamb, for all the good it did. When the Moors
entered the ruins, he followed, and stumbled in a heap of
snow-covered rubble. He caught himself against a stump of
crumbling wall, just short of falling headlong across what
remained of a roughly square beam, half buried in frozen mud.
He was swearing with a passion when Bilqasim turned to smile
at him.

"Do not worry, my friend," he soothed. "If there is no roof,
it means it will not fall on our heads." And with that, he took
from a decorated pouch a flat, round object, large as his palm
and gleaming dully, and bent to pore over it — a compass!

Wild thoughts sprang up in Tom's mind — thoughts of
Spanish spies studying the lay of the land, of bloodthirsty *tercios*
scouring the countryside… Wild and idiotic — for what
Spanish spy would study the lay of the land right before Mr.
Secretary's own man? And perhaps the same thought came to
Bilqasim, for he held out the instrument for Tom to see.

"A *Qibla* compass," he said. "There is a very sacred place, far away in Arabia. We always pray facing that way, and a compass like this tells us where the Qibla is, wherever we find ourselves." And then he called to al-Awar, who bowed and went out.

With an apology for keeping His Excellency from his prayers, Tom followed. A part of his mind wondered at what it must be like to have a physical direction for faith and prayer, some place that a compass might mark — even as he scanned the yard for the guard. Where on earth could he have disappeared in such a short time? But no: there he was, crouching in the snow, half hidden behind the abandoned dovecote.

Farras al-Awar was gathering handfuls of unblemished snow in a small brass basin. So absorbed was he in this task, that at first he didn't notice Tom approaching on his blind side. When he did, he straightened, quick and wary, watching as Tom came to stand between him and the barn.

"I must go, *Sayyidi*," he said, showing Tom the snow-filled basin. "We wash with pure water before prayers, and the Raìs is waiting..." He stiffened when Tom crossed his arms instead of giving way.

"He can wait a tad longer, while you tell me why it is that you always watch me. Again and again I keep catching you at it. What is it that you're hoping to spy? Unless..." Tom took a step closer. "Unless it's something that you want to tell me?"

There was no other word for it: al-Awar squared himself. Shoulders, back — even the misshapen face rearranged itself into a stony mask. "I am no spy, *Sayyidi*. I am a soldier."

"Yes, a disgraced one — and I've only ever known disgraced men to seek one of two things: are you after redemption or revenge?" Not that it was quite true, in spite of being Sir

184

Francis's wisdom, for there were also those who, under the weight of disgrace, sought death. But this fellow had had all the time to seek death between Fez and Cornwall, and yet here he stood, looming tall and lifting his chin in that proud Moorish denial.

"Perhaps this is true of Christian infidels, *Sayyidi*. I remain al-Sultan al-Mansur's servant, and pray for the day my Lord will be again pleased with his soldier."

How very noble! "A soldier who does a good deal of watching, though."

"I have eyes, *Sayyidi*." A twitch rippled from his mouth up his scarred cheek. "Or one eye, at least. So I watch and see — as others had better do."

"What do you mean?"

For the first time the guard looked away, fingers tightening around the basin's rim. He shifted his weight, like one ready to bolt, and peered over his shoulder, towards the barn first, and then towards the byre, for all that the dovecote hid them from both.

"Farras al-Awar," Tom prodded, "heed me: what do you mean?"

The man fixed his gaze on Tom. "Men make mistakes, sometimes, and sometimes they are pushed to —"

And then there was the slam of a door thrown open, and young Galvam's voice shouting, "Mr. Walsingham — Master!"

"Here, Lucas!" Tom called, and al-Awar took it as leave to step away.

Head tilted, he held up his basin, where the snow was beginning to melt. "I must go, *Sayyidi*. It is late for *Asr* already." And he walked away, with shoulders straight and head bowed.

Frowning at the retreating figure and then at the dovecote, Tom tried to gauge each shadow's length — but the light had changed to a golden greyness, too dim to make shadows at all. How had they reckoned their prayers all this time without the sun? But that was an idle thought, as soon formed as chased away by others far more pressing — such as that, if the Moors didn't make it short, it would be a chore to get to Whitchurch before dusk...

And then Lucas Galvam came around the dovecote, with much stomping in the snow and panting.

"What is it?"

"What's to be done with the horses, Master?" The youth skidded to a halt, as breathless and red-cheeked as though he'd run half a mile. "They won't all fit inside the byre, no matter what Dunne says — and I said it's for you to decide. Are we staying long? For Mr. Roberts wants a fire..."

When Tom went to pinch the bridge of his nose, the glove's frozen leather was most unpleasant against his forehead. Curse the fire, the horses, and them all! Wasn't it enough that he should contend with roads, and Moors, and spies, and dangers, and all sorts of things? What did they take him for — a housewife?

"Fates willing, we won't stay long enough to need a fire!" Tom groused, and steered them both back towards the byre.

The inside of the byre was dark as soot after the glow outside, and thick with horse-sweat and smoke, because someone had tried to make a fire — with middling success. The one good thing was, it was also somewhat warmer — although this likely was more from the lack of wind and abundance of horses than from the sickly, hissing flame. Roberts stood by it, bent down to warm his hands. When he looked up, his ruddy countenance seemed to float amidst the wisps of smoke. He glowered at Tom with scant benevolence.

"Now, lad —" he began, and all but choked when Tom waved him silent to ask:

"Where's Rolston? And Harker?"

"Harker — ha! Sleeping in a stall, that's where he'll be... Says he has a fever." Roberts squinted around in the dimness. "And where your cursed Rolston is, I don't know. Tried for the loft, the ladder broke under him at the second rung, and then he disappeared. He's not to know, I take it?"

Ah, that now! Galvam wouldn't have tattled, and Andrada had promised, but... "Supposing he hasn't sniffed it out already, the less he knows, the better..." Tom stopped when the door opened again, squeaking on neglected hinges, and a blast of wind shoved in Dunne carrying a bucket. Close behind came Galvam, all but taking the door in the face as he ran in with an armful of wood. Both men made for the fire, revealing that Dunne's bucket was full of snow, and young Galvam's loot was made of wet branches and broken scraps of furniture.

"Fire and water, Master," the soldier said. "You never know. The rest of the horses are in a shelter behind this one."

When he crouched to blow bellows-like on the small flames, he raised a cloud of smoke and ash.

"Sink you, Tolly! You want to choke me?" Roberts waved to clear the air, upon which Dunne, rising and brushing straw bits off his breeches with his sooty hands, blamed Galvam for gathering damp wood — but, he informed his master, they ran no danger, the byre possessing a forking hole up above.

"Ay, so the cold will kill us if the smoke doesn't!" Roberts grumbled — and, as though spies and bad fires were all of a piece as ills went, he turned to Tom. "But I can't make myself conceive it. Are you sure that Harker...?"

This being a subject best discussed out of hearing, Tom steered them both away to the furthest stall, where the farmer had stacked a few charred old wheels.

"Are you truly sure?" insisted Roberts, as soon as they were ensconced in the grey gloom.

"He himself admits it."

"Ay — and he's never lied before!"

"Galvam recognised him as Manuel d'Andrada, whom I know for Dom Antonio's man."

"And this Galvam ... you trust him? Isn't he Portuguese, too? Dunne says he's a Papist..."

Not that anyone growing up in the Lopes household was likely to be much of a Papist — but this Tom wasn't going to point out. "He's no such thing. He was born and raised in England and has nothing to do with Dom Antonio."

Roberts harrumphed. "Curse King Antonio! Can we trust his fellow?"

"As you said, he's been so frank and open-hearted!" Tom regretted his testiness at once, for surely God had never meant Henry Roberts to deal with spies. "He says he won't make himself known to the Ambassador — but... Do you know what's in the Sultan's letter for Dom Antonio?"

"You have it, and all the others — all bound and sealed — but..." Roberts's small eyes glittered as he peered around and, with an air of great secrecy, breathed, "Bilqasim says his Sultan would like a Portuguese king in Portugal."

It was hard to be patient with this fellow. "Well, he would, wouldn't he? A Spanish Portugal is to no one's liking but Spain's own. Is that all Bilqasim has to say?"

"I don't know that he ever *read* the letters, but the Raìs used him as a secretary, too, and talked to him —"

"And quite what did he tell him about King Antonio, I'd like to know!"

Roberts sniffed — and whether he'd even thought to ask was neither clear nor of great matter now. "And so would your Andrada, I'll wager," he muttered.

"Indeed…" A new thought stirred inside Tom's head, a glass tile of a new colour. "Could *he* have bought Hakim? Bribed him to let him see the letters — and then the Moor took fright at what he'd done, and tried to run…"

A frown, a hum. "I saw no Portuguese coins in the purse. *Cruzados* are easy to tell apart, for they bear no saints. A cross on one side, a shield on the other — nothing like a ducat."

"But would you bribe people with *cruzados*, in Andrada's place? *Mark well, Englishmen: here a Portuguese did foul play!*"

And truly, truly Tom should learn to rein in his impatience, as his mother had preached often and at length, and to curb his sarcasm…

See how Roberts harrumphed, surely thinking unkind thoughts about Mr. Secretary's high-handed pup. "Well, then he bribed him with ducats, though why he'd do that, I don't know — nor what it matters, seeing as the Raìs's case is still sealed!"

"So it is, yes." Or so it seemed. Would Andrada have the skill — and the time — to deal with the seals? There was a man among Sir Francis's people, a master at opening seals and putting them back in place so perfectly that no one could tell: he'd know if someone had tampered with the Sultan's papers — and he'd open and reseal them at need. But this was still two days and many miles away, and only if no word got out that the Ambassador was not the Ambassador.

"You think that Bilqasim will make friends with the Portuguese?" asked Roberts, with the suddenly ill-used manner of one seeing his only chance of glory going up in smoke. "Better he doesn't know he has one of them right here!" And trust the fellow to only see his own interest in this disaster!

"What I think..." *What I think is that al-Mansur would like a king of Portugal beholden to Morocco more than England, and if he finds Dom Antonio well disposed...* But what was the use? Life must be easier to men like Henry Roberts, who only saw the surface of things — and the surface nearest to them, at that. "Mr. Roberts, once and for all: I don't know what will be done in the end — but, if your charade is to work, nobody else must know of it!"

And why must Roberts grow angry, he alone knew. He poked a hard finger at Tom's arm. "Ay, and to keep Bilqasim away from the Portuguese, we tell him: look, there goes one — don't talk to him?"

Which, put like that, sounded even reasonable, *prima facie* — especially when one didn't know of the turciman's private motives. "Or we tell him: look, the Portuguese are spying on you — there's no trusting them; they'll endanger —"

Then it happened all at once: the afternoon light flooded in with a gust of wind, as the door swung open, and Dunne's violent coughing signalled the entrance of Bilqasim and Khalida. Could it be hoped that they might leave now?

Dunne pointed to where Tom and his master could be found — and, having left Khalida to seek the fire's scant warmth, Bilqasim sauntered to join the two Englishmen.

"*Señores,*" he saluted, lowering his pointed hood — and then dropped his voice to a whisper. "You will forgive me if I ask: have I been charitable to a Spanish spy, after all?"

It was all Tom could do not to burst out laughing. At his side, Roberts blew out his cheeks and stomped away a few steps, before he circled back.

It was little wonder that these singular doings should perplex Bilqasim even more. "Because it seems to me," he said slowly, "that if I have, then this plan of yours is ruined." *And you need me no longer*, he didn't say.

"Isn't it strange that you should ask?" Tom tried, for no other reason than that he wanted to know.

Even in the dimness, there was no missing the creased brow and searching eyes as the turciman slowly answered, "Perhaps I am mistaken."

And what was that? *We'll talk when Roberts isn't about?* Or, *I'd better never trust any of you?* Or perhaps it was just plain confusion, even a touch of fear — but Roberts had already jumped to his own conclusion. See how he sprang forward to stand nose to nose with the Moor.

"Reckoning your chances with the Spanish, are you?" he hissed, grabbing the man's front. "Well, you corner-creeping fox-dog, that's no Spaniard — he's a Portuguese!"

"Roberts!" The one who'd wanted to keep secrets! When Tom dragged him off the Moor, Roberts shook free and threw up both hands.

"Oh, what's the use?" he grumbled, and stalked away again to kick at the wheels.

Devil pinch the fellow! Of course, heads turned their way — Khalida half-crouched by the fire and poised for a fight, and Dunne, who looked up from his bucket, while Andrada peered out of the darkness at the byre's far end, just as the door opened again and Rolston strode in, rubbing at his arms.

"Sweet Jesu — but it's cold!" he said, loud enough that everyone would hear him. "I, for one, am not riding on today."

Who'd ever thought the day would come when Tom would be grateful for anything that Rolston did or said? There was the low rumble of Dunne answering, and all went back to their business. At least, thank the Fates, Roberts's ire had been of the sort that chokes instead of shouting. Could it be hoped that the bystanders had seen the disagreement without catching its object? Tom wasn't much surprised to find Bilqasim gaping.

"A Portuguese," the Moor repeated.

Ah, well… "Sent by King Antonio — to spy on you."

The turciman shook his head like one dazed. "I have a notion that I should be incensed," he said. "Or is it that I am incensed in my innocence, while I should be much interested?"

This time Tom couldn't help the laugh, which brought a fuming Roberts back from his circuit.

"Ay, young fool, laugh!" the man griped. "What if this jackanapes has given himself away?"

Poor Bilqasim, beset with ever new perplexities! "I thought that the King of Portugal…" he started, and then stopped short.

Being used to imagining the workings of his mind as the movements of coloured glass tiles, Tom could almost see the same going on inside the Moor's head. Better to set him straight at once — or as straight as he was going to be set for now.

"King Antonio is England's fast friend," Tom said. "It's only a misguided wariness that had him send this man. Let's not make him even warier, shall we?"

And, if he thought that too much truth about himself would make King Antonio as wary of England as of Morocco, Bilqasim didn't say so. Instead, he considered, tapping a fingertip to his lips.

"I do not think that I betrayed myself. I have spoken very little to him. He…" A halt, a stutter — and Tom could have sworn what the man was thinking: *He saw us come back to the inn that night in Salisbury…* "He cannot have seen through me, I should say."

Had Roberts caught the hesitation? Perhaps not, for what he asked was: "What of your men, though?"

"They know what is at stake," said the Moor — and again he paused. Thinking of Salisbury again? Or perhaps of the slippery ways of Farras al-Awar? "And they have had little to do with him. Why, Farras himself told me to be wary of the man. Does he have Arabic?"

"Most likely not — but…" Tom hesitated, thinking of the catalogue of Andrada's perfections. Harker had been riding double with one of the Moors when Tom had met the party. Had it been Farras who spoke Spanish, or Hakim who did not? And the fact remained that not talking to someone wasn't the same as not giving oneself away. Would pointing this out be of any use?

It was a decision Tom never came to make — for the big doors flew open again, as though the snow-laden wind had blown them, and Galvam rushed in.

"Mr. Walsingham!" he cried, eyes raking the shadows.

Lord — what now? What else? Tom hastened to meet him, before the lad shouted whatever it was for all to hear. He was too late, of course — for, having come close enough to grasp Tom's sleeve, young Galvam cried, "The Moor … Farras — he's dead!"

A heartbeat of stunned silence, a hubbub of exclamations, and then they all spilled out in the yard, Tom at the head with Galvam leading the way to the ruined barn.

"How dead, Galvam? What were you doing outside?"

The lad was trembling with impatience, with cold, with horror — it was hard to tell. "Dead — dead! I was gathering wood, and I thought perhaps there was something in there — and..."

Stopping in what had been the doorway — so suddenly that Tom walked into him — he pointed.

It could have been a bundle of rags, but for the boots. Farras al-Awar lay curled on his side between the downed beam and the heap of rubble Tom had stumbled on.

"He was sitting up," Galvam said, pale to the lips. "Still praying, I thought. I was going away, but I caught my foot on a stone and nearly fell, and swore — and he never stirred. He sat there in the snow, so still..." A shudder. "I went to see. I touched his shoulder, and..."

But this journey was cursed! Picking his way across the uneven ground, Tom went down on one knee. The guard's face, marked by the scar, had stiffened into a livid mask. The dark band had slipped, revealing puckered clumps of flesh where the right eye had been. There was no mistaking that the man was dead — or was there? Drawing his cheap dagger, Tom put the blade against the parted lips — if only the way the body lay, the cursed cold, and the wind weren't making it so hard. No fog formed on the blade — but who could tell?

"The pulse..."

Looking up, Tom found Bilqasim bent with his hands braced on his knees. "Our physicians have a way to tell — by feeling the wrist, or the neck, I do not know..."

So said Ambrose Lopes, the son of the good doctor and Tom's friend — but how it was done, was another matter. Tom leant lower, the snow seeping through his breeches, and slipped off a glove. Though what he'd feel, with his fingers all but numb... The wrist first, because it was easier — and then, when he found nothing, he dug under the headscarf until he found yielding flesh.

"He's still warm…" he began, and then stopped. Wouldn't everything feel warm to his chilled fingers? As for a pulse… "I can't tell. I'm sorry."

But in truth, nothing in the guard spoke of life. Bilqasim knelt down and fussed with the cloth band, hitching it up to cover the mangled eye. Standing over him, the Lady Khalida stared, fingers to her lips.

If only they had some more light…

As if summoned by the thought, Dunne came to stand by Tom, hand cupped around a burning torch of sorts. Not that it helped very much: by the time Dunne bent to shine it on the body, the wind had buffeted it down to a smoking ember.

"Dead as a stone," Roberts pronounced.

"Killed by the cold, I'll swear!" This from Rolston — a prelude, no doubt, to some tirade of how he'd said so, and how they should have stayed back in Andover… Only, Bilqasim straightened sharply, mouth open to gainsay the English words he shouldn't understand.

What a good moment for the Moor to lose his head! Tom spoke before he could, as if translating into Spanish. "*Señor* Rolston thinks that your man froze to death, Excellency — and, I'm sure, he also thinks that it's my fault."

Now see how Bilqasim swallowed hard. When he spoke again, he was Marzuq Raìs — although a perturbed one. "But it has been such a short time, *Señor*," he protested. "Al-Awar was hale when we finished our prayers. He only stayed behind to dry the basin…" He stood, casting around for the basin. It lay in the mud, half a dozen steps away. The false page went to recover it, clutching it to her chest.

Bilqasim never took his gaze from her as he asked again, "Does your English winter kill a man in so short a time?"

Did it? It had been asked in disbelief — and Tom had no answer. He'd heard his share of tales, as a boy, of people getting lost in the snow and being found dead, come morning. But this hadn't happened overnight, and al-Awar hadn't been lost at all, only a few steps from a fire. Why would he sit in the snow instead? Unless he'd taken ill somehow. Was there a way to tell if a man had suffered an apoplexy? Oh, for Ambrose Lopes's vast and quiet knowledge!

The sight of Bilqasim murmuring with lowered head brought to mind the other death in Bridport. Back then it had been al-Awar to ask for... What had it been? Water, and a length of cloth. It would be harder to find a shroud this time — and harder still to bury the body.

"Shall we bring him inside, *Monseñor*?" Tom asked softly — and see how the turciman startled, shuddering and lost. Small blame to him, in truth, for England's land and waters were strewn with the bodies of the Ambassador's men.

CHAPTER 12

The choking little fire had never been much to begin with. Left untended, it had all but gone out by the time Galvam and Dunne brought the body inside the byre.

"Where do you want him, Master?" asked Dunne, subdued for once.

Ignoring Rolston, who griped that why it must be Walsingham's to decide he didn't know, Tom had the corpse carried to the last stall under the loft — as far as possible from the fire, and from the place where they'd all have to spend the night. Having revived Dunne's makeshift torch, the Lady Khalida lit the way.

And all the time Bilqasim's question ran round and round in Tom's mind: did winter kill a man so swiftly? It made him uneasy. It made him want to observe the corpse. It made him wish he knew just what to look for.

With the others gathered around the fire, Tom sought the turciman and found him preoccupied with the burial: the cloth, the urgency…

Had they not done the same three days earlier? This was like running inside a bad dream: no matter how hard one tried, the same kept happening again and again. Only, this time it was worse than it had been in Bridport.

"You must see that we've no shroud and no spade," Tom said. "I'm not trying to belittle your faith. It's just…" *It's just that this damned journey grows more disastrous with each hour, and I wish to God that you'd gone down with your ship before I ever saw you!* A most ungenerous thought, and all the worse because all the man did was give that slow, grave nod of his.

197

"Al-Awar's own cloak will do for a shroud. And we can carry the body to the next village on horseback, surely?"

"Yes — yes, surely." Tom wanted to close his eyes but didn't. Once in Whitchurch they'd have to wrangle with the locals for permission to bury a Moor, and lose another half day, at the very least. But then, it *was* his own fault. Rolston wasn't wrong, much though it galled him to own it: had they stayed in Andover, they'd have lost less time, in the end. A sudden pang of guilt bit at Tom. What sort of unchristian, hard-hearted thought was that? Had they stayed in Andover, Farras al-Awar would have been still alive. Or would he? Again the question reared its head: how long could he have sat there, freezing in the snow?

Full of misgivings, Tom followed the turciman to the last stall, where the Lady Khalida knelt by the corpse. Where Dunne had found two candle stumps was a minor mystery, but by their light the woman had begun the bleak work of undressing the dead guard, so that he lay naked to the waist.

Having moved to the headcloth, she looked up sharply when Tom stayed her hand.

"*Monseñor*, would you let me observe the body?" he asked of Bilqasim, and the turciman narrowed his eyes.

"What are you seeking?"

Proof that I haven't killed this man with my reckless haste... "I ask myself what you asked before: winter kills, yes — but so swiftly?"

When Bilqasim nodded and murmured to her in Arabic, the Lady Khalida sat back on her heels with a brisk gesture that could only mean, *Go ahead, if you must, since pageboys can't gainsay their masters.*

Tom lowered himself onto one knee, thinking hard. How did Ambrose Lopes conduct his observations? For one thing, not in half darkness.

"Do you have more of these, Dunne?" he asked, and the soldier went for his pack. For a wonder, he didn't seek permission from his master, who watched from some distance in the company of Andrada and Rolston. In a moment, Dunne was back with a piece of greased rush, and proceeded to light it from the remaining stump.

"Always keep some bit of candle in my pack," he said, the brief flare showing his scowl for a heartbeat. "But this is all I have left."

Now Fates send that the Lady Khalida didn't know how rushlights were made... A foolish hope, for there was no mistaking the greasy stench. Fates send, then, that it was mutton fat, and not bacon. Tom would certainly say so if asked. The rushlight spluttered and hissed, and it was plain that it wouldn't burn for long.

"Hold it aslant, will you?" Tom ordered. "And close."

The soldier sidled close and knelt, holding the rush between two shards of wood.

"What are you after, Master?" he rumbled.

Didn't Tom wish he knew! "I have a friend, a physician who says that death has its own ways of telling tales," he said, for lack of a better answer. Armed with one of the stumps, he shone it along the sprawled, half-naked body, feet to head. It hadn't grown stiff yet, but it soon would in this cold — not that it mattered, since they knew when al-Awar had died. The breeches were wet at the back, where the guard had sat in the snow, and on the side where the body had collapsed under Galvam's touch. Thick, whitish mud crusted the knees, though, and the front of the boots. Perhaps the man had fallen to his

199

knees in one place, and then had dragged himself to sit in another? *Or been dragged*, Tom's mind supplied of its own accord.

A pall of deep quiet had settled on the eight living and one dead in the byre.

When Tom and Galvam rolled the body onto its side, the flames showed scars and marks of all sorts on the back, ribcage and shoulders — witness to al-Awar's soldierly life: it might have lacked glory, but not incident. Dunne hissed when the light washed over a web of thin, white marks across the shoulders.

"Whip marks," he said. "In disgrace, indeed!"

That — or the traces of that long-ago conversion. "And these...?" Tom pointed at the fading bruises on the left shoulder and arm. "From the *Consent*? When the yardarm fell?" *And he failed to save Marzuq Raìs?*

Pursing his lips, Dunne raised a shoulder with all the unconcern in this world.

Poor Farras al-Awar, naked for all to see, exposed in death to unfriendly strangers who passed judgment on his life, with the marks of his last useless feat of valour faded away and unremarked ... and not a shred of pity to be glimpsed among them all! Conscience stinging again, Tom rolled the body back onto its side as gently as he could and motioned for Dunne to light the head.

Dark-lipped and slack, the face appeared wax-like in the flickering light, the colour of old parchment against the black headcloth, while the ugly scar stood out less starkly. The missing eye was covered again now that Bilqasim had tugged the band over it. No marvel that the guard had kept that mangled socket securely covered... Securely, yes: very much so. Tom fingered the band. It clung tightly to forehead and cheekbone, and Bilqasim had struggled to hitch it back into place. Strange how it had slipped…

The bits of glass in Tom's mind stirred as he looked up at the hovering turciman. "What was he doing still out there?" he asked.

"Cleaning the *Wudu* basin," was the answer. "That is for the ritual washing. Why?"

Instead of answering, Tom turned to Galvam. "How did you say that you found him?"

Brows drawn together, the lad lowered himself to the ground, leaning against the stall's partition, legs angled before him and head hanging forward. "Like this. I thought he was praying at first, but in truth, who would sit like this in the snow?"

No one in their right mind, no… "What if he'd fallen, though, and hit his head? There's all sorts of rubbish on the ground: I very nearly took a tumble myself." And how easy would it have been to crack his head on that half-burnt beam. For appearance's sake, Tom hastened to translate into Spanish. "A broken head would have killed him much faster than the cold." He turned his attention to the headcloth that the guard had always worn wound around his head. It seemed tight and tidy, but for the end that looped loosely around the neck and shoulders. That piece, too, had been wound snug against the raw air earlier, as both Bilqasim and Khalida still wore theirs. Had it come loose in the fall? But if it had, why not the rest? What sort of fall would loosen the scarf, and displace the band over the eye without disturbing the turban itself? At a word from Bilqasim, the Lady Khalida began to undo it, unwinding coil after coil, uncovering a bald scalp the colour of wet chalk, and, on the side above the blind eye, the mark of another scar. This, too, was old, but neater — the ghost of one single blow from the top of the head, down to a scrap of grist where the right ear had been.

"That is not from today," said Bilqasim, quite uselessly, just as the flame of Tom's stump sizzled and died. Dunne leant closer with his rush, and the small movement was enough to make the flame dip.

"Make haste, Master. Won't burn long," the soldier whispered.

Tom felt the skull. There were no wounds, no swellings, and no discolouration that he could see. The scalp was intact, and so was the bone under his fingers. He scooted to observe the other side, and it was just as intact.

"He never broke his neck, did he?"

Looking up, Tom found that Roberts had wandered by to watch — and was right. He should have thought of the neck himself!

"It would take a longer fall for that, I'd say…" All the same, he caught al-Awar's chin and rolled. The head turned smoothly enough; nothing felt broken, nothing ground like the broken bones in Hakim's neck, back in Bridport.

Was it selfish and unchristian to feel disappointment? Here was another confession for Frances to hear: this poor man was dead, and all Tom could think of was a way to assuage his own guilt!

And he'd found none, so far. What now? Tom hesitated, studying the corpse, trying to recall Lopes's ways: the eyes, the mouth, the teeth… Oh, but this was gruesome work! Hissing through his teeth, he lifted the left eyelid and studied the cloudy apple. What was he even seeking? Oh, for more light… And even before Tom's thought was quite formed, the Lady Khalida — who must be a reader of men's minds or a very sharp-witted woman — moved to his side, having somehow revived one of Dunne's candle stumps, and shone it steadily, making the guard's dead eye gleam. With a sharp breath, she murmured an incomprehensible word — but for once her meaning was plain: *look! Look at the white, the dark specks staining it, a thin streak below the iris...*

There! Tom would have wagered that in daylight the marks would show red.

"*Petechiae*," he murmured to himself. Another of Ambrose Lopes's ugly erudite terms. *A sign of suffocation, most often. Which can occur by strangulation* — but there were no marks of that on the bare throat and the neck — *or else by smothering.*

The headcloth lay in the matted straw like the spires of a dead snake. Tom snatched it up and rubbed it between his fingers. It was thick, and rough enough to scratch.

"Light, Dunne!" he commanded — and, also taking the stump from the false page, he leant low over al-Awar.

"What on earth are you doing?" This from Rolston, and then someone shushed the man.

Ignoring it all, Tom bent still lower, hissing when a drop of molten wax guttered on his fingers. But there — there it was... Could it be? He touched a careful fingertip to the dead face: the skin was a little scraped on the left side — under the eye, on the cheek right by the nose, on the nostril. Faint marks, slanting down to the corner of the mouth, too shallow, and too wide to have been scored by nails.

The glass bits moved again, clicked into place, made pictures in Tom's mind — that of a man crouching in the snow, another coming up behind him, unseen. Hadn't he himself walked unnoticed on the guard's blind side? And there was also the mangled ear... *Imagine now that man approaching al-Awar from behind, grabbing at this cloth enough to undo one end, pressing it over mouth and nose...*

And al-Awar, in life, always tilting his head when he listened... "You were half deaf too, weren't you?" Tom made as if to fling the cloth over the blue-lipped mouth — and that was when Ahmad Bilqasim sprang to his feet, stiff and narrow-eyed, with a sharp Arabic exclamation that made the Lady Khalida jump. She hissed something — a caution, perhaps — and rose to stand at her lover's side. They had forgotten Dunne, though, who clambered to his feet to confront the two across the dead body.

"What's that?" the soldier barked in Spanish, and then switched to English: "Capt'n, they speak of murder!"

Oh, Jove — was this where it all went to the devil? "Is it true, *Excelência?*" Tom cried in Spanish, sounding rash to his own ears. "You say that your man was slain?"

One thing to say for the turciman: even in his agitation, he was quick-witted. In a heartbeat he went from a trapped deer, backing away and glancing at the Englishmen, to haughty Marzuq Raìs — and, if his gaze remained wary, it was in Spanish that he spoke. "What I say is that *you* think he was."

Chaos broke out at that — Rolston demanding explanations, Roberts snorting in disgust, Dunne growling half in Arabic and half in Spanish, Galvam gaping and questioning... And all except Andrada — who stood back in wide-eyed silence, still playing the hapless Harker — were closing in on the two cornered Moors, a pack of copper-faced shadows in the fitful light.

And then, Sir, all went mad, and tore the Ambassador to pieces...

"Peace!" Tom roared, putting himself in front of Bilqasim. "You fools, what do you think you're doing?"

Not tearing the Ambassador to pieces, after all. The din subsided into shrugs and mutterings so swiftly that Tom felt a little ludicrous, standing there, square-shouldered and loud as

Tamburlaine himself, with Galvam loyally at his side. At least he hadn't even touched his hilt — and, if it came to small mercies, the others all looked just as abashed. Save for Rolston, who of course just had to grouse.

"A fine one you are, Walsingham, ordering us all about, and throwing accusations."

But this man was a penance! "I'm throwing nothing!" Tom snarled, and ruined it all by stopping short — struck by the fact that perhaps he should, if not throw accusations, at least mention his new suspicions ... but to these men of Essex and Dom Antonio's?

And as he hesitated (*be deliberate in speech and in action, Thomas — but never hesitate*) Bilqasim finished gathering his wits, and took things into his own hands by stepping forward to confront the bickering Englishmen.

"*Señores,*" he said, "what it is that you discuss before me in your own tongue, I will ask once we have reached the inn — but we would do better to leave now, while there is some light left."

Which, of course, only roused more tumult. Rolston's protestations were the loudest, but Roberts was no less displeased, with Dunne shaking his head and grumbling.

"It's far too late to leave, now," Tom tried to say. "It will be dark soon..."

Ignoring him amidst the continuing ruckus, Bilqasim joined the Lady Khalida, who had begun to gather their bags.

Lord, how Tom would have liked to shake some sense into the man — or at least to give him a piece of his mind. There being all around a byreful of Spanish-speaking watchers, though, there was nothing for it but to swallow one's fury and mind one's words.

"*Monseñor*," he ground out, striving for a tone of quiet reason, "this is no season to travel at night. There are still a few miles to Whitchurch, and —"

"There is a moon, and the sky is clear." The man snatched a bag from his pretend page. "There will be no difficulty."

"There will be danger a-plenty!"

"Not half as much as in staying a whole night in this forsaken hovel!" the turciman cried, eyes blazing. "And with a murderer among our numbers! You will do as you please — but *Billahi*, I will not rest unless it is at an inn, where other people are, and doors that can be bolted!" And with that he strode out into the yard, with the false page on his heels.

Oh, Jove — what now? Calling for Roberts, Tom followed them out, and around the byre to the half-covered shelter, where he found the two Moors saddling their horses in a rush.

"You promised!" was Bilqasim's welcome.

"Yes — when you promised to travel to London and wait for Mr. Secretary's decision. And now…" Tom lowered his voice. "And mind: I know what all this great show of fear is for!"

The man's eyed gleamed, round enough to show the whites — and he would have retorted, no doubt, but at that moment Roberts joined them — chin jutting and elbows large.

"What is it now?" he thundered — and, before he gave them all away, Tom informed him, in Spanish, of the Ambassador's whim.

"It's our Christian duty to talk His Excellency out of it," he concluded, with a warning glance at Roberts as the others descended on them, Rolston insisting that it was madness to leave now. For once, Tom agreed with the man — not that he was going to admit it — but, just to be safe, he ordered Galvam to saddle the bay.

"If you dissuade Marzuq Raìs, it will be more than I can manage," he told Rolston. Over his shoulder he saw Roberts and the Moor arguing, while the pageboy worked at the saddles, brisk and close-faced. "He's taken it into his head that he'll be murdered in his sleep, if he stays —"

And then there was a string of curses from Roberts, and the two Moors hastened out, each leading a horse by the bridle. Once out in the yard, they mounted and trotted away in the purple dusk.

God plague them both! Tom followed at a run. "You don't even know the way —" The wind snatched away the shout and flung icy powder into his mouth. Swearing, he ran back to the shelter, met by a spluttering Roberts.

"To put the body on the man's horse, he says, to follow…"

Tom pushed past, and Galvam, bless him, was there with the saddled horse and Tom's cloak, though not his hat.

"Follow, Lucas — quick!" Tom shouted. Throwing the cloak around his shoulders and leaping into the saddle almost in one motion, he tore off, bare-headed and gloveless, as fast as he dared after the two fugitives.

Bare as the trees were, the coppice had afforded some shelter. Out in the open the wind grew furious, cutting and tugging, and kicking up the snow in a haze that stung like ground glass and gleamed against the last rays of the setting sun. If nothing else, between one fierce gust and the next, Tom could make out the hedges that lined the road not so far ahead, and along it, two black shapes heading north-east. There was no use in shouting, nor in spurring the horse too hard, for the ground was uneven, and now that the sun had all but set, there was no discerning the ice that lay in treacherous sheets. The only good thing was that, if Tom could not go very fast, neither could his quarry.

Did horses swear at their riders? For all his snorting and tossing, the white-faced bay trudged valiantly enough, climbing at last through a gap in the hedge and over the road's shoulder. Not that the packed snow and the deep rut made for much better going, and yet see how the two fugitives sped up — the fools! It was no more than a small trot, and yet even that was dangerous in the failing light. Didn't they have bad roads, in Morocco?

There being nothing for it, Tom spurred on the bay, for ahead lay a denser murkiness that could only be a patch of trees, and he very much wished to catch up with the two Moors before they entered it. As though hearing his thoughts, they tried to speed up again.

"Cursed idiots!" Tom growled, not that it sounded like it, through his stiffened lips. Not only was he hatless and gloveless but, in his haste, he hadn't fastened his cloak, so the wind had no trouble finding its way inside the flapping folds. Al-Awar's dead visage appeared in Tom's mind. Surely winter would kill a good deal faster out in the wind? It was a great relief when the fugitives' idiocy was repaid before that of the pursuer — in the shape of one of the ghostly horses ahead swerving with enough violence to spill its rider into the snow. A great relief — and very short-lived, as Tom's thoughts tangled with each other: yet another Moor dead under his charge, Sir Francis's treaty gone to the devil — and, with a distant jolt, the discovery that he wanted neither Bilqasim nor the Lady Khalida to be dead. He reached the figure sprawling in a snowdrift at the road's edge, and found it stirring — Lord be thanked!

"Are you hurt?" he asked, bending down to offer a helping hand. All he had in return was a torrent of shrill, if breathless, gibbering as Khalida grabbed his arm and dragged herself to sit up.

The next moment, Bilqasim was there on his knees, shouldering Tom aside to snatch the woman to his chest. She sounded aggrieved, rather than hurt, as she squirmed free, brushing snow out of her collar — and, while it was hard to tell by now, Tom had the impression that she was glaring both at himself and her short-winded lover. The little shrew! Whatever she said made the turciman stand in haste and peer down the road, where the clop of horses could be heard plodding closer and closer.

Well, if these two ever made it to freedom, it would be thanks to the young lady's sharp wits.

"This was the maddest, the most reckless and witless thing... What were you thinking?" Tom hissed, before he straightened and hailed the approaching riders.

Galvam joined them first, and leant from the saddle, squinting in the wind, and shouting, "Are you well, Master?"

"Let's go back to the farm," Tom said. And then, because two other riders were joining them, he called, "Is that you, Mr. Roberts?"

Roberts, yes — and the taller figure at his side was Rolston. Not much of a surprise, perhaps, for Essex's man was loath to be left behind — but what of the rest?

"I left Dunne to follow with the packhorses," Roberts said — and lowered his voice to add, as though it were some secret thing not to be discussed aloud, "And ... the body."

Never mind the body: Andrada, too, was back in the byre... What a marvellous notion! What *had* been left behind? What papers, what evidence of what? At least Dunne was there too

— but truly, Tom would be glad to see London and the end of this! "There's no need for that," he said. "We go back: I think that His Excellency has learnt the perils of night-travel."

For all that Roberts seemed greatly relieved, trust Rolston to throw back his head for a mirthless laugh. "And what we'll eat for supper in that place, God knows!" he exclaimed. "And how we'll keep warm. Not to mention that, if you are right, one of us is a murderer…"

All of it truer than Tom cared to admit — but, for a mercy, Rolston didn't harp on again about how much better off they'd have been back in Andover.

It was in the grimmest silence that they all made ready to seek the farmhouse in the last of the dusk — and look at Bilqasim: bent low in the saddle, the turciman was reaching down to help up the supposed page…

So they could have another try at bolting? The gall of those two! Tom strode up just as the Lady Khalida stumbled back from an attempt to put her foot in the stirrup. She bit back a cry as she found herself caught from behind. Was she hurt then? But no, it had been surprise and anger, not pain.

"The boy can ride with me, Excellency," Tom said, glaring up at the turciman. *Try to gainsay me now!* "My horse is much stronger."

It would take a cat's sight to read miens in that gloom, but oh, how Bilqasim's shoulders slumped in defeat, and how the Lady Khalida's slender arm shook in Tom's grip!

And then Galvam, having appointed himself Tom's man in the Minotaur's absence, arrived, leading the bay. "Marry, but these Moors are a penance!" the lad grumbled, trading black looks with the one he thought a pageboy.

And you don't know the half of it! Tom all but tossed the woman up into the saddle and mounted behind her, an arm tight around her waist. A great impropriety, surely — but at the moment he didn't care a straw.

CHAPTER 13

They broke down one of the ruined stalls for firewood and scraped together what little hay had been left behind. Dunne tried for the loft, but the ladder was too ruined, and they had to make do with what could be found in the hayrack. It was a pittance, and mouldy with it — but still, once stabled in the wooden shelter behind the byre, the horses fared better than the men.

Dunne, with a soldier's eye for lean times, had done some scavenging at the inn — but he wasn't half as thorough as the absent Skeres. In the end they only had half a loaf of coarse bread to share among eight men.

Well, seven men and a woman in truth — but it could be hoped that no one knew that yet, beyond Tom, Bilqasim and the lady herself ... or could it? So it had seemed this morning; so it had seemed until they'd stopped in this cursed place — but now it was a good deal harder to be sure of anything. This had to be true for all: eight wary shadows slinking around the byre, eyeing each other, each reckoning, no doubt, whether more safety was to be found in light and numbers, or in some solitary corner. It was not long before the prevailing notion drew moth after anxious moth around the fire, where two of the emptier stalls, made into one by the lack of a rail, afforded room enough for a loose circle. The two Moors huddled together in a corner, a little away from the rest, while Roberts sat against the trough at the back, listening morosely to Rolston, who talked too loudly of miles, and hours, and London. Andrada, rolled up in his cloak, lay curled up across from them, as still and quiet as the corpse in the last stall.

Only Dunne was still moving about, gathering fuel, if the cracks of broken wood were anything to go by. As for Galvam...

The boy fidgeted by himself, close by the doors. It took a couple of false starts before he came to sit a few steps from Tom, with his arms around his knees and his brow creased.

"Is it true, Mr. Walsingham?" he asked. "The Moor... Was he killed?"

Was he truly? Tom thought back to his examination: there was no other answer, was there? "I very much fear that he was."

The boy's mouth twisted, nostrils flaring. "But that... But then..." He peered over one shoulder and then lowered his voice again, speaking so softly that Tom would not have caught the words, had he not known what they would be. "Then it was one of them..."

Earnest as daylight, and all of seventeen. See how he startled when Tom corrected him, just as softly: "One of *us*, yes."

The lad opened his mouth and closed it again. The firelight limned one side of his face copper and left the other in the blackest shadow, making him as one-eyed as the dead guard — and that eye studied Tom for a while.

"Master Ambrose says that you chase murderers for Mr. Secretary," he said. Whatever commendation Ambrose Lopes's assurance was to this boy, it certainly carried a good deal of weighty expectations. The question, when it came, sounded reproachful: "Don't you know who it was?"

If I knew... Tom bit down the curt answer. Dr. Lopes trusted this scrivener of his with rather grave errands. Could the boy be this innocent? Young Toby Chandler came to mind: their own scrivener in Seething Lane, now learning to be a cypherer, had been very young once, and very raw, and round-eyed with awe and importance — and yet had been trusted with messages of importance now and then. And reed-thin, serious Toby had never burnt with half of this one's earnest fire.

"All I know for now, is that I haven't killed him," Tom said — and the boy's deepening frown made him smile a little. "But then, that's what I'd say if I had, isn't it?"

Whether he was innocent or not, Galvam was no fool. With a stiff nod, he rose and walked away.

Settling back against the railing's post — which was deucedly uncomfortable — Tom watched him resume his former place, just as fretful as he had been. Was this the fretting of unease, of honest fear, of guilt, even?

Lucas Galvam as a murderer, now... Tom poked at the idea, the way he would at a reluctant fire. Supposing he'd had reason to kill Farras al-Awar, could he have done it? He was a sturdy lad enough; if he'd surprised the crouching Moor from the blind — and deaf — side, caught him unbalanced, clutched the scarf over his mouth and nose from behind... The violence Tom could believe, perhaps also the jumping at the chance that offered itself; it was the stealth that sat ill with what he'd seen of the boy. But then, one thing he'd learnt: there was no telling what most men — and women — were capable of. But had young Galvam had the time to do it? Had he been inside the byre when Bilqasim returned from his prayers? No — nor had Rolston...

Tom tried to picture the scene in his head: Dunne had arrived carrying the bucket, and Galvam with an armful of wood, and after that the two Moors. But Galvam had gone out again at some point. What of Dunne? What of Andrada? When Roberts had all but choked Bilqasim, Dunne had been there, while Rolston hadn't, and the Portuguese had walked into the firelight, but not from outside, had he? He'd come from the byre's far end, under the loft — one of the stalls, most likely.

Tom blinked — for a man was emerging from the darkness, just as the Portuguese had done. Or not just, for Andrada hadn't been laden with broken planks, nor had he tiptoed around the others, and dropped his hoard between his master and Tom.

There were scraps of rough planks, a chair's legs, the spokes of a wheel, some firewood, and a few broken handles.

"Where did you get that, Tolly?" Roberts asked.

For a moment Dunne sucked his teeth, rolled his shoulders, and looked from his master to Tom, and back again. "Over there…" He jerked his head towards the dark end under the loft, where the farmer must have piled what was neither quite destroyed nor salvageable. "There's lots of rubbish, and…" With all the manner of a decision made, the soldier ducked his head and whispered just loud enough for both men to hear. "And a door."

The hairs on Tom's neck stood on end. "A door," he mouthed, and Dunne nodded in the way of one who knew what another door meant.

And so did Roberts, who stared and breathed, "Sink me! But then…"

"But then, indeed. Keep them here, if you can." Before the man could protest, Tom climbed to his feet and followed Dunne. Roberts's grumbling followed them, as well as half a dozen chary stares… Oh, let them! They'd all know soon enough.

Just when Tolly Dunne had dropped his contrariness and decided that Tom was in charge, it wasn't clear — but he led Tom under the loft and around the last stall, where the fire's glow barely reached.

"Mind your step," he warned when Tom stumbled into something wooden that rattled against the wall. A ladder, perhaps, or a rack of some sort.

All sorts of clutter lay there, heaped and propped at sixes and sevens, and draped in cobwebs. It took steering from Dunne as Tom felt his way through the chaos, in a gloom that grew denser as they moved away from the fire.

"There!" said Dunne at last, and all but shoved Tom against a narrow oblong that looked blacker than the surrounding stone wall. Roughly planed wood, a waist-high horizontal plate — a door, indeed.

"Does it open?"

In answer, the soldier put his shoulder to it and pushed with all his might.

"Dunne!" Tom warned — too late, as the door flew open, banging against the outer wall, and then banging again as the wind caught it.

It did open — and no mistake.

By the time they had grasped the damn thing and jammed it shut again, there were calls, and all the others came spilling around the stalls, young Galvam first, carrying a burning firestick like some modern-day Prometheus.

"What happened?" Roberts wanted to know.

At the same time, Rolston asked, "What have you done?"

Rolston, it was worth noticing, had his rapier drawn, while Bilqasim held his strangely shaped dagger, and was that a knife flashing in Andrada's hand at the back of the group?

It was the charitable view to take that perhaps Dunne was rattled by his encounter with the door. Otherwise, why would he point and blurt out, "There's a door!"

Ah, well. Tom watched as comprehension made its uneven way around the circle of faces.

The first to take a step forward was Rolston. "You cannot mean…"

When he hesitated, Roberts took it up. "He means," he said in slow Spanish, "that anyone could have gone out there and killed the Moor — and who would know?" And see how smugly he folded his arms. "Anyone but myself, eh, young Walsingham? For I was right there, talking to you."

And then bedlam erupted, with Galvam protesting fierily, and Rolston asking what of Roberts's man, then, and Andrada playing a bewildered Harker, and Dunne grim and indignant, and the false page gibbering at the speechless Bilqasim… Roberts alone stood, square-shouldered and smug, in the midst of it. One would think he enjoyed the brewing row, until Tom roared for peace.

See how they all gaped — angry, frightened, wary. And again it was Rolston who broke the silence and slammed his rapier back into his scabbard for emphasis — having circled back to the beginning: "You never mean…"

"*I mean*," Tom said, glaring at Rolston and then at all the others, "that anyone could have gone out that way. You're all protesting very much, I think. After all, even that the fellow was killed at all is still only a suspicion." *Never show all you know, Thomas — and even less of what you think.* "The door opens — you all heard that. Bring that light, Lucas."

In the glow from the improvised torch, the door swung open easily enough, with only a slight scrape against the ground, and the softest groan of well-used hinges.

"It makes noise," said Galvam, stammering in his relief — but Tom shook his head.

"Very little, and we were all moving about and talking, and the wind was blowing. Done with a whit of care, who would have noticed?"

He motioned for the lad to shine the torch outside. The flame dipped and danced in the wind, and Galvam shielded it with his hand — but, even dimmed, the smoky light revealed, of all things, a stretch of rough gravel.

Damn all the gravel in England! Couldn't these people have left alone the mud, or grass, or anything that would show footprints? But no — it had to be gravel! See how mockingly it glimmered here and there, glazed with ice! Crouching on the threshold, Tom reached out to touch it: it was frozen hard. Besides, this must be the building's more sheltered side, and there was little snow at its foot. The door itself had scraped away what drift there was in a semicircle — but when had it happened? Under Dunne's mighty push, or earlier, when someone had sneaked out with murder in his heart? Not before that, most likely, for the edge of disturbed snow hadn't firmed yet, unlike the coarse-grained crust that glittered beyond the door's reach. Straightening, Tom took the torch and stepped out, with Dunne and Rolston following so close on his heels that they stumbled into him when he stopped. He raised the sputtering flame, and it flickered briefly, showing that, just beyond the corner, between the byre and what remained of the house, the snow lay thicker, and much marked with dark footprints.

"We all went about, this way and that, searching for wood," said Dunne. "Me, and young Lucas and, and…"

Ay — and Farras al-Awar, and Tom himself, and who knew who else? What good would it do to ask them all where had they been all the while?

"So, you see, it means nothing," was Rolston's triumphant conclusion.

As triumphant as it was ungrounded. "It only means that we *know* nothing." Just then the flame lost its battle, leaving behind only embers — and a shudder crept down Tom's spine with the sudden darkness. Was either of the men behind his back a murderer? The wind was chasing thin, ragged clouds across the sky, hiding and showing a sickle-like moon. Bilqasim had been wrong, for they would never have found their way by its light; there was barely enough to silver the black-pocked whiteness. The chill air was full of the scent of smoke and snow.

"Let's go inside," Tom said. "There's nothing more that we can do out here now."

Dragging their feet, looking askance at each other, each shuffling to be the last — that was how they all went inside, and began to settle around the fire in an uneasy circle where everyone could see everyone else.

Galvam dithered, watching as all went back to the places they'd claimed earlier. He looked startled when Tom beckoned to him.

Did the boy think that Mr. Secretary's man would murder him in his sleep? Perhaps he did, judging by how slowly, how crabwise he inched close.

"Did you kill the guard, Lucas?" Tom asked — and, as the youth gaped, "Well, neither did I, I tell you — and I won't kill you either."

For a little longer young Galvam gawped like a sturgeon at Billingsgate Market — likely thinking how Tom himself had said that the murderer would certainly deny his guilt. Or perhaps that Dr. Lopes and his son trusted the Walsinghams… In the end he knelt down at Tom's side with the graceless suddenness of his age, knee-bones thumping on the packed dirt.

"I went out to see to the horses in the shelter, Master," he said, "and then I thought I'd find some more wood. The Moor was dead when I found him!"

And wasn't it interesting that, of them all, Roberts and the boy alone had felt a need to protest their innocence?

"We'll see," Tom said. "Now settle down and let me sleep."

Settle down he did, poor Galvam — curling up against the railing, quiet if not reassured in the least: did he think Tom wouldn't catch him fumbling under his cloak to slip out his knife? But then, Tom himself had his own dagger drawn and concealed, and could have sworn there wouldn't be an unarmed hand — or a truly closed eye — in the abandoned byre that night.

Of course, there was no question of sleeping. Tom sat wide awake, too chilled and too jittery, even if he'd been of a mind to doze — and he was not. He listened as the fire crackled, the unquiet men around it rustled and held their breath, and the wind blew outside, now a gentle sough, now a howl. Most of all, though, he listened to the clicking of the glass bits inside his own head, as he tried to sort facts and thoughts.

It shouldn't have been difficult, considering how little he knew...

Item: Farras al-Awar was dead.

Item: While he *might* have died of natural causes, a number of things pointed to the contrary — namely:

Item: the brief time the man could have spent sitting in the snow.

Item: the lack of any wound on his head and body that a fall might have caused.

Item: the unnatural displacing (or not) of both headcloth and eye-band.

And, most noteworthy and suspicious…

Item: the bloodshot eye, a mark of suffocation.

Item: the scrapings on the cheek and nose that matched the rough headcloth.

Also, a consideration of a different nature:

Item: the death occurring just after al-Awar had been talking to Mr. Secretary's man.

Not so little, after all, was it? In fact, far too much to rule out foul play.

Therefore, *quæstio*: who could — and would — have played foul?

Those were, in truth, two *quæstiones*, the first sure to whittle down the number of suspects. Not much, perhaps, when it came to physical ability: the guard had been a trained soldier, a veteran of battles — but half blind and half deaf, poor fellow, no matter how he'd tried to hide it, out of either pride or prudency. Tom himself had all but walked on him unnoticed without trying. What could a foe have done, with both malice and stealth? The scene played itself out again in Tom's mind: a shadowy figure creeping up from behind the Moor, as he crouched down with his basin. Caught unawares, al-Awar would have toppled backwards, flailing, easy to grab from behind, to smother with a fold of his own headcloth.

Strangling a fellow creature is hard work, Ambrose Lopes was fond of saying. *Smothering, now — that's easier, quieter, swifter.*

Ergo: any of the men could have done it quite easily — not least the sturdy young Galvam. All but Khalida — who, of course was no man at all.

Ergo again, there was very little whittling done: excluding himself and Roberts, Tom was still left with Dunne, Rolston, Andrada, Galvam, and Bilqasim, all of them capable of killing.

Another side of the same question, though: who among those five would have had the time to do it?

Suppose it had happened between the end of the prayers and the time Galvam found the body — or so he claimed. A short time — and, within it, where had each of the five been?

In primis, Dunne and young Galvam had certainly been outside, though they'd come inside before Bilqasim returned from his prayers — but Galvam had gone out again, and Dunne could have done the same and come back.

In secundis, Andrada had been inside the byre, according to Roberts — although out of sight for most of the time: who was to say he hadn't gone out?

In tertiis, no one knew for sure where Rolston had been and when. He'd come back inside after Bilqasim — but when had he gone out? Given the hidden door, it could have been at any time.

In quartis there was Bilqasim himself — who might well have known of al-Awar's deafness and had had more time than all the others. He could have murdered his guard just after the prayers and then come back to the byre playing not just innocent, but ignorant. It must be an especially grievous sin to kill during prayers, and it meant that the Lady Khalida was complicit in the deed. Besides, only the two lovers had tried to run after the murder was discovered.

Eyes narrowed, Tom peered at the two Moors where they lay in the corner — the Turciman sitting up, with the false boy's head resting on his thigh. Anyone could look innocent when slumbering — but these two had broken quite a few of their laws already — both divine and human — and given a reason strong enough...

Which led to *quæstio* the second, and the crux of it all: why would Bilqasim, or any of the others have wanted Farras al-

Awar dead? Or perhaps not so much the crux, for time and again Tom had seen people kill for reasons so well concealed that they had seemed at first no reason at all. But here…

I watch and see, the guard had said just before being killed. He watched on his Sultan's behalf, whose favour he wanted to gain back. And one thing he'd watched was how Roberts had put the turciman in the dead Marzuq Raìs's place. Roberts had much to lose, if al-Awar were to denounce the imposture: a false ambassador, a puppet whose strings the English held… The Sultan was sure to make a row about it, and England wouldn't be thankful to the man who had caused it all. Roberts had set all his hopes on this mission. When facing ruin instead, would he have ordered Dunne to rid him of the threat? Perhaps, yes — though why now? Why not between Ireland and Bridport? What had changed?

Tom had joined them, and then Rolston, and Galvam, and then Andrada had been revealed as Dom Antonio's man…

Andrada, too, whose master would never want the treaty to be delayed, and with it his chance at the throne. Andrada should know nothing of Bilqasim's true identity, but who could tell? And the same went for Rolston — but then why would Essex's man do murder to protect the treaty? Dr. Lopes, on the other hand, had much at stake in this matter. But Galvam didn't know of Bilqasim, either — and, had he somehow found out, would he take it on himself to kill a man for the sake of those stakes? And yet the boy had been so reluctant to discover Andrada. Could he be in the pay of Dom Antonio — whom he called *the King*? And then there was Bilqasim himself, who had little to gain from the scheme's success, but much to lose from its failure.

Ergo... Tom rolled his stiff shoulders and groaned inwardly: if the murder had been done over the charade, four out of his five suspects had good reason for it.

Unless... *I watch and see — as others had better do.* How many times had Tom caught Farras al-Awar watching him? Wanting to talk to him, perhaps, and never doing it? What else had he watched and seen?

With a sudden harrumph, Dunne lurched to his knees — and see how all jumped! Eyes flew open, and cloaks shifted to show the gleam of blades.

"Someone has to mind the fire," the soldier growled, as he fed the languishing flames. He poked at his handiwork once or twice, whipping up swarms of coppery sparks, and then retreated to his master's side, muttering to himself as he sought a measure of comfort against the rough wood.

See how slowly all the others settled down — or didn't, like Andrada sitting upright, and Rolston moving so he could better watch the others. The actions of innocent and prudent men, or the instinct of wary guilt?

Although, Tom thought sourly, show him an innocent around that fire! If ever there was a company of liars, this was it, to be sure, but who had told lies worth a man's life? While neither Andrada nor Rolston were what they'd claimed to be, Rolston had been called out on his lie soon enough, and Andrada knew himself discovered. And yet there must still be some undiscovered secret, and al-Awar had dithered about it for long enough that someone had killed him to keep that secret. To keep it from Mr. Secretary's man, surely: it could be no chance, could it, that Tom had uselessly pressed al-Awar for answers, and, not an hour later, the man was dead? And, apart from the imposture, there was only one secret that would need to be protected that fiercely: the identity of the Spanish spy.

A piece of wood crumbled to embers — very softly, and yet all stirred again, including Tom, much though it galled him to admit it. Lord, what a dreadful night. At least he'd kept his startlement to himself — unlike the Lady Khalida, who'd come awake with a gasp.

Oh yes — that one. Another impostor with a deathly secret of her own, who'd been arguing with al-Awar, who'd called him a thief... But it could have been something else entirely. Al-Awar had travelled longer with the Ambassador's party, lived more closely with them. And he had been around that night in Salisbury. So had been Andrada, in truth, but perhaps the Portuguese had no interest in what the Moors did among themselves, nor much to gain by revealing it. Farras al-Awar, however, had been desperate to gain favour again. Would two punished adulterers count towards redemption in the Sultan's eyes — or in those of the Moors' God? And while it was rather late to disclose that particular truth to Tom, al-Awar hadn't known that. However one looked at it, Bilqasim had all sorts of reasons to get rid of a guard who was both long-eyed and loose-tongued. It had to be him, and never that small, slight woman? Though back at that ford, she'd shown such unexpected strength...

With a sigh, Tom rubbed at his eyes, wishing he could grind out both smoke and drowsiness — and even that slight movement made young Galvam lift his head at once.

"Sleep," Tom ordered, and the boy lay back down, unassuaged and taut.

A discovered impostor, an adventurer facing ruin, a Spanish spy, two lovers in danger... Nobody would call it a well-reasoned conclusion, but there it was: any of the people around that fire could well have wanted the death of Farras al-Awar.

CHAPTER 14

They would not bury Farras al-Awar in Whitchurch.

To think it had looked such a pretty little place as they'd approached it, gleaming white in the sun, with its frost-garlanded trees, the neat cottages, and the clear little river chuckling between rims of sparkling ice. Surely to live in such a cheerful village would make, if not for open minds, at least for open hearts?

Which thoughts Tom squarely blamed on the sleepless night, as he tried to glare the young vicar into submission — and tried in vain. With his rabbity face as white as the limestone of his church, the man barely kept himself from wringing his hands, and yet stood his ground most manfully, and cinched his refusal with the argument that a Moor couldn't possibly be buried in consecrated ground.

"I'm not suggesting that he be, Sir," insisted Tom, whose patience hadn't benefitted from a wink of rest or a morsel of food since dinner the day before. "But perhaps a place outside the graveyard could be arranged, out of Christian charity?"

The wrong thing to say, plainly: see how the oxymoron of squandering Christian charity on a Moor darkened the little vicar's pasty brow. See how he pursed his lips and said, "There is no precedent for it, I'm sure."

Yes — yes, there is, you prating coney! We ourselves did it not a week ago in Bridport — and what do you think is done with the merchants from Barbary and Levant when they die in London? Mince pies? More than any unseemliness of calling a clergyman names, what stifled the rant in Tom's throat was the way the clergyman spoke of precedent: with lessons learnt by heart, there was no reasoning — Jove rain on half-lettered provincial clerics! Explain the way things were done in Dorset and in London, and they'd raise a brow — *and, pray, what has this to do with us here?*

Even the paper with Mr. Secretary Walsingham's seal achieved little. The vicar tapped the page with an ink-stained nail, nibbling at his lower lip and stealing glances at Tom and at his companion, repeating over and over how there was nothing in these writings about the burial of Moors — until inspiration struck and he said that he couldn't possibly make a decision on his own. The Parish Council might, he suggested — and, bidding the alarming visitors to wait, he disappeared inside the church.

To barricade the door and sound the tocsin against the invaders? To summon the Parish Council at once?

Not that he was entirely to blame. Eight men, all mad-eyed and dishevelled, demanding to bury a Moor! And, to make the demand still more sinister, Tom himself had presented it, invoking near almighty authority, and with him Bilqasim, not only a Moor, but a most Friday-faced one.

Gone was the amused manner, gone all urbanity and whim, as the turciman scowled at the church's shut door. "Could it not have been done the way you arranged for Hakim?" he asked — in English, and not for the first time that morning.

And, it not being the first time, Tom took in a lungful of crisp air and let it out in a white billow before answering in Spanish, "I thought you'd want it done as soon as can be. Even if I were to find one soul in this place willing to have a Moor buried in their land, we'd have to wait for night —"

"Too long — too late!" Bilqasim's voice grew harsh. "Is it not enough that he should be murdered in infidel land — must

227

he also have his body dishonoured, and his soul wandering untethered?"

As though Tom weren't doing all he could to have the fellow buried! As though he were to blame for the murder; as though anyone in this cursed party were any help at all, all juggling lies and secrets, beginning with Bilqasim, and al-Awar himself, ever watching askance and speaking in riddles. "Had he been a tad less secretive, his soul would still be in his body, wouldn't it?" he retorted. And why must he sound this sour and peevish he didn't know, especially when he was in the right, for al-Awar's secrecy had done him no good.

And therefore it was the peak of unfairness that Bilqasim should draw tall so severely to say, "Perhaps he saw no reason to trust you more than he did anyone else."

This now! "I never expected him to trust me in particular —" Tom began, and stopped at a familiar bellow of, "Oy, Master!"

There, across the churchyard, came Nick Skeres, puffing, sweating, and milling his arms as he trotted up — and glory be! Here were Sir Francis's instructions at last, and a great weight off Tom's shoulders.

"Dolius — at last!" he called, lighter of heart than he'd been in days. "Do you have a letter?"

But what was a letter when compared to the lad's curiosity? "Cuds-me, Mr. Tom!" was the breathless greeting. "Young Lucas says the guard's been done in!"

Why should the Minotaur have learnt discretion in two days, when he hadn't in six-and-twenty years? "A town-crier, that's what you should have been!" Tom groused, more on principle than anything else. "You do have a letter, don't you?"

"Ay, ay…" Pointedly turning his back on the silent Bilqasim, Skeres sat on the nearest tombstone to yank off a boot. "Galloped all the way to Richmond and back to get it…"

Which Tom didn't much credit, considering the roads — but in the end the letter was dug out of the boot: a small, folded square, creased, stained, and none too fragrant.

"But, Master…" Ducking his head, the lad peered askance at the man he thought was the Sultan's envoy. "'Tis true? They did in their own guard?"

Not that it would avail much, but Tom answered in as quelling a tone as he could: "Someone did, yes — but who *they* are is a horse of another colour. Don't babble about it." And, as Skeres tugged his boot back on, muttering and un-quelled, Tom walked away a few steps to break the seal and read his letter.

It was just one line, in Sir Francis's own hand, uncyphered but couched in the simplest of codes: *Dear Cousin, I find it best to keep the hives well covered. We'll sort bees and hornets.*

Which was all well and good when it came to keeping the secret, and a great relief that Mr. Secretary would deal with the imposture. But there remained the fact that meanwhile, someone had been stung to the death — but that would have to wait, because then the vicar emerged from the church. He'd fetched reinforcements in the form of a thickset, fully bearded man, a more impavid fellow, judging by the way he planted himself, wide-legged and cross-armed, between the strangers and the church — although he had a chary squint for the newly arrived Minotaur. What did he think — that they'd use force? Perhaps he did, for he proclaimed himself a churchwarden and, in that capacity, announced that no heathen would be interred in the graveyard of All Hallows. What about it would make Whitchurch the talk of the county, he said most severely —

and all the while Bilqasim seethed, while Skeres glowered equally at the Moor and churchwarden.

And there they were, back at the beginning. When not even the prospect of money worked in the least, Tom asked to speak to the Lord of the Manor, only to be told that Whitchurch had none. There was a mayor — who, however, was in Basingstoke for the day, and whose clerk, when consulted, deemed it all a Parish matter for certain... Why didn't they try the vicar?

It was with little love to spare for Whitchurch and its inhabitants that Tom urged his party into the saddle again — and why he hadn't aimed for Basingstoke in the first place, he didn't know.

"Basingstoke is a larger place," he assured Bilqasim. "A market town. They're bound to have, if not more charity, at least less prejudice." Or were they?

It was plain as day that the turciman shared the uncertainty rather than the hope.

"Don't speak as though this were my own whim, *Señor* Ulsingam," he said, favouring Tom with a burning stare. "To you it makes no matter, but to us delaying a burial is not just to dishonour the dead, it is to offend God himself. Surely even an infidel must understand that?"

Why, just where had this thankless heathen been while Tom strove to do his outlandish bidding? "Tell me this, Excellency," he retorted, "would it be much easier to bury a Christian *infidel* in your land? To bury him in a way that we judge decent and proper?"

And, petty as it must be, Tom had the satisfaction of seeing Bilqasim lost for words.

There was something to smithies — the roaring of the fire, the vapour of smoke and of heated iron, the hissing of water, the clanging pulse — something Tom had always liked, even as a child. A sense of preparation, of imagined battle... How his father had laughed to hear little Tom, all of five, declare that, if he hadn't been a gentleman, he'd be a blacksmith. A cuff to the shoulder had gone with the laughter — and then the hand had lingered. It was perhaps the warmest memory Tom had of his father, and it surged unbidden to his mind as he waited for Basingstoke's placid farrier to tighten his mare's loose iron.

What the late Sir Thomas would have had to say of this plight in which his least unfavoured son struggled, though, was the sort of contemplation from which Tom tore himself without regret the moment young Galvam showed up, all but dancing with impatience.

"They're still at it," the boy announced, the way he would a great personal offence.

"They would be." Basingstoke had barely lifted a brow at the business of a dead Moor, and a burial in daylight might prove less hasty than one done at night under the snow. "By the time they're done, we'll be ready to go," Tom said — with more equanimity than he felt, and more than the boy liked, judging by his restless shuffling.

"But I could ride ahead with a message, Master," he offered — all eagerness. "I could leave at once, never having to stop for the Moors! You see how fast Skeres rode to London and back!"

Oh very, very eager... "Indeed — and he just brought my answer. If and when I have another message to send —"

"If and when!" A sudden flurry of hammer blows from the forge made a good music for the boy's stare: Outraged Disbelief in person, an arm flung out at the world at large, where Moorish soldiers were smothered to death, and slaughterers rode and ate together with good people.

And, before Disbelief turned to Loud Indiscretion, Tom steered the lad out to the little yard. "*If and when* I send anyone ahead, don't you think it will be Skeres, who wasn't here when al-Awar died?"

It was a maxim of Sir Francis that one should watch men closely, and read their thoughts in their transparent faces. Lucas Galvam would have made a good hornbook for a novice of this art, for every thought was spelt clear and wide in his mien. See how incomprehension flickered briefly, chased away by disbelief again — but only until anger flared, in battle with resentment.

"You —" To his credit, the lad choked down the half cry, to resume in a hunch-shouldered whisper, "You think that *I* did it!"

But did he truly? Tom wished he had a better answer to that. "You could have, for all I know. You or anyone else."

It might have been betrayal twisting the boy's mouth, or disappointment. Both, perhaps: plainly young Galvam had expected better from Walsingham's hound — not this admission of disgraceful ignorance. It had the effect of sending the lad into a narrow-eyed sulk.

"You too, then," he said. "For all *I* know, it could have been you."

This surprised a huff of laughter out of Tom. "The cheek of you! But yes: I could have done it. I haven't, though. Ask Mr. Roberts: I was with him in the byre."

A brisk nod. "I saw you there, both of you — but all the time? And what of Dunne? And Rolston, and ... Andrada?"

"It must be said, none of them is raring to ride away on his own all of a sudden."

This was waved away most impatiently. "And the Raìs? He tried hard to ride away last night, didn't he? He says the guard was alive when he last saw him, but —"

"True — and you say he was dead when you found him, but…" An idle retort, if ever there was one. What murderer would answer other than by denying?

"And dead he was!" young Galvam exclaimed, and then sniffed. "But then, I'm not Mr. Secretary's kinsman, to say what I will and have it believed."

There — there went another thinking marvels and prodigies of the Walsingham name! "Not that it's yours to question — but you'd be surprised."

"Even if they called you a murderer, you have people in London trusting you, and believing you, and taking your word. You're like a son to His Honour — everybody knows that!"

Philip Sidney was like a son to him, not I… It was more than Tom could do to keep the bitterness from his chuckle. "His kinsman, his loyal servant — that's what I am, earning his trust, day by day, since I was your age. And still you, and everybody, will think that I have it all gifted to me because of the name I bear!"

What an unspeakable fool! Tom could have kicked himself — pouring out the bitterness of his heart to a child he hardly knew, a child who, moreover, was shaking his head, hard-faced at once.

"*I* am a servant, Master," he said. "A servant with no family and no name — or none they'll let me claim…" And he swung away, swallowing hard.

What on earth was this now? Tom waited to see if more would come, but the boy seemed taken of a sudden with the noises from the smithy — the rasp of a file, the great whoosh and rattle of the bellows.

"Who are *they*? What name would you claim?" Never that of Dr. Lopes? That it was hard to imagine the physician fathering bastards didn't make him incapable of it — but... "Lucas, who is your father?"

Unsurprising as the shrug was, the quivering little laugh was another matter. "My mother was a maid in the house of Dr. Rodrigo's cousins, back in Crato. When she became big with me, they sent her over to England. Oh, they meant well. How could they know? It's God who should have brought my father elsewhere."

Oh, Lord above! Dr. Lopes's cousins back in Crato — and who had been there seventeen years back, with a roving eye for pretty *converso* maids, and then come to England?

"Dom Antonio..." Tom murmured. What had been Lopes thinking, bless him with hot water, that he never saw fit to mention this little fact?

"*King* Antonio!" was the choked-out retort.

Poor Lucas Galvam! To know himself abandoned by his father would crush a boy; to know this father to be a king of sorts... Or at least to believe it. Tom observed the lad. How to put this delicately, now?

"You know, he has half a dozen children..."

"All of them bastards, yes — and all of them he raised. All but me."

After all, Dom Antonio was illegitimate himself — though nobody ever mentioned this. So why reject yet another son, unless... "Do you think he knows?"

A shrug. "Dr. Rodrigo was angry the one time I asked. Angry with me, and angry with my mother — but..." The boy looked up sharply. "She never told me my father's name, and she always went quiet when there was talk of the King. When he came to England, she was ill already and found no peace when she heard that he'd live here. Why, unless I'm his son?"

Oh, for all sorts of reasons — first of all that the father might have been someone in the King's ragged court. Here was why Lopes had never mentioned Galvam's royal blood: there was no such thing. Not that it would make much difference to the boy.

However things stood, it was not Tom's trouble but for one matter. "I don't know what King Antonio's son would do with the Moors," he said, turning stern, "but perhaps he wouldn't have willingly discovered Andrada."

What he should make of the lad's scoff, he wasn't sure: was it for himself, for the Portuguese, for Galvam's own clumsiness? Before any explanation could be asked for or offered, the farrier's apprentice ambled out of the smithy, leading the mare, who kept stamping her foreleg, as though disliking the new shoe… One more irritation to add to the many curses of this journey — but then, what was an ill-fitting shoe, compared to a scrivener who imagined himself of royal blood?

Handing the apprentice a penny, for all of his misgivings, Tom would have left, but young Galvam called after him.

"You're right!" Raw as the file's rasp inside the smithy — and just as grating to say, by the sound of it. "When I saw the King's man, I didn't know what I should do… But you are right, Master. I should have told you at once, for Andrada is a liar. Perhaps he's here of his own counsel. Perhaps the King doesn't even know." He must have read the doubt in Tom's manner, for he stamped a foot, making the mare twitch. "The King is grateful to Dr. Rodrigo, and Mr. Secretary, and the Queen!"

And pray nobody was eavesdropping... "The gratitude of sovereigns doesn't work like that of us mere mortals." Sir Francis's wisdom, in truth, spoken long ago — and little consolation for a sore-hearted boy. "Andrada does what his master tells him, Lucas. I hope you see where your loyalty must lie." But did he? The half-formed shrug was far from reassuring. "And if you're thinking to earn the King's favour in some way —"

The bitter, skew-mouthed laugh aged the youth ten years. "The noble *Senhor* d'Andrada — they say that *he* has the King's favour for all he's done. Nameless scriveners, all they can hope to earn from a king is a vail. Leave me the horse — I'll walk her for you and see if she limps." And taking the mare's reins from Tom, off he strode.

Very, very far from reassuring. Because, when it came to acting, there was little difference between a bastard prince and a boy who thought himself one. And King Antonio's son might well have thought it a noble deed to kill ... whom? The man who threatened his father's chance at the throne? The Spanish spy?

The Spanish spy, indeed... One bit of glass moved inside Tom's mind, catching the light. Hardly a new bit, but different now that someone had murdered this maimed and disgraced soldier — bitter and watchful...

It struck Tom at once that he didn't know half enough about the late Farras al-Awar.

Of the nature of the dead man's disgrace, Roberts had no idea.

"It was the other guards who talked of a punishment. We had three of them when we took ship, and then one died out at sea, and another in Cornwall." He stopped, thoughtfully gnawing on a piece of cheese. "Come to think of it, Farras always stayed by himself. I thought he didn't like the other Moors, but maybe the others didn't like *him*. Eh, Tolly?"

Dunne sat back and considered. They were sharing the corner of a table at the inn, the three of them — Tom breaking his fast in earnest at long last, and the other two keeping him company while the Moors buried their fellow, with Skeres playing both gravedigger and guard.

It was a little while of tooth-sucking before the soldier leant forward, both palms on the table. "Ay — and Hakim gossiped. Farras used to be an officer, Hakim said. Then ... I don't know, he broke some oath, or lied, or the like. He was full of spite, that Hakim — and besides he jabbered like a jackanapes. Didn't understand half of what he said."

Al-Awar, the One-Eyed ... and the one-eared. "Perhaps Farras had lied about being half-deaf. Would that keep him from rising through the ranks?"

"Not of a necessity," said Roberts, but Dunne put a hand to his temple, splayed to both cover his ear and make a blinker.

"Wouldn't want a man like that covering my side in a battle," he said. "See how it got him killed."

"Did it, though?"

If Tolly Dunne thought he'd betrayed himself, he showed none of it. One struck with sudden fear wouldn't just pull a face. "A well set fellow, was Farras, and one who'd done his fighting. If he was caught from behind, as you say..." Dunne rose and went to stand at Tom's shoulder, who looked up at him — and suddenly found an arm snaking around his neck from the other side, pressing his throat, choking.

It was a white-blind moment — every muscle stiffening, one hand grabbing the woollen sleeve, the other going for the dagger at his back, and finding a sturdy arm blocking the way...

"See, Master?" Dunne released his hold and slid back onto the bench.

See, indeed! Tom fingered his throat, which could so easily have been crushed, had the soldier been in earnest — and waved away the alarmed tapster who hurried close.

"More ale, if you please," he ordered, as a sign of normality for the youth, who sidled away narrow-eyed and unconvinced. By the fire where he stood, Andrada had turned to observe the proceedings, and so had Rolston, who sat by himself, playing both sides of a game of tables.

"Are you ever a dunce, Tolly!" Roberts grumbled. "All we lack is the constables slapping you in gaol for brawling!"

There was no heat to the reproof, though, nor much contrition to Dunne's ducked head.

"Wanted to show Mr. Walsingham, Capt'n…" he said.

And shown him he had — but what, exactly? That he could well have killed the guard? That he had not — by doing it the wrong way? "You're rather bigger than I am, though," Tom said. "And al-Awar was smothered, not strangled."

"Maybe it's even easier — can't rightly say. Couldn't cry out, though…" The soldier scratched a stubbly cheek. "If you ask me, once the poor bugger lost his footing, even one of the boys could have done it."

Even one of the boys — as opposed to only a trained soldier… Had Roberts missed his man's intention, or was he very good at feigned innocence? "Ay — but blind me if I know why one of the boys would do it." He squinted at the other two. "Or anyone else, come to that. Do you think Farras was the Spanish spy?"

But, if he was, wouldn't someone else be dead instead? Or else, wouldn't the murderer have claimed his fine deed? "You never trusted al-Awar, did you?"

"And what of you, lad? Never say you liked the man."
Roberts sat taller. "Where has that dolt gone with our ale?
There isn't one of these Moors you don't suspect, dead or
alive! Hakim first, then Farras — not that either of them
disposed one to trust."

"I saw precious little of Hakim, but if al-Awar was a spy, he
was a dismal one. It's only at the play that spies skulk about
and talk in riddles." *Sometimes men are pushed...*

There was a snort from Dunne. "Oh, Hakim never skulked
— as brazen a scoundrel as you please."

And yet he was dead just the same. *First Hakim, then Farras.*
Sometimes men are pushed!

Tom sat up straight, bits of glass clicking madly in his head,
so loud it was a marvel the others couldn't hear them. "What
did you say?" he barked at Roberts.

"What did I say?" The man blinked. "That you suspect all
the Moors..."

"Yes — Hakim first, and then Farras! Ah, but I'm blinder
than that poor fellow, blind on both sides!" Tom leapt out of
his chair, all but running into the tapster with the three
tankards. Heedless of the youth's yelp and of Roberts calling
him back, he strode for the door. He stopped with his hand on
the latch when Rolston looked up from his tables, smiling
askew.

"I'll never understand your method, Walsingham," the man
drawled. "If you have one, that is. Yesterday, you had us trot
ahead at dusk; today we go two miles, if that, and then we stop,
go ten more, and stop again. Ah, well, you'll know best, and I,
for one, like to sit by a good fire."

Wasn't it a shame that, at once, Anthony Rolston couldn't be
the culprit?

"Take your ease while you can," Tom retorted. "We'll be on our way soon enough."

He stepped outside into the glassy sunlight and took a lungful of stinging air, tinged with smoke and middens. A blind fool, that was what he'd been — and a deaf one when al-Awar had tried to warn him! Rolston couldn't be the murderer, and nor could young Lucas — for neither man had been with the party the night the unpleasant Hakim had fallen to his death — or rather... Tom slapped his gloves against his thigh. Men *are* pushed sometimes — and not as a figure of speech: Hakim had been pushed out of the window — the murderer's first victim, made to seem like a fleeing thief.

"And you fell for it!" He rubbed at eyes that stung and teared in the cold glare. Well, he *had* thought Hakim might have been the spy — for all that Mistress Peters's candlesticks spoke rather to the contrary — but now? If both Moors had been murdered, did it mean that the spy was still with them? The murderer was for certain — and now only Dunne, Andrada, and Bilqasim remained ... and also the Lady Khalida, say what you will, with those strong hands of hers and her wilful heart. But was the murderer also the spy?

One thing Tom's Service years had taught him: when he was chasing a murderer and a spy, he could never assume that they were one and the same. Men — and women — killed for more reason than the secrets of princes, and, out of Tom's four suspects, three had good reason to get rid of two loose-tongued servants, even without Spain: Dunne to protect Roberts's charade of the false ambassador, the false ambassador and his lady to protect themselves. Andrada, though ... would the Portuguese have killed Hakim over his false English name? And even if he had, what of al-Awar, then? No: only as the Spanish spy, and threatened with discovery, would Andrada have killed the two men. But would King Antonio's faithful champion turn spy for Madrid? Even young Galvam, who disliked the man, only had wonders to say of his loyalty and valour. What a tangle! And that was without considering that there may be two murderers — one being the spy. But then, what of al-Awar, dead right after all but denouncing Hakim's murder? Too great a stroke of venture, surely?

A logical mind is a great gift, Thomas, but one that not all mankind owns or acts upon. Don't let yourself be blinded to possibilities just because Aristotle would scoff at their shape. Sir Francis had smiled as he told this, in the middle of a reminiscence of his younger days at the University of Padua. What would he say now? What would he think when Tom arrived in London and dropped in his lap this whole cursed armful of thorns?

I have a false ambassador for you, Sir, and a double murderer, and a Spanish spy who might or might not be the same man. Or else two murderers, one of them a spy. And if the spy had only killed once, didn't this bring Rolston and young Galvam back under suspicion?

Oh, Lord! A pity that the snow in the yard was so filthy, grey with soot where it wasn't trodden to mud — or Tom would have scrubbed a handful of it all over his face. It had to be the long, sleepless night catching up with him. Once he was rested, his thoughts would stop clattering around his head and settle down in a pattern ... as long as the murderer didn't strike again, while Tom waited for his wits to wake up.

And there went Galvam, leading into the yard Tom's becalmed mare — Galvam, who hadn't killed Hakim, for sure — but what of al-Awar? On hearing that the mare was well enough to travel, Tom dispatched the boy to recover Skeres and the Moors.

"What if they aren't done?"

"Tell them I said to cut it short. They've had time enough to bury a trained band."

Which was unlikely to go down very well, but Tom wanted to be on the road again — as though, by making haste, he could outrace spying stealth and murderous intent. A foolish notion, in truth — but behind it, much less laughable, stood another: killing once with a push could happen in rage or fear; killing a second time, though, and by stealth, showed a different, far more dangerous sort of mind at work. One he'd rather not tackle on his own — but who was there to trust? He'd better keep this latest illumination to himself.

For all of Tom's misgivings, there was no trouble for the rest of the way. In fact, the road was good enough to canter now and then — a great relief after days of walk and trot — so that they made it to Bagshot in time for the sunset prayer.

Or they would have, but the Red Lion, where he and Dunne had stopped on their way west, was full to the eaves, the innkeeper claimed, for his own just-wed daughter and her new husband were being feasted in the great hall with many guests. Couldn't His Honour hear the music? There was no room for men and beasts and, most of all, there were just four horses to hire. Which was how they ended up at the White Hart — the sorriest, dampest, draughtiest, most rickety place in the whole of Surrey — and, while the two Moors claimed the one parlour for their *Maghrib*, Tom had to comb through the whole of Bagshot, and hire fresh horses piecemeal. It was a good couple of hours before he found his way back to the White Hart — chilled, much vexed, and less than satisfied.

Given the day, given the previous night, given it all, he felt justified in sitting by the taproom fire and having some claret

— which, he compromised after a brief tussle with his conscience, he wouldn't put down in his expenses. Then again, when the wine came, it was middling at best and watered down to within an inch of its life. It was all of a piece that Rolston should saunter by and stop with a hand on his hip. And, to see him smile, wouldn't one think them the best of friends!

"Wine!" he exclaimed. "Ah, but Mr. Secretary's men are creatures of indulgence!"

Oh, were they! Beckoning for another pot, Tom pushed it towards Rolston. "Be my guest," he said. After all, there would be a point to the wretched claret, if he inflicted some on Essex's man.

Essex's man winced at the first sip and decided to set aside this particular indulgence in favour of needling. "Would you believe that your Moors are at prayer — again?" he asked.

Tom raised one shoulder. "And they'll pray some more when it's quite dark."

"And they had the funeral this morning," Rolston said. "Never tire of it, do they?"

"Worse than Papist monks."

"And you always let the Raìs have his way. How much time have you lost over this?"

"Well, he's the Sultan's envoy. What would you have me do, truss him up and throw him across a saddle?"

Even Rolston had to concede this, surely? But no: the fellow propped his head on one hand, lips parted in a show of sudden comprehension.

"Ah, so that's how it works! You let him have his way and, in exchange, he heeds you, and you alone?"

And wasn't it a pity that Hakim's death must clear Anthony Rolston of most suspicions? There a measure of consolation in that he could still be the Spanish spy, though…

"He told you himself, Rolston: did you expect to be trusted, coming here under false colours?"

For once, Rolston grimaced. "I'd told His Lordship that it was a risk... Still, the Raìs took against me from the moment I arrived."

"A lack of winsomeness on your part?"

"That — or he feared he couldn't hide from me that he has English."

How the devil...? Tom made himself not blink — and here was another thing with bad wine: it roiled in a man's stomach, all the worse when the stomach's owner was taken unawares. "Has he?" he asked, raising a brow — and could it be hoped that he sounded amused? "He turned down your offers of friendship in Spanish, I think. Very flowery, at that."

"Oh, he's careful with me, but with you he speaks English, doesn't he?"

How many times, *how many times* had Tom warned Bilqasim to be wary of what he spoke and what he understood? Railing inwardly at the turciman, he made himself huff and shake his head. "Perhaps it's no great loss that you changed masters, Rolston. I don't know about young Essex — but Mr. Secretary would have little use for a man so fanciful..."

Of all the things Tom disliked about the fellow, the worst must be the way he threw back his head to laugh. So merry a laugh — and, under the merriment, so wolfish.

"Ah, you are not surprised! Did you find him out and let him get away with that too, or have you known all the while? And does Roberts know?"

Too close for comfort! Too precise to be just a stone thrown haphazardly... Oh, Roberts knew, Roberts was to blame for the most part, so there were no secrets to discover — but would the man keep his head if he was confronted? And could

Tom, at least, keep Rolston guessing? "Truly," he said, as lazily as he knew how, "I don't know what came into your head —"

"What came into my head —" all false amiability gone, Rolston leant forward, lowering his voice to a hiss — "is to wonder: is there some reason that you're raring to reach London, that you watch the Ambassador like a bandog, that you hide that he has English?"

Much cry and little wool, that's what I call it. And what's the rush? You know and I don't... Skeres, grumbling about the need to guard a Moor and complaining of the haste. Skeres trusting the Moors better for speaking English. Skeres sitting with Rolston and drinking in Tarrant Monkton and squirming when asked about it... Devil pinch the blathering halfwit! Having managed a sip of the wretched claret as he fumed to himself, Tom succeeded in sounding passably diverted. "Have you been bribing my man, Rolston?" he chuckled. "I wish you joy of it: there's very little that Skeres wouldn't make up for the sake of a vail!" Fates be thanked for the flicker of uncertainty, for the furrowed brow. Rolston covered it with another of those bright grins, but there was no mistaking it: the doubt had been sown — and, as though summoned by Tom's unkind thoughts of him, see who must be drawing close, face knotted in a scowl like a storm brewing. Had Nick Skeres heard himself disparaged by his own master? It served him right — and besides, he had much worse coming.

Even as Tom dragged him out of the door and into the small kitchen yard, the Minotaur tried to grumble about the one room they'd all have to share.

Someone had lit a fire in a corner — to burn what, best not to ask — and now the flames sputtered and stank, a greenish yellow in the sharp evening air. It was towards that dubious heat that Skeres moved, shoulders up to his ears and bottom lip jutting — Mutinous Guilt in person.

"Not that you'll believe me," he groused, rubbing at his arms. "There's naught I wouldn't make up."

The gall of the man! "Well, I had to make Rolston chary of you, hadn't I? Since I can't make you chary of him..."

And see how the curly head flew up. "Strike me blind if I — !"

"Soft, you dolt!" Tom glanced around. Across the little yard, yellow light glowed in what had to be the kitchen window, and shadows shifted past the horn pane. On the long side a set of curtains made ruddy another window, while the faint halo of a candle danced to and fro in a room upstairs. Was someone eavesdropping? Just to be safe, Tom leant close to whisper in the servant's ear.

"I warned you back in Blandford, well before Galvam came to discover the fellow. And I was right, it turns out — and yet you told him ... what?"

"Told him? I didn't give 'im the time of day, since young Lucas arrived! And 'e keeps being jolly, mind, but I know better..."

Oh, the overabundant explanation, the weight shifting from foot to foot... Tom had known the Minotaur too long. "And before that?" he prodded. "The night we spent in that cider-house, when he was so friendly he bought you a pot of cider?"

Having taken a sharp breath to speak, Skeres stopped short when the kitchen door slammed open, and a woman stepped out carrying a pail, the snow crunching under her feet. They must have seemed alarming, for she took care to approach the fire from the other side and, having dumped whatever she was carrying on the dying flames, she scurried away. The fire disliked the treatment: with a billow of oily stench, it sizzled down to embers, and they were left in all but darkness.

"What did he ask you?" insisted Tom.

"Nothing! 'E just…"

In the sudden silence, one could almost hear the stones grinding uneasy thoughts inside the Minotaur's head: how much trouble had he got himself into? Could he gab his way out of it? Before too much grist could come of it, Tom grasped the lad's arm. "What did you tell him about the Ambassador?"

The Minotaur undone — and then it all came out in a torrent: "What was there to tell? 'E knew already! 'E said you'll be in trouble when we get to London, for the Ambassador's a queer bird — and that 'e is, say what you will, Mr. Tom. It's queer birds as 'ave English and 'ide it…" And there the torrent dried up with a thick swallow and a gasp of: "Cuds-me!"

There — there! Tom's stomach clenched into one sinking leaden ball. Did nothing teach the loose-tongued fool? "He didn't know a thing, you gudgeon! He angled, and you took bait!"

"Spit and scorch 'im, always with a good word and a slap to the shoulder — and a farthing for ale…" Like many who are in the wrong, Skeres sought refuge in bluster. Tom had grown accustomed enough to the gloom to see the lad stomping around in a circle, arms milling as he chuntered that Rolston had cheated him, and ay, call him a fool, but he'd never known — for, had he just known…

"Known what, you halfwit?" Tom snapped. "Didn't I tell you to keep quiet about the Raìs?"

"Ay, to the inn-folk, and to 'Arker — as isn't even 'Arker — but Mr. Rolston? Odd rat, 'im — 'e said 'e came from 'Is 'Onour!"

"Well, he didn't."

"But I didn't know!" Skeres exploded at last, wheeling around to kick the embers into a shower of sparks. "You didn't know yourself, back then! 'Ow was *I* to know?"

And if this was a fairish objection, Tom was past fairness. "You knew enough to lie when I asked what you and Rolston had talked about!" he seethed. "*Nothing*, you said."

To this there was little that even Skeres could object. He stood there with hunched shoulders, breathing heavily. "'Tis that I don't know what's what these days, Master," he murmured at length, softer than Tom had ever heard him speak. "What's secrets, and the like..." A shrug. "You used to tell me things, before."

And thank God I didn't tell you more... Even through the simmering anger, Tom felt the cold biting at him, seeping through the soles of his boots. "Go and find some supper for all," he ordered. "Hot — and not a whiff of pork meat. And Skeres..."

Having half spun away, Skeres stopped, head hanging. The Minotaur dejected — as though it made up for anything!

"Lie to me again," Tom said, "or shout at me, and you're out of wages."

What the lad was mumbling as he trundled away, Tom didn't want to know. After all, he couldn't even truly turn him out — at least not until they reached London, and he found the money to pay him his dues ... which, without Skeres himself as a broker, he'd be hard put to do. And that begged the question of what would happen with all the loans the lad had lombardeered for him already. Just how tightly was he stuck with his servant? For the first time in their acquaintance, Tom truly wished himself rid of Nick Skeres — and uneasy of what a resentful Skeres might do with his knowledge of his master's troubles. Ungenerous thoughts, for the Minotaur, blabbing and rough-edged as he was, had never proved himself less than loyal.

Wrapping the cloak tighter around himself, Tom went in search of fire, wine, and supper. Now Fates just send that Rolston… He huffed in laughter at himself, the vapour of it white even in the murk. Who would have thought the day would come for Tom Walsingham to pray that anyone might truly be Lord Essex's man?

CHAPTER 15

There was less snow in the fields, and hedgerows to line the wide, well-tended road, and more traffic on it — all welcome signs that they were drawing near the journey's end. Let only the weather hold and the Fates smile just a little, and by night they would be in London.

A little more perplexing was that Andrada made no sign of parting company. Not that Tom was eager to see one of his suspects leave — but...

Things being the way they were, Tom decided, Andrada could hardly resent some curiosity, and so he drew abreast with him, and asked, "You are bound for London too? Because it strikes me that, if you were for Eton, you'd have left us a good deal earlier."

For the first time since shedding the pretence of Harker, Andrada seemed uncertain. "For Eton and the King, yes, but ... I crossed at Maidenhead, on my way out, and travelled via Reading — and I lost my way, and the ruts, and the mud ... *caminho dos diabos!* So I'll cross when you do, and from there..." He looked at Tom sideways, one brow arched.

"From Staines, it's just a few miles to the road to Eton," Tom said. Could the man truly be unfamiliar with this part of England? Then again, before this matter of the Moroccan envoy, he would have had little reason to travel west on Dom Antonio's business. "You've learnt all that you wanted to learn for your king, I take it?"

His white teeth flashed amidst his dark beard. "Mr. Valsingam, the King greatly wishes to be more open in his dealings. He just doesn't understand why your master — and, even worse, your queen — won't trust him a little more."

"But you do?"

There was something in Andrada's eyes as he threw up his chin and asked, "You ask if I trust my king?"

Something, yes — and Tom couldn't give it a name. "I ask if you understand why we don't," he said, and could have sworn the man's grip relaxed minutely around the reins.

It might have been an impression, but the rueful smile was not. "Perhaps I do, for trust begets trust — and the King is…" He made that plucking gesture he had when seeking words. "How do you say? *Desconfiado* … mistrustful, yes. What you do not see, though, is that this is as true of him as of you. The King mistrusts because he is mistrusted."

And he is mistrusted because he mistrusts, Tom didn't retort. Mythical snakes biting their own tails apart, it wasn't quite true: Dom Antonio was mistrusted because he'd tried to run to the French, and would likely run to the Spanish as well, if they offered him his throne.

"That he sent you under a false name won't beget much trust, you know," was what Tom said instead — and, when Andrada nodded thoughtfully, he added, "Whether what you've learnt is worth it is for you and His Highness to decide."

Not that he truly expected an answer — not from this seasoned and sharp-witted fellow — and, indeed, all this shot in the dark earnt him was a small chuckle. Then, of a sudden, the man caught his breath and hunched in the saddle, slope-shouldered and a little lost, half-bowing to Tom as he let his horse fall back. Harker again of a sudden — and only then it struck Tom that, as they spoke, the man had let the mask slip to show a glimpse of Manuel d'Andrada. A nobleman of very old blood, Galvam had called him, and there was no doubting it: even unkempt and plainly dressed, with the faded bruises yellowing his face, there was something to the man, something beside the lilting accent. What had caused the slip now, was another matter. *You ask if I trust my king?* Had he misunderstood the question as some impugnation of Portuguese honour?

And then a bellow came from ahead: Dunne, announcing that there — there lay Staines.

"There, see?" he said, sweeping an arm towards the horizon as though he'd made the landscape himself.

A few soft hills rolled on the right, like white-furred beasts slumbering in the winter sun; ahead, the road made a broad curve around a village, a causeway snaking across a stretch of mist-cloaked fields, down to the wide, dull gleam of the Thames, and, just across it, a handful of brown rooves and a belfry or two.

Staines — and then no more than fifteen miles to London. It should have been a cheering thought, but for the fact of the eight men — no, seven men and a woman — and each of them could well be either a spy or a murderer or both... *And, Sir, I don't know just what snake I've brought with me in my precipitation.*

It was with a very jaundiced humour that Tom watched his fellow travellers take the causeway ahead of him.

Dunne first, who would do anything his captain said, and Lucas Galvam, who thought himself a king's son. After them Roberts, ruined and bitter, clinging to this embassy as his last chance, never taking his eyes off Bilqasim, whose fears grew with every step that took them nearer to London. Then the Lady Khalida in her baggy disguise, alert and frightened in equal parts, and at the same time shrewder than all the rest of

252

them put together. After her rode Rolston, who was likely no murderer, but had lied once and could well be lying again, and Manuel d'Andrada, still wearing the mask of Harker the clerk. And last, disgraced and much offended, plodded Nick Skeres, tugging along the pack-beasts, man and horses equally ill-humoured.

Well, the lad could have drawn some consolation from knowing that, of all that ill-assorted, false-tongued company, he was the only one Tom didn't suspect of either murder or betrayal.

Not that it had ever been an especially merry party — and the murder had spread on each and all a pall of general distrust — but nearing Staines made them all glum as wet crows. It was a quiet ride across the marsh, with the mist creeping up from the fields and over the road, so that the horses seemed to wade through a bank of knee-high clouds, their unseen hooves plashing in the mud, and the murmur of the Thames growing louder as they approached it.

Once or twice they crossed paths with a single rider trotting towards Bagshot, and once they had to stretch into a single file to pass by a carriage — but even that was done in all but silence.

Were they each asking themselves: what now? Or was Tom's mind just painting them all with the colours of his own dejection?

As they came within sight of the riverbank, the road widened and became gravelled — and there was the head of the bridge, with a fringe of winter-bare trees on either side. A magpie was startled into flight as they drew near. Like an arrow of crisp black and white, the bird soared over their heads, cawing in protest — or, someone fanciful could have thought, in mockery. From the other bank, the bells of Staines's Sunday piety carried on the water.

A week earlier, in the midst of a snowfall, the wooden bridge had seemed a rickety thing, its piers gracelessly planted on gravel islands like a wide-legged animal on uncertain ground. What a difference the sun made: now the bridge looked sturdier and larger, almost noble as it strode across the expanse of lazy, winterish water. It was a toll-bridge, with a tollhouse sitting on the Middlesex side, and Tom fingered his dwindling purse. With any luck, this toll, an early dinner and a change of horses would be the last he'd have to pay for the whole group.

It being Sunday, there wasn't much in the way of traffic. Still, they had to wait as another party crossed the other way, slow as a sunless Lent, for they carried a litter.

"It will be easier to wait, and quicker in the end," Tom explained in Spanish when Bilqasim came to stand at his side. "Were it just horses, the bridge is large enough, but that litter…" He trailed off when he observed that Bilqasim's attention wasn't on the bridge at all, but on the man in the green hood.

"Will the King of Portugal make pretence that he never sent his spy to us?" he asked under his breath.

"Most surely, yes — and you'll never see the fellow again."

Bilqasim shook his head. "God did not make me for these games, *Señor* Ulsingam. Do you think he is the one who killed Farras?"

And Hakim… Tom looked the turciman in the eye. "I don't know. He could have done it."

Such a great sigh, such a forlorn gaze… "If I had not insisted on taking him with us…"

"Would you have abandoned a man, injured and horseless, to die in the snow? He counted on the fact that no one would."

"So he would at least have until the morning to watch us. To think…" Bilqasim clicked his tongue. "Do you know why I had him travel with us?"

Was it truly only five days since they'd argued over this in Bridport? "Charity is a pillar of your faith, you said."

"And I thought that my many sins called for a greater act of charity."

It struck Tom that he might have laughed at this, only a few days ago. Now… "You couldn't have known the man for a liar," he said. "Wouldn't your God count the good deed, rather than the misjudgement?"

"Even if my misjudgement caused the death of a man? Even if poor Farras paid the price of my charity?" Bilqasim hung his head. "*Ya Hasrati*! It's a regret I'll carry to my grave."

Now, if he truly was a murderer, this fellow had missed his calling: what a superb player he'd have made! But perhaps he wasn't. "That, too, you couldn't have known."

"Are we innocent because of ignorance, then?" A wan smile broke through Bilqasim's frown. "I am not sure how our learned men would regard the matter — but you possess a kind soul, my friend, for all your suspicions. Oh yes, you do suspect me — and still you offer kindness: to a lost sinner, kindness is more than a fountain in the desert."

Kindness, now! "I hope, then, that you'll repay the kindness by not trying to disappear again, Excellency!" Tom retorted, and quenched a temptation to regret the gruffness when the man's face fell.

"You have little cause to believe me when I promise, have you?"

His gaze strayed to Tom's cheap rapier, and Tom's left arm moved of its own accord, as though to conceal the commonplace hilt... Fool! Had he been doing this witless thing for two days without noticing?

And besides, the question: did Tom believe Bilqasim? The silence stretched, and would have grown uncomfortable, but the turciman sought no answer, and had more to say. "Your fine sword... I'm sorry, *Señor* Ulsingam. Another piece of idiocy, if not quite a sin, to add to the burden of my soul."

If he'd gone out seeking on purpose, the man couldn't have chosen a surer way to irk Tom. He was irked at the turciman, and at himself that, in the midst of all that had happened and might happen still, with a vital alliance at stake, he should sulk so about Frances's lost gift. The flare of impatience was more for himself than Bilqasim as he spurred his horse on and joined Dunne at the bridge's head, where the litter-bearers touched at last the Surrey bank.

They crossed in single file, hooves drumming on the wooden planks, the Thames below running an oily blue. Only as they neared the Middlesex end did the river awake a little from its winter slumber, as it sloshed against a watermill wheel and surged over the piers. The large-timbered mill and a tollhouse sat on the bank, guarding each side of the bridge like mismatched sentries. The creaks and groan of the wheel and the gurgling of the water filled the air. It took some shouting to summon the keeper, and Tom paid the toll for the whole party — even for Andrada and Rolston. Out of the corner of his eye he caught Skeres scowling as the coins changed hands, most likely reckoning men and horses and shillings in his head.

"Yes, Skeres — all of them!" Tom groused at his servant as he remounted — not that the lad was wrong, for he'd just bought passage for a murderer and a spy among the others. Then again, he'd fed and lodged and horsed them for a whole week — so why old tales of bridges bought from the devil with a price of souls must come to mind, he didn't know.

And then the keeper, so bundled up against the cold that there was no telling the age or build of him, swung the toll-gate open for them, and they entered Staines.

A fairly large inn by any reckoning, the Angel had that lively briskness about it that was often found in bridge-boasting towns. Or was it? Tom wasn't sure if he was still spinning fancies as he dismounted in the well-swept yard and left the reins to a young groom. But there was nothing fanciful to it, for the power of bridges came of traffic, and commerce and control of the land, and not of fiendish intervention — unless one was a Puritan, bent on calling power and money the devil's work... A most idle inner disputation that Tom was happy to set aside when Andrada approached him, cautiously watching over his shoulder.

Oh Lord — he couldn't be coming to raise more trouble, surely?

Something gleamed in Andrada's gloved palm, and his mouth had a displeased skew to it. "You paid the bridge toll for me, Mr. Valsingam," he said in that tilting, awkward English of his. "It sits ill with me to accept."

Buying back your soul? The wild thought flickered across Tom's mind like distant lightning — Lord, but he must be tired! — followed at once by another: *You had no qualms in accepting all the rest, though.*

And then Andrada uncurled his fingers, showing a good deal more than the bridge penny. "The toll, and much else before," he said.

Petty and small-minded — that's what Tom felt of a sudden, and a little weary of himself. It was small consolation to decline, to say that Dom Antonio was a friend and an ally. "Even when the King forgets it, Her Highness does not."

What was it, fleetingly changing the man's countenance? A moment's darkening, as soon gone as come, and more than Tom could put a name to — like a foreign word overheard. Not even the Moors were as hard to read as this man. Had he taken offence? There was a strange, stiff gravity, almost a sadness to the slow nod.

"My thanks, then, *Senhor* Valsingam, for this, and for rescuing me from that pit…" Andrada stopped, face twisting briefly. "*Deus vo lo pague.*"

Portuguese was enough like Spanish that Tom understood some of it: *God reward you.* With this most curious valediction, Manuel d'Andrada turned about — straight-backed as no clerk would ever carry himself — and strode away, his green hood vivid in the sunlight until he disappeared inside the inn.

One of these days, Tom decided, he'd have to ask young Galvam or Ambrose Lopes about the workings of the Portuguese mind and Portuguese pride — if either could be of help, for both had been born and raised in England, after all, and neither as a nobleman. *God reward you…* Hardly the salutation of a murderer, was it? But then, if murderers went about gnashing their teeth like villains at the play, life would be much easier. Tom followed the man at a more sedate pace. Now for an early dinner, and promptly changed horses, and then the road again. No matter what, he meant to be in London by night, and to sleep in his own bed in Seething Lane.

After the sunlit yard, the Angel's passage was a sudden greyness, and a smell of fresh sawdust and cooked onions. Tom paused, blinking as he waited for his eyes to adjust. There was a door at the far end, and another on either side. The one on the right stood open, and from it came a lilting voice that could only belong to Andrada, too soft to catch the words. The answer, though, there was no mistaking: "That ain't no good English silver, my fine Master! Papist saints won't get you no horses here!"

A peek through the door showed a corner of the stables, and Andrada arguing with a cross-armed groom. Were wars born of this mistrust of all that is foreign, or did Mankind learn mistrust from warring with foreigners?

And then someone came noisily through the farthest door, and philosophy was cast aside when the innkeeper appeared to enquire what the gentleman lacked.

The wits to uncover a murderer and a spy, a real ambassador, the finest of rapiers, money while we are at it, and land of my own... But, since for the moment a quick meal and fresh horses would do, that was what Tom asked for of the solicitous landlord, for himself and the party that would soon cease to be his trouble.

"*Him* you're letting go," Lucas Galvam muttered — so softly that, hopefully, Tom alone heard him, for all that they were all squeezed together around one table in a snug, just apart from the crowded taproom: the two surviving Moors close together at one end, Roberts with Dunne at his side, Rolston and Skeres each on his own — the Minotaur a figure of Maltreated Innocence — and young Galvam at Tom's elbow. Three times the lad had started to speak, and twice he'd made no word. Now, it seemed, he'd found the courage.

Not even bothering to ask for patience from above, Tom kept to his cheat bread and cold meat. If he ignored young Galvam for long enough, would the boy give up?

Seemingly not. See how he squirmed on the bench, glaring at the townsmen in their Sunday best that crowded the room, as though each of them were Manuel d'Andrada — or perhaps Tom himself. "Is it because you've found he's innocent?" he asked. "Or is it just that he's a nobleman, and —"

"It is that he's Dom Antonio's man," Tom broke in. "What would you have me do — hit him over the head and lock him in a cupboard?"

The brown eyes blazed like murder. "But if he has —"

Oh Jove! Tom straightened, half twisting around to loom over the boy. "Whatever he's done, I have no proof," he said with all the quiet sternness he possessed. He'd have to speak to Dr. Lopes, if he meant this lad for Service work.

For a whole minute Galvam sat in cowed silence, head bowed as he sliced a bit of cheese rind into smaller and smaller pieces. "Not that you've proof against me, either," he said eventually.

"Over you I have authority, though," Tom pointed out. "Or I should have, and you shouldn't talk back."

Oh, the bitterness as the lad looked up, likely biting back more impertinence. "Ay, Master," was the flat-voiced answer. "And then I'm only a scrivener, am I?"

Little fool, dooming himself to a life of misery, if he kept this up! What had his mother thought, with her talk of kingly fathers — even if it were true? And meanwhile, couldn't he unburden his bitter soul to someone else?

"Scriveners thrive better when they don't pity themselves," grumbled Tom. "Since you've no stomach for dinner, though, go and see whether the horses are ready."

With such vehemence the boy sprang to his feet — half offended man, half child released from the table — that all turned to watch him. He remembered himself just enough to duck his head in apparent obedience before he stalked away.

It's my station in life that I've no stomach for, said every line of his body as he elbowed his way past a harried maid.

But truly, how did the Lopeses stand such a spitfire? Tom sipped at his ale, ignoring his companions' stares, until all went back to their dinners — all but the Lady Khalida, who kept staring from behind Bilqasim's shoulder, and Dunne, who scooted onto the bench to sit in front of Tom.

"I've had cockerels like that under me on the field," he said, jerking his head towards where Galvam had disappeared. "Boys playing at being grown men. Some make it, some don't... And you never know which, 'til they go into the fire."

It vexed Tom that the man seemed to be fishing for something — but for what? Then again, most things vexed him these days, and all raised his suspicion. And, because in uncertainty it served better to appear dull rather than too shrewd, he said, "There's a good thing about being a scrivener. For the most part, they never see fire at all."

With a little grunt, Dunne sat back and sucked his teeth like one pondering some choice morsel of wisdom — which Tom's remark hadn't been. He picked a piece of cheese rind from the trencher. "And ... Harker?" he asked. "Gone his way?"

Offhandedness didn't come any more naturally to this soldier than subtle inquiry.

"As was to be expected," Tom said. There had been just enough of a pause before Andrada's false name to show that Dunne knew better. In other times, Tom would have trusted his own servant just as much.

But the soldier wasn't done — why, far from it!

"Young Lucas is Portuguese, ain't he?" he asked — of the cheese rind, one would have thought — and there was the bone the man had been gnawing at all the time. Had Roberts sent his scout ahead with his doubts, or were they Dunne's

261

own that Roberts wouldn't listen to? The latter, perhaps, judging by the side-glance the soldier shot not quite at his master. Roberts, busy eating his fill, took no notice.

"Young Lucas is Dr. Lopes's man," Tom pointed out, because the more he thought about it, the less minded he felt to suspect the boy. "And he was the one to discover our Harker."

With a sniff, Dunne braced himself upright with both palms on the table. "Well, it's for you to say, Master. Myself, I never trust a Papist if I can help it."

Was it worth pointing out that Galvam's master had come to England fleeing the Inquisition? Likely not. "You're hardly the only one in this," Tom said instead, and rose in turn, half wondering at the boy, and half thinking back to the groom, who had refused Andrada's Papist saints...

Oh Lord!

Tom's innards clenched around a stinging nest of sparks as the glass tiles shifted and clicked inside his mind. There was the pattern at last — and he'd never thought...

The landlady in Blandford greeting Harker like an old friend.

Al-Awar searching the cloaks, and Harker snatching his away.

Harker, drenched to the bone, carrying Roberts's smashed box.

A glimmer of gold, the Christ on one side, on the other a haloed saint. *Ducatus Venetus...*

Cruzados have no saints on them.

Papist saints won't hire you no horse here.

Because he'd given the wrong coin...

"Are you well, Master?"

Tom found himself blinking at Dunne and caught the Lady Khalida's stare fixed on him again. But Spanish spies weren't magpies to be startled into flight; they were popinjays one tended carefully, and fed, and taught words to repeat.

"All's well, Dunne, I just want to see the horses," Tom said as evenly as he could. "Finish your dinner: the sooner we leave, the sooner we'll make London."

Skeres made to rise and join him — but, the Minotaur having his own notions on how to deal with spies, Tom pointed at the leftovers. Not that they'd need them, with any luck, but Skeres could never resist a bit of scavenging, and he set to work as Tom made for the door.

Only when he was in the passage did he take off at a run.

Now Fates send his man hadn't taken flight yet!

In the quiet stable, five horses waited, already saddled. Four of them were quite placid, while the fifth shook his head at some annoyance, with much rattling of bit and bridles.

"Galvam!" Tom called, looking around, and called louder when there was no answer. "Galvam!"

The noise of steps came from the hayloft above, and the groom's head appeared in the trapdoor. "You want the other horses, Master? Out in the yard." He leant lower to point to the doors, sending down a rain of hay dust.

"And my men?" Tom asked.

"Out there." The man pointed again. "The boy just arrived, and they went outside. Speaking in tongues, Master, and the boy's mad as an adder —"

Tom didn't stop to listen, and rushed out, half expecting to find the two men fighting in the yard...

The yard was empty, but for three more horses. On two sides stood the stables and the inn; against a third wall stood half a dozen barrels and a small cart. Along the fourth was a row of low, rough doors — three of them, and the farthest stood ajar. Were there voices filtering through it? Tom sidled close — and yes: Manuel d'Andrada, speaking in Portuguese. He spoke slowly, as though each syllable weighed greatly on his tongue, breath hitching now and then... Which was a good thing, or Tom would have understood even less than he did.

"What does he know of gratitude, young fool? Even if you truly are his son..." There was more that was incomprehensible, and then something like a choked laugh. "All the years I served him, all that I gave up for his sake! My blood, my lands, my family — and he takes all as if it's just his due, and when you've no more to give —!" Andrada cut to an angry halt and, when he resumed, he sounded much gentler. "Nobody should want to be his child!"

There was a string of soft, fierce words — oaths, perhaps. Was this Galvam retorting?

"Nor mine, yes!" Andrada again, voice thick with bitterness. What came next Tom didn't understand, but then the man grew louder: "Serving this worthless, thankless man, then going over to Spain — and I make a poor traitor! One Moor caught me, one saw through me, and now you..."

There was a weak, gurgling gasp that turned Tom's blood to ice.

"If you'd waited a while, boy — only a little while!" Andrada's sigh hitched.

Go and see whether the horses are ready... Tom closed his eyes. He'd sent Galvam away out of pique and impatience! And now... His fingers cramped around the hilt.

A spy exposed, Thomas, is but a petty satisfaction...

But, Sir, what of the weight of a man's life?

As noisily as he could, Tom stepped in front of the door. "Galvam! What are you about?" he called, shoving at the rough planks.

It wasn't Galvam, of course. It was Andrada who whipped around in the sudden flood of wintry light — nostrils flaring, dagger bloodied. The arm he held up against the glare was crimsoned too, blood staining sleeve, wrist, palm and fingers.

"What the devil —?" Tom surveyed the narrow room — an empty pigsty that the stark light cut in two — and there, in the shadowed half, sprawled on the packed dirt... "Lucas!"

Shoving Andrada against the wall, Tom went down on one knee by the boy. Lord God have mercy! Young Galvam lay on his back, his stare empty, his face ashen but for the thin line of blood that escaped the corner of his gaping mouth. His bare hands were half-curled into fists, the left bloodied, clutching at the tear in his chest, the other flung out, where it had scrabbled at the dirt.

"He attacked me..."

Soft as the words were, Tom was startled. He'd forgotten Andrada for a moment — long enough that, had the man been minded to strike him and run...

But no, he'd sheathed his dagger and had a tale ready behind that grim manner.

"He attacked you," Tom repeated in slow disbelief, watching the ground for ... there! The boy's own weapon lay by his outstretched arm, the blade stained with blood.

And the murderer was holding his left forearm, where blood leaked from a tear in the sleeve. "A thief, a spy, a murderer — whatever he was."

Bitter laughter burned in Tom's throat, sour as bile and hard as quarried stone. Oh, but this man had his wits about him!

"I caught him —" Andrada began, and then Roberts barged through the door, with Dunne on his heels. Both came to a halt two steps inside, blocking out the light.

"Walsingham? What...?" Roberts squinted into the gloom, taking in Andrada bleeding, then Tom on his knees, and at last the boy's body. "Save us all!"

"He attacked me!" Andrada started again, holding up his wounded arm — and then stopped, eyes narrowed at the newcomers.

"They know," Tom said, and Andrada's shoulders fell.

When he began again, it was the nobleman speaking: "I caught him searching the bags —"

Dunne broke in bluntly: "In here?"

"Back in the stables. He said that he would tell, that there were things the King must know. But the groom was coming and going, so he led me outside first, and then here..."

Yes, it had all happened, no doubt — only the other way around. Galvam happening on his countryman with his hands in a bag that wasn't his own, the boy calling out, and then... Had Galvam seen his chance at a noble deed at last? Or had he been flattered that the King's man would take him into his confidence? It mattered little enough — and it mustn't be known.

When Roberts sought Tom's eye, what could he do, but shrug?

Roberts grimaced. "Never much liked the boy, did you, Tolly?"

"Never thought he'd know how to best that Moor, either," the soldier said, "or one who ain't no clerk."

"He caught me by surprise. It is dark, this place, after the courtyard. And he was *muito forte*." Andrada made to lift an unsteady hand, frowned at the bloodied fingers and lowered it. "Not very skilled, but strong."

The finest liar — curse him! One would think that he was truly upset.

"You'd better have that arm bound," Tom said — curt, but who would blame him? Failing to find the murderer until it was too late...

And then there came a bellow of "Master!" and Skeres pushed his way inside, and Rolston behind him, and both stared at the dead boy on the floor. The innkeeper waddled in next and broke into lamentation.

"You've ruined me, my masters!" the man wailed. "What am I to do with a dead man in my poor inn? I must send for the constables —"

"No you must not." All they lacked now! Leaping to his feet, Tom grabbed the man by the arm. "Not if you value this place of yours."

How the innkeeper sputtered that he knew the law, and was taking no threats — until Tom shoved under his nose the papers with the seals.

"Mr. Secretary Walsingham's business," he said. "And Her Majesty the Queen's."

It had long ceased to be amusing, the way those few words and a piece of figured wax affected man, woman, and child. The landlord's cheeks went the damp yellow of butter, and all spluttering died down to a bleat.

"But the constables will hear of it..." The man inched backwards until he bumped into Skeres. "Please, Your Honour, what shall we do...?" He jutted his quivering chins towards the dead youth — several times, in minute, birdlike jerks — this fellow who'd thought to play the lion.

Yes, what would they do with Lucas Galvam? Poor boy, who'd called himself a king's son — and now would have to be remembered as a spy... Roman Virgil sprung unbidden to Tom's mind: the young king slaughtered in an uneven duel for the greater good, his offended soul fled in anger... He'd have liked the lofty poetry, this child who lay killed in the dirt.

"There was a row, one of the Queen's men was badly hurt, and his fellows brought him away — that's all you know," Tom ground out. He sought Andrada's eye to make sure the man had heard the hasty tale, and found him leaning against the wattle wall, holding his bloody arm, pasty-faced but very much alert. He needed tending, though, which the flustered landlord was tasked to see done.

Where was Skeres, now? The Minotaur hovered by the door, glowering at the world in general. His scowl didn't clear one jot when Tom told him to find a cart for the conveying of the body, and follow with it as best he could.

"A row!" the lad snorted. "'Ope the law's mighty dull-witted 'ere around, Mr. Tom!"

"I'll leave enough papers with you that they'll swallow it whole."

For a moment Skeres just dithered, studying his shoes and sucking his teeth — all signs of deep soul-searching with him, which Tom would have waited out or ignored at another time. As it was, he went for the easy misunderstanding.

"Just play dour, Nick, and wave the papers about: they *will* swallow it," he insisted.

"Ay, and the more fool them — for I —" The Minotaur stopped short and threw a savage glare at the landlord leading Andrada away, and then at Roberts and Dunne where they stood over the body. "Say what you like, Master: if that stripling did in the guard, then I'm a sugar poppet!"

"Well, then mind the rain, or you'll melt away," Tom warned sternly. Must the Minotaur turn astute at the most inconvenient moments? It was a good thing that Roberts and his man were so busy muttering to each other — although

Tom would have wagered that the gist of their muttering must be just as inconvenient as Skeres's doubts.

And then at last the lad shrugged in defeat.

"Ay, Master. The boy was a murtherer, if you say so."

"Not that you'll tell that to anyone who asks. A row — that's all there was to it. The boy was hot-tempered…" Which was true enough, for there had been a fire to Lucas Galvam, who now lay cold and sallow as a lump of old wax. And why the expediency weighed so unpleasantly on him, Tom didn't want to question. With a last reminder of carts and promptness, he fled Nick Skeres's reproachful gaze.

Half a population had gathered in the yard by then — inn-folk and customers, men and women shifting their weight, and gaping round-eyed as Tom emerged from the pigsty and took a lungful of clean air.

"They's killed a man!" a vixen-faced scullion shrilled, half tickled and half in fright.

Tom ignored her — and the murmuring her outburst raised — and went to the two Moors, who stood clinging together, away from the little crowd. Or rather, Bilqasim clung with an arm around the not-boy's shoulder; she held on to the man's sleeve as though to anchor him, and frowned at Tom with steady eyes.

"It was the lad, then?" Bilqasim asked in soft Spanish. "He was the spy? He killed al-Awar?"

It stuck in Tom's craw to call Galvam a murderer, a spy… But nobody must know of Andrada — much less these two liars, so desperate for money.

"Spy and murderer were one and the same," he said — and Fates send the turciman blamed the strange utterance on Tom's unskilled Spanish, rather than his uneasy conscience.

CHAPTER 16

Tom was relieved when the innkeeper's wife took charge. Just as cowed as her husband but more active, she sat Andrada by the window in her kitchen parlour, fetched him a cup of well-sugared wine, and busied herself with water and strips of white cloth, working with purse-lipped alacrity. She only had a fleeting glance for Tom when he perched on the windowsill to watch the proceedings — but, innkeepers being what they are, both men kept quiet as she cleaned and bandaged.

The cut was sizable, though not deep. Had poor Galvam truly managed to inflict it, or had Andrada wounded himself, after murdering the boy, to lend more credit to his tale? There was very little that Tom would put past Andrada, for all that he sat hunched and ashen. He'd bled, after all — although not half enough for Tom's reckoning.

Pray God this man would prove of true use to Sir Francis, to the Queen and England, because otherwise...

At length the landlady was satisfied with her work and eased the sleeve back over the bandaged arm. "There you are, Master," she announced, as she tied the last knot.

Andrada smiled uncertainly at her, and fumbled one-handed at his side — only to stop short. Was he foolish enough to still wear the purse that had never been Hakim's? He cursed softly, dazed eyes wandering between Tom and the landlady.

And Tom did what any unsuspecting man would do in his place, and fished out of his own purse a vail for the woman — a generous one, in the vague hope that silver would buy some discretion. Perhaps it would, judging by the slow deliberation of the landlady's curtsey. After that, she gathered her pail of bloodied water and stained cloths and bustled away — eager to leave the Queen's men to their secrets and their quarrels.

There was a moment's silence, thick as curdled milk, but for the clucking of poultry outside the window. From his perch, Tom watched as Andrada picked at the bandage peeking from his cuff.

At length the man heaved a sigh. "Whatever made him kill the guard, he was still searching for it today, wasn't he?"

Clever, clever fellow. Calling the boy no worse than a thief — and yet sowing the doubt that there might have been more… And a taker of risks, for the same went for him as for Galvam.

"My man is checking al-Awar's bag," Tom said, which he meant to make true as soon as possible. Not that they'd find anything … or would they? Whatever the guard had been seeking — and perhaps found — back at Blandford? Or perhaps Andrada hadn't been rifling through the bag; perhaps he'd been planting some suspicious item in it. One of the cursed Venetian ducats? Or would they find one of those on Galvam's person? Surely this snake had had the time, while Tom — God forgive him — eavesdropped on the poor boy's death.

See how the murderer turned round and round the cup of wine he hadn't touched.

"Lopes must —" he began, but Tom broke in.

"Lopes will hear about it at length — for all that Galvam travelled under my charge." And then another thought made him cold to the marrow. "And you'll inform your king."

Oh, the care Andrada would take in informing King Antonio of the spy in Lopes's camp! Sowing distrust, covering his own dealings with Mendoza, and who knew what other birds he meant to down with this one stone. And poor Galvam's name would at last come to the ears of the man he called his father — as the name of a traitor. Tom pretended to watch out of the window, where half a dozen chickens scratched around in a little yard, just black and ruddy spots when seen through the thick leaded glass.

"*Que idade tinha?*"

Tom stiffened at the softly spoken, foreign words, and turned slowly, as blank-eyed as possible. Better to pretend he had no Portuguese, in case this was a trap, in case the man wondered if he'd been overheard...

When the silence stretched, Andrada repeated the question in English, just as softly and sadly — as though he were discussing an acquaintance, instead of the man he'd just murdered. "How old was he?"

"Seventeen," Tom said, and then Manuel d'Andrada looked up.

God smite this murderer — must he twist his face in such raw-eyed anguish?

"My son is of an age with your Galvam," he murmured. "I have not seen him in eight years. I all but abandoned him. If I were to learn that he..."

Or he that you... It was all too easy to imagine fiery, artless, loyal Galvam meeting this nobleman's betrayal with the most stinging revulsion, bristling at all persuasion, rejecting all bribes, answering any threat at dagger-point. *You think I'll let you betray the King, my father?* Or some other high-minded nonsense.

And, of a sudden, Tom found that he could take no more of it — not another heartbeat — and pushed himself briskly to his feet. "Well, Galvam had no father to learn of this — or anything else," he said — and let Andrada make what he liked of it. If he had a shred of conscience left, he wouldn't make it a lie. "We part ways now, Mr. d'Andrada — and I wouldn't tarry if I were you: the innkeeper is silenced for now, but the constables, when they come, may prove a different matter."

Andrada blinked and sat straighter on the bench. "I'll leave at once," he said, jaw set and shoulders squaring, until there was nothing left of Harker.

And this fellow, carrying himself so nobly, was a murdering traitor… "I hope your master comes to see how ill-advised your errand was," Tom threw over his shoulder — a prayer under the guise of a parting shot. Thrown to the wind, most likely — or perhaps not, who knew? All Manuel d'Andrada had for it was the shadow of a grimace.

Having been charged an unconscionable sum by the landlord — and having paid it all with no protest, Tom was eager to leave before rumours of the Queen's men brawling reached the constables. He walked into the stable yard to find that Dunne had ridden ahead with news of their arrival, and all the rest of his travellers were ready to go, if very grim. Even Rolston had grown thoughtful as he studied Galvam's body across the yard, where it lay on the bottom of a tumbrel, covered with his cloak. As soon as Tom was mounted, Essex's man nudged his mare close, still fixing the cart.

"If ever I needed proof that you can never tell…" He shook his head. "Who would have thought?"

Angling — which was not unexpected, for Rolston, though no great wit, wasn't entirely mindless. Tom had his lie ready by then — one of several to be distributed according to what each listener knew and must learn. "He believed the Moor had stolen who knows what from him. He'd told Skeres, it turns out, and the fool never thought to tell me before now."

"Was it true?"

"Who knows?"

"And when the clerk caught him, he lost his head?" Rolston tapped a knuckle to his lips, like one weighing the notion. Was he disappointed? Had he hoped to solve the matter himself? Not that they'd ever discussed a Spanish spy, but the chance of one must have crossed even Essex's untrained mind. At any rate, poor Galvam hadn't made a likely intelligencer.

"One of Lopes's fellows, was he?" Rolston mused, in a manner Tom disliked very much. The manner of one who stored away at least one titbit for his master who, it was no secret, had little liking for the good doctor.

"A most unwisely hot-tempered scrivener," Tom said — and, as he spurred his horse to leave the Angel, he would have gladly left behind Essex's man as well.

What the Dolphin Inn looked like on a Sunday evening when no foreign ambassador was about, Tom didn't know. At the moment it was all astir, alive with hasty steps and voices. Yards and hall, and parlours, and stables all glowed with light, and the doors stood wide open to the damp, nipping air as men came and went, and called orders or scurried to obey them, so that no flame — candle or hearth — was left to burn undisturbed.

This was the largest inn by Temple Bar, just without the City, where travellers from the west must pass to enter London, be they poulterers or kings' envoys. The inn-folk must be used to bustle — although perhaps not quite to the degree of having the Barbary Company take over.

From where he stood by the taproom fire, sipping warm ale in the company of John Cardenas, Tom tiredly watched an anthill's worth of finely attired merchants and busy servants go about with much noise, and a manner of the greatest purpose. Now and then one of them would find Mr. Secretary's men, and ask some question of no discernible relevance, and then rush away again…

"They've been at it since your Dunne arrived," Cardenas said as the latest such messenger disappeared up the oaken staircase. "Flocking here in a frenzy, running around…" He stopped, raising one brow as a great peal of laughter sounded from the upper gallery. "Fortifying themselves."

"And they've mounted this Bartholomew fair since this afternoon?"

Cardenas huffed into his ale. "Well, these past ten days — ever since they got wind of the Ambassador's coming. They've stabled horses all over Fleet Street, they've sent criers to raise an audience for the solemn ingress, and you wouldn't credit the coach!"

In truth, Tom had seen the coach — how could he have missed the lumbering affair that took up half the inner yard? And it was unreasonable to dislike the thought of Bilqasim paraded across London in that great open cage of gilt wood and green velvet. The man had looked lost as Roberts whisked him away, presumably to show him off to his masters. Fates send that he kept his head, and bless the Lady Khalida, who never left her lover's side, wide-eyed but steady.

It was Cardenas's elbow to his ribs that dragged Tom from these thoughts — for they were to enjoy more attention from the Barbary Company. Not a servant, this time, but one of the merchants, a long-shanked young fellow, clad in the finest burgundy velvet, a bejewelled high-crowned hat, and tall boots so gleaming they couldn't have ever seen an honest day's riding. But it must pay well to be a Barbary merchant…

Tom stood as tall as he could in his mud-spattered buskins, and endured as he was told, for the third time, that the

Company's escort numbered fifty mounted men, all with torches.

"Perhaps you would like to ready your people for the ingress?" the fellow suggested, and, tilting his long chin at Tom's travel-stained attire, added, "And to ready yourself, Master?"

Jove rain on the stiff-necked popinjay! "Walsingham," Tom snapped — not that he'd been asked. "It's Mr. Walsingham — and I'm all my people at present, and I've no intention of readying myself for anything. I've escorted His Excellency across a good half of England — surely your Company can be trusted to see him from Temple Bar to the Cheap?"

Be it the Walsingham name or the brusque address, the man was struck speechless for a moment. He blinked twice and then recovered enough to blurt out, "Well then!"

Blessings be on the head of John Cardenas, who stepped forward with his smoothest smile and an orator's hand spread in placation. "Mr. Staper, is it? What Mr. Walsingham means is that we've done our part — for now — but the honour of leading the Sultan's envoy into the city was always meant for the Barbary Company."

The best that could be said for fools: most of them were easily mollified. Young Staper, or whatever he called himself, was one such man. A look of appeased dignity spread across his horse-like face, and he nodded to Cardenas and, if a little more stiffly, to Tom.

"Of course, my masters," he conceded. "We could have done with an earlier warning of your arrival — but Mr. Roberts tells us that you had a harrowing time of it... I'm sure, Mr. Walsingham, that you had your hands full."

And, with more equine nodding, the man went to bother someone else — leaving Tom a-gape.

"A harrowing time!" He turned to find Cardenas wincing. "My hands full, had I! Had you not come between…"

"Call it an act of charity. Little Staper thinks much of himself, because his father is a senior man in the Company — but he's never had to deal with a Walsingham before."

"Oh, Jupiter!" A huff of laughter escaped Tom. Of a sudden all the soreness of ten days in the saddle, the cold, the constant tension, all of it was catching up with him. "Sir Francis wouldn't have liked it, if I knocked the dunce on the head."

"Only because he's never met him," Cardenas said, with a little smile that didn't quite mask the worry beneath. "But … you think that Roberts is gilding his tale?"

"Oh, let him. He'll want to paint himself a hero's part: the fearless soldier, shepherding his charges amidst dangers and torments…" Tom stopped when he caught just what he was being asked. Lord — but his wits were dull this evening! He frowned at the fire, making himself think: how far would Roberts go in his eagerness? It was a relief to find himself, on the whole, reassured. "He promised to keep the matter of the murders small — a row over a theft and nothing more. The first murder, back in Bridport, he still thinks an accident."

"And will he keep his word?"

"I impressed on him the weight of both Mr. Secretary's gratitude and his displeasure — but I think he'll keep quiet for his own sake. *In primis*, imagine that you're angling for all the credit you can snatch for the mission: how would you like to admit you let a Spanish spy travel with you and kill one of the Moors?"

Cardenas hummed in acknowledgment. "I'd be only too content to leave this particular bone for Mr. Secretary's man to gnaw."

"And, *in secundis*, and most importantly —" Tom dropped his voice — "there's what Mr. Secretary's man knows."

This, also, Tom had taken care to impress on Roberts and on Bilqasim separately: one wrong word, and they'd be the first to suffer for it. And if uncovering the false Ambassador could prove very awkward for Mr. Secretary too, that would protect neither man: both had seen it at once.

So had Cardenas, judging by his brisk nod. "As long as Roberts believes that the scrivener is the spy," he murmured.

Didn't it come as a piece of cruel good luck now that Tolly Dunne had never taken to poor Lucas Galvam? "He and his soldier both are of those who will believe the worst of any soul from Lopes's household," Tom said. "Like Rolston. You remember Anthony Rolston?" And he told of the turncoat who had taken his leave outside the bar — headed to Essex House, no doubt. Cardenas was not overly surprised.

"Essex thinks he's astute. Buying away a few of His Honour's men, waiting for the rest to fall into his lap…" *When His Honour dies and we're left adrift*, the Spaniard didn't say.

And Tom said nothing of Rolston's fancies of the earl courting Frances, and only groused that Essex was welcome to the Rolstons of this world. Some of his black humour must have shown, though: see how Cardenas studied him aslant, like one mulling over an awkward question. But surely he could know nothing of Tom and Frances, could he?

But he did not — or, if he did, it wasn't on his mind at present. "Especially if they bring to him the wrong conclusion," he said, still with that slantwise wince. *Because it is the wrong conclusion, and there's no chance that the scrivener could have been the spy?*

It was all Tom could do not to laugh. Did he seem moon-sick, that Cardenas should worry and mislike to ask? Perhaps he did — at least when he dwelt on Frances. He could only hope the rueful huff he let out would sound sane, if not quite reassuring. "Yes, John — quite the wrong conclusion. I'll tell you in Spanish, in Italian, and in Latin, if it convinces you that I'm in my right mind."

They shared a chuckle and backed out of the way as half a dozen servants trooped past, carrying a trunk and several boxes that belonged neither to Bilqasim nor Roberts. The Company's welcome gifts, or had the merchants decided that no ambassador could lack a baggage train? With any luck, the Company would also dig up some Moorish jewels for the Queen.

"If they knew of King Antonio's man, wouldn't they all jump!" Cardenas whispered.

"Not quite King Antonio's — but yes, Heaven forbid!" Abandoning his empty cup on the mantelpiece, Tom went to sit on the settle and surreptitiously rolled his shoulders. "A traitor in Mendoza's pay, ruthless enough to kill three men…" he mused when Cardenas joined him.

"Not very good at it, though, if he risked being exposed three times," said the Spaniard. "What will Mendoza do with one who leaves behind such a trail of death?"

One Moor caught me, one saw through me, and now you, Andrada had told poor dying Galvam. But was this true? Tom had been mulling over this on the journey's last leg. "I don't know that the first Moor discovered him at all. We all thought him a harmless sick clerk, back then, and perhaps Hakim just caught the false Harker snooping where he should not, looking far healthier than he'd made out… But Andrada couldn't hazard the slightest suspicion, so he drew the fellow up to the garret, or perhaps found himself followed there." He groaned. "I wish I'd thought to check Hakim's skull, for I'd wager you that

Andrada hit him on the head to daze him — and only then planted the purse and shoved the poor fellow out of the window."

"Come now, what reason had you to suspect foul play?"

"I'm Walsingham's hound. I should always suspect foul play on principle."

"That would be a grim life to lead," Cardenas said, soft and solemn-eyed.

It was one of those times when the Spaniard in him showed, Tom thought, in the form of this austere gravity. "Well, it should be my job, shouldn't it?" he retorted in sudden irritation. "Instead I called it an accident. Oh, I had the wit to suspect that Hakim might have been a spy, more than a thief — but when the damn purse was lost in the Tarrant, did it give me pause? Not a jot! I kept wondering, and running in circles, and stumbling into ever more lies, more pretences, more... What a fool!" With a groan, Tom sat forward, elbows on his knees, and rubbed at his eyes. "I kept misdoubting each soul in that pack of liars of being a spy — but a murderer? Even after the guard died, and that *was* a murder, it took me a whole day to put two and two together. What will Sir Francis think?"

"That you found out all there was to find, I think. And the guard didn't help you — or himself — by not coming to you with whatever he'd seen."

"I'm not sure he knew what it was that he'd seen."

"Andrada in the wrong place, just like the other servant?"

"That — or something else, so slight he didn't think I'd believe him." *A man who does not expect to be believed*, Bilqasim had said of al-Awar. "Still I think he meant to tell me... Why, he even tried, and I didn't understand, but Andrada saw it. If only I'd been less ready to suspect him..."

"And then what? You'd have had to let Andrada go all the same, and I don't think it would have made any difference to that scoundrel: he'd have killed the guard anyway, and the boy, too."

"That we cannot know," Tom sighed.

"Yes, because the boy knew of the Spanish spy. When he caught Andrada with the bags, there was no other conclusion he could draw — whatever it was that he was searching for."

It irked Tom that he still had no certain answer. "Perhaps he wanted to make sure that al-Awar had had no proof against him ... and then Lucas Galvam happened by — a gift from the devil! The perfect culprit who could never defend himself."

"Jesu..." Cardenas stopped short at the sudden ruckus from the door to the street.

Oh, was there no end to this hot water? Tom jumped to his feet and rushed for the nearest window, Cardenas at his elbow, and pushed the casement open to find Fleet Street invaded by clamouring apprentices in thin cloaks and blue caps. "Ye Moors and valiant men of Barbary!" they jeered, clubs held high, until a dozen between Dolphin grooms and Company servants rushed out to disperse them, armed with clubs of their own, a few daggers, and even one or two of the much-famed torches.

Tom wished them joy of it. "Aren't apprentices a plague and a penance!" he exclaimed, raising his voice over the din for Cardenas's ear. "What the devil do they want?"

The Spaniard tilted his head in mock disconsolation. "How many times have I told our Barbary friends these past days? If you raise a crowd, the crowd is likely to raise hell. If you give them money to be in the street, what do you think they'll do with it — offerings to the church? But did they listen?"

And see the man's catlike smile widen as he contemplated the fray in the street, only stepping back when a chunk of horse-dung sailed through the open window.

"You've had your share of torment from these fellows, haven't you?" Tom asked.

Still, there was something to be said for the Barbary Company's discipline, if a gang of roistering apprentices thought it wise to retreat before them. Not that they went far — at least not all of them: a dozen still pressed together across the street, doing no worse than hooting and yowling, "Ye Moors and fine asses of Barbary!"

Which sounded very familiar. "That's never...?"

"Your friend's *Tamburlaine the Great*," Cardenas laughed. "They go to the play, these imps."

Tom joined in with the laughter. Oh, how Kit Marley was going to love this!

And then there were hasty steps and a string of curses, and Tom found himself all but shoved aside as little Staper strode towards the door, an ornate rapier half out of the scabbard.

What did the popinjay have in mind — to go outside and gut a few apprentices?

"If you barge out there armed —" Tom began — and again Cardenas stepped between.

"I wouldn't if I were you, Mr. Staper," the Spaniard all but purred. "Your men have things well in hand, I'd say."

"Well in hand!" The young merchant waved towards the street. "Don't you hear those... those..."

"Yes, well. With your calling in life, you must know what apprentices are like: go out armed, threaten them, and you'll have a full riot — hardly the right welcome for the Raìs..."

Upstairs the gallery was filling with well-dressed men, the senior merchants, wanting to know what the matter was.

Let Cardenas enjoy himself with this — for he'd had practice. Tom went back to the bench, and, undoing his sword belt, he placed his cheap blades beside him and sat back in what comfort he could, legs spread before him and crossed at the ankle. Not that it was restful, for the merchants were unhappy, and calls and shouts came from the stable yard, and the facts of the last days kept whirling inside his mind — although the glass bits had settled into their pattern now. No matter what John Cardenas said, though, he could have done more and better. He could have been quicker to understand. He could have saved at least young Galvam — who now was not just dead, but a dead traitor for all most would know.

One day, he started to vow, one day he would... And there he stopped. Could he ever hope to bring Manuel d'Andrada to justice, and clear Galvam's name? It was most likely a good thing that, before he could even begin to answer, Cardenas sauntered back, with the air of one pleased with himself. Past the Spaniard, young Staper was trotting up the stairs to join his fellow merchants.

Cardenas was chuckling as he made to sit down — and stopped halfway. "What's that?" He picked up Tom's discarded rapier. "You leave wearing the finest blade I ever hoped to borrow, and come back with this?"

Ah, yes — there was that too. Tom very much disliked his own peevishness as he told the story — and yet, he couldn't stop himself. He was still at it when a voice boomed behind him.

"Just the men I sought — Mr. Secretary's lads!"

Oh, Jupiter — there *was* no end! Tom scrambled to his feet as Sir Christopher Hatton, Lord Chancellor of the Realm, descended on them, loud, fierce, and cheerful. Too cheerful, surely — please Lord — to have caught Tom's indecorous whining?

At least there went one half-answered prayer: the Lord Chancellor clapped Tom's shoulder hard enough to topple him, had he not braced for it, and boomed, "So, what is it, young Walsingham, that these sugar-mongers cackle like jackanapes, and you mope? Haven't you brought the Sultan's man?"

Well, that he had, hadn't he? For Bilqasim was no less the Sultan's man than Marzuq Raìs had been. "I have, Sir," he said with a bow — and he'd worry about all but lying to a Privy Councillor later.

"Good lad!" Hatton squeezed Tom's shoulder. "So why do you mope still?"

Oh, where to begin, Sir? With three murders? With the spy? With the small fact that the Ambassador —?

"He's had the devil's own journey, Sir," Cardenas put in — who must have appointed himself the guardian of half-witted friends that day. "It's a feat that he managed. Would you believe it, Sir —" and, to Tom's horror, he held up the ugly weapon — "that he had to sell his own new rapier when he was robbed and ran out of money? A very fine rapier."

It was often said — though not to the man's face — that when Sir Christopher laughed, the whole of Surrey knew it. It struck Tom that they could have told him square, for the man looked quite pleased when his explosion made the whole inn startle and stare.

Another clap on the shoulder. "Now there's a tale, eh, lad? I'll have it from your uncle — but for now, let it never be said that faithful service should cost a man his sword. How much was your own worth?"

Cardenas never missed a beat. "Ten pounds," he said, smooth as you please. Truly, the man's gall!

But perhaps that was the way to go about these matters, for Hatton chuckled most heartily. "Then ten pounds he'll have, by George," he exclaimed — and then turned around at the sound of many steps on the stairs.

There came the Barbary Company at its most splendid, parading down to meet Hatton in various degrees of wariness and expectation. At once the jollity was gone, and it was the Lord Chancellor who strode to meet the fellows.

"Master Staper," he called, "far be it from me to steal your thunder. I only come to convey Her Highness's appreciation."

The man who stepped forward with a bow and a smile of icy welcome — an older, steadier, much shrewder version of the pup in burgundy — didn't seem all that reassured.

There was a soft moan from Cardenas. "His Honour will want to know this. I'd better go and hear," the Spaniard said, pushing Tom back down onto the bench, and dropping the rapier into his lap.

Oh yes — that. Tom grabbed a black sleeve. "Ten pounds! Are you mad?"

A shrug. "I'm not saying that you should profit — but I wouldn't like to see you lose too much. Besides, I very much doubt you'll see *ten* pounds." And with that, Cardenas left to join the Lord Chancellor.

Shaking his head, Tom sat back down. Oh, he'd lost quite a good deal on this cursed journey that no money could buy back. Three men under his charge — at least one of whom he could have saved — and any last hope that he could, by his work, serve Justice as well as Sir Francis. But then, he always strove for that — and every time found himself bitter again that he could not, which made him consistent in his fond delusion, if nothing else. Whether he'd also lost his servant, he couldn't say. Did he still trust the Minotaur, so loose-tongued with Rolston, so careless at times, so resentful of being kept in the dark? Did the Minotaur still trust him? It would be hard to dismiss him now, because of the money, and harder to keep him. And then there was Frances's rapier — although perhaps he could ride back to Dorchester, if and when Hatton kept his promise, and find the swordsmith's shop again, provided that the man hadn't sold the fine piece already.

And in the middle of this wool-gathering, Tom had the sense that he was being watched. Sitting up straighter, he took in the room. The Barbary Company's men had grown in number, while he reckoned losses in his head, and moved with the Lord Chancellor towards the back door. From the yard came a glow, redder and redder as the torches were lit. And, among the little throng, stood a much different figure, black, and white, and straight, and quiet — and watching Tom.

When he saw he'd been noticed, Bilqasim moved towards the fire. A couple of the merchants took note of the movement, but made no sign of objecting: to them, this was Marzuq Raìs, after all — the Sultan's envoy, rightly impatient to enter London and to start his mission in earnest, eager for all the honours he could receive on his master's behalf. Well, the merchants could not be blamed for thinking so: who would have guessed this grave fellow with the noble bearing to be a humble turciman? He seemed taller in a huge turban and robes of the most dazzling white, several layers of them, under a woollen cloak dyed the deepest black, and draped in abundant folds. Under the cloak, hanging from a gold-encrusted baldric, he wore a gold-hilted Moorish sword with a long gold tassel.

So this was what Moorish finery looked like: not the peacockish glitter of the stage, but unadorned and austere, and all the more imposing for it. Even the man's lean visage had taken on a new hardness against the turban's white folds. This was Marzuq Raìs — until the stern mouth twitched, and Ahmad Bilqasim showed through.

It was the weakest curl of lips, though. "You do not know me anymore, my friend?" the Moor asked in soft Spanish. "I do not blame you, for I hardly know myself."

"It's a great change," Tom whispered back. "I see Marzuq Raìs — or rather…" What was it Bilqasim had said? "The man Marzuq Raìs should have been."

"I wish to God that he were here, and I no more than a turciman and a free-hearted poet!"

Why he'd thought he couldn't read the hawkish face, Tom didn't know, for of a sudden it was plain as daylight: all that straight-backed gravity was nothing but fear. And why shouldn't it be? The man was entering a great capital now, and tomorrow a royal court under false pretence, embroiled in a game whose players had shown themselves ready to kill.

It would be unseemly for anyone to offer overt comfort to the Sultan's envoy, so all Tom could do was to bow, as though receiving thanks. Still, he caught Bilqasim's gaze and held it. "Nothing will befall Your Excellency," he murmured under his breath, "as long as it *is* Your Excellency. You are under Mr. Secretary's protection — whatever is decided." And, as he said it, it struck him belatedly that the decision must have been made already, for otherwise Sir Francis would never let the Barbary Company's welcome make it irrevocable.

Not that the promise seemed to afford Bilqasim much comfort. "Nothing will befall us?" he repeated. "Not even afterward?"

"Nothing," Tom repeated — and wished that he believed it more than he did.

At that moment the Lady Khalida slipped towards her lover's side, attired in a suit of deep green velvet with a wide tunic, and a bejewelled poniard at her hip. She would have made a most handsome boy, but for the far too knowing frown.

"I'm sure we never carried all this finery," Tom said, mostly to shift the talk towards less grim subjects, and Bilqasim's wan smile reappeared, though with a bitter twist.

"Oh no, poor Marzuq Raìs lost all of his luggage in the shipwreck — but the Barbary Company is well versed in aping the Moroccan manner. Among them they possess, it turns out, trunks and trunks of our finest clothes."

Would they also supply more Moroccan jewels to accompany the medallion? Before Tom could ask, one of the merchants came to respectfully fetch His Excellency, for all was ready for the ingress into London. Before this elderly man, with his shrewd, wizened countenance and excellent Spanish, Bilqasim was quick to become Marzuq Raìs again.

"I hope we shall meet again, Tomàs Ulsingam," he said, with that slow, lordly, graceful nod Tom had first seen under the snow in Dorset, and then he glided away with the merchant, head tilted as he listened to the old man. The pretend Ambassador in borrowed finery, going to take to the stage for this, his first play-day in London.

They filed out into the torchlit evening: Hatton and Staper escorting the Sultan's envoy, the page following closely, the merchants on their heels. It had started to snow again, if only slightly: walking to the threshold, Tom watched the flakes dance like moths in the halo of each torch to the sound of calls and cheering. Only when a hand closed around his elbow did he turn around.

"Well, lad? It's done, eh?" Roberts beamed — a much brushed and brisked-up Roberts, in velvet and tall boots. Tom suspected that the Company had attired him no less than the Moors. It was a shame to dim the man's pride…

"Done, Mr. Roberts? We've only just started — so don't let your guard down."

Not that Roberts took heed. "Pah!" he exclaimed. "I never let my guard down in the war in Ireland, nor in all my years in Barbary. I daresay I can keep it up a while longer, eh?" Which would have been reassuring but for the gleeful smile that went with the words — that of a child promised a prize. "I must go now: I'm to ride in the coach with His Excellency."

"Are you? Then see to it that…" The rest Tom swallowed. What was the use? All that could have been said, he'd said already, and Roberts wasn't even listening to him. See how he smiled as the servants handed a torch to each mounted man…

"It was just like this that night, in Marrakesh," he said contentedly. "Last summer, when tidings came that the Armada was sunk. Little did I think, back then…" He shook his head and squeezed Tom's elbow. "Say what you will, young Walsingham: it's done! Please God, we've confounded Spain again."

And he walked out, to reap the first of his rewards in the form of a coach ride in a torchlit pageant — or, rather, a play.

HISTORICAL NOTES

A man had arrived from Fez to see the Queen and Don Antonio, and in order to beguile the people they had christened him ambassador of the Sheriff and asserted that he had brought a great sum of money for Don Antonio. They caused the merchants of London to go out and meet him with 200 horsemen, and the Queen received him with the ceremonial of an ambassador, Don Antonio doing the same, sending him a coach in which to visit him.

When, in late February 1589, the Spanish ambassador Bernardino de Mendoza wrote to King Philip from Paris, he obviously thought the Moroccan envoy a fraud, or at least a visitor of no account dressed up as an all-important diplomat. He owed the notion to the spy he codenamed David, someone with access, if not to the English Court, at least to the motley entourage of Dom Antònio, Prior de Crato — an illegitimate prince who, after a very brief stint on the Portuguese throne, had fled from the invading Spaniards to find refuge in England. Under a veneer of courtly courtesy, Elizabeth and her councillors — Sir Francis Walsingham among them — regarded Dom Antònio as nothing more than a potentially useful pawn in the long game to eject Spain from Portugal, this most important square in the chequerboard of transoceanic trade. Dom Antònio knew this very well — at least most days — but didn't much care, convinced as he was that he could play the English into giving him back his throne.

The Queen's ambitious physician, Dr. Rodrigo Lopes, hailed from Portugal and could boast some remote kinship to Dom Antònio. Thinking himself the perfect man to liaise between the two courts, and relying on his own intelligence network, he stepped into the game — working mostly for Sir Francis, but with an eye to his own gain: the step from royal physician to kingmaker must have seemed like a smart career move.

That said, nobody took Dom Antònio very seriously: not Sir Francis and Elizabeth, not Lopes, and certainly not Mendoza and King Philip. Everybody knew that England would need another kind of ally to threaten Spain's hold on Lisbon. And England, in a rather bold move, looked to the Muslim world: after all, the Ottoman Empire and its North African vassals disliked Spain's commercial, military and religious power as much as England did. Even siding with a non-Christian country seemed worth the political danger: strange bedfellows, and all that.

As was always the case, all had begun with trade: in 1580 a treaty with Sultan Murad III had granted safe passage for English ships in the Eastern Mediterranean and the Barbary Coast, which amounted to de facto trading privileges, and soon after that English merchants and investors began to establish trading ventures licensed by the Crown, like the Turkey Company and the Venice Company. In 1585 the Barbary Company was created, meant to further English trade on the Western coast of Morocco.

To be honest, the Barbary Company never worked too well. Headed by Lord Leicester, the Queen's own favourite, it lacked the structure and focus that made the other companies so successful. Loosely ordered and rather vague in its protection of the interests of its members, it didn't even officially call itself the Barbary Company. And if it's true that it was meant mostly as the means to prepare a political alliance with Mohamed al-Mansour, King of Morocco, even in that it achieved little. Henry Roberts, the military officer Leicester had put in charge of the operation *in loco*, often complained in his correspondence that the King of Morocco all but ignored him. Now, Henry Roberts was neither a merchant nor a diplomat, and it's entirely possible that he wasn't the right man for the job — but I'm not sure that anyone else could have done much better in his place. Al-Mansur, just like Sultan Murad in Istanbul, was happy enough to trade with England but, when it came to this tiny island undermining the power of Spain? Let's say that the Muslim world was highly sceptical.

And then, in the summer of 1588, everything changed when the large armada King Philip had sent to teach England her place in the order of things was thoroughly routed through a combination of naval skill, reckless courage, and bad weather. Well, Sir Francis Walsingham had helped a good deal, by both gathering knowledge and feeding false intelligence to Madrid — but this King al-Mansour didn't know. What he saw was that Spain had been taught a humiliating lesson, and clearly there was more to this small nation of merchants than met the eye.

Enter Marzuq Raìs, who travelled with the returning Roberts in late 1588 and, after "much torment at sea" made land in Cornwall on New Year's Day, and entered London on the twelfth of January. There he received the welcome Mendoza describes, and proceeded to meet the Queen — and, in due time, Dom Antònio. Who was he, really? Mendoza's fraud? Roberts's "gentleman and captain"? The full-credited ambassador received at Court? He certainly carried letters from King al-Mansour, offering 150,000 ducats and military help in an expedition against Spanish Portugal. While it came with conditions and requests, it was the kind of support England had been cultivating — but it's hard to tell just how far the ambassador's mission influenced the organisation of the so-called Counter-Armada later that year. The trouble is that in exchange, al-Mansour expected English military support, should Christian countries attack Morocco — something that Elizabeth simply could not grant.

So, while the negotiations dragged, the Counter-Armada launched in late April, enthusiastically supported by the Queen's new favourite Lord Essex, and was not a resounding success. Certainly, no Moroccan help materialised: the only Moroccan member of the expedition was Marzuq Raìs himself, passing himself off as a Portuguese gentleman aboard Dom Antònio's own flagship. Eventually the English ships sailed back home, having accomplished very little. Dom Antònio was furiously disappointed: Portugal has not risen in his support, and his English friends had grown vague. As for the Moroccan ambassador, we last find him on a ship bound for Morocco, in the company of Sir Francis's not-quite-Spanish secretary, John Càrdenas, who calls him by another name: Ahmad Bilqasim. Afterwards, whatever his name, the man disappears.

Does this lend weight to Mendoza's claim that the ambassador was a fraud? Much as he must have liked it, the idea was not his own. It came from "David", the spy who wrote from England, in Portuguese-tinged Spanish. We know that "David" was Mendoza's codename for Manuel d'Andrada, a Portuguese nobleman who had espoused Dom Antònio's cause, fought, risked and lost much for him, suffered ruin and exile, become an agent and courier — and then … gone over to Spain. At one point he just approached Mendoza and offered his intelligence and even a plan to kidnap Dom Antònio. Mendoza refused at first, then declined the kidnapping, but gladly accepted the intelligence. Spain paid well, we know that — but I like to think that Manuel d'Andrada had grown disillusioned with his petty, greedy, self-centred, small-minded master; having given all he had to give for Dom Antònio, perhaps he came to truly wonder if the man was fit to hold a crown — and the answer turned him into Mendoza's spy.

It's one of those things we'll never know — but it makes for a good story, so I snatched it up.

Regardless of his motives, Manuel d'Andrada is real, and so are Henry Roberts, Marzuq Raìs/Ahmad Bilqasim, Anthony Rolston — who went from Walsingham's service to that of Essex — John Càrdenas, Dr. Lopes, Sir Christopher Hatton, and Staper, the Barbary merchant. The difficult journey from Morocco to England comes from Roberts's report to the Company — basically a litany of complaints and claims for compensation, which the Company rather pointedly refuted. The ambassador's torchlit entrance into London on the twelfth of January 1588/89 also comes from Roberts, and from "David".

The rest is of my own making. I combined Càrdenas's renaming and "David's" scepticism into the idea of the translator posing as the dead ambassador. I made up the Lady Khalida and the murders, and, of course, Tom's involvement in it all. Or, at least...

We know that, in February 1588/89, "Thomas Walsingham gent" was paid a hundred shillings on a warrant signed by Sir Christopher Hatton, "for his paynes and chardgs being ymployed [...] aboute speciall services for her majestie wherwith her heighnes was acquainted." So ... why not the Moroccan ambassador — and a lost rapier with sentimental value?

And, while I was at it, I made John Càrdenas right: of those ten pounds fictionally mentioned to Hatton, poor Tom only sees the half.

A NOTE TO THE READER

Dear Reader,

Thank you for reading *The Man From Morocco*. I hope you enjoyed it.

A very young friend recently asked me what it is that I like so much about history. Well, quite a few things, I said — but one favourite is the glimpse we get sometimes of someone who lived long ago. We catch a habit in a worn kitchen tool, or a predilection in a well-thumbed book, or a quirk in a peculiar way of spelling words…

As a young girl, I first experienced this at the Museo Egizio of Turin, where I saw a bread loaf that had been perfectly preserved inside an Egyptian tomb. It wasn't all that different from the bread we bought and ate every day, and it still carried the imprint of that long dead Egyptian baker's fingers. For a short moment, I could almost see this man, smiling as he handed his piece of bread to me across the millennia.

And sometimes it is a voice, like that of Marie Mountjoy, Shakespeare's Huguenot landlady in Silver Street. I learned about her in Charles Nicholl's *The Lodger* (a book I recommend, by the way): Marie once consulted Dr. Forman, the astrologer, about some missing money and jewels. Forman's detailed notes contain Marie's description of her servant Margery, "a tall, freckled wench". It's a bit of a voice from four hundred years ago, unfiltered by the conventions of literature, law or ritual. It's a small window thrown open across the centuries to show us, to make us hear this long dead woman. Nicholl loves it just as much as I do: *Whenever I try to conjure up a sense of Marie*, he writes, *I imagine her while she pronounces "freckled" with a French accent.*

Well, something like this happened to me in this book with Manuel d'Andrada, the Portuguese nobleman turned spy. We have his letters to Don Bernardino de Mendoza, his Spanish contact — and when he writes, he always begins a new paragraph in Spanish, only to slip into Portuguese more and more as he nears the paragraph's end. Then he begins again in Spanish. Like Nicholl with Marie Mountjoy, I can never think of d'Andrada without hearing in my head his Portuguese-accented, Portuguese-flavoured Spanish.

It's from these glimpses that I endeavour to build my characters — historical or fictional — trying to combine what belonged to their time, and what hasn't changed too much across the centuries, into (hopefully) well-rounded characters.

If you think that I succeeded in this, if you "heard" the voices of d'Andrada and my other characters, I would truly appreciate it if you'd drop by **Amazon** and **Goodreads** to post a review and let other readers know that you enjoyed this novel. I'd also love to hear from you, if you like, through my through my **website** or **via Twitter**, where I tweet under the handle **@laClarina**.

Thank you, and we'll meet again in the pages of Tom Walsingham's next adventure!

C. P. Giuliani

Sapere Books is an exciting new publisher of brilliant fiction and popular history.

To find out more about our latest releases and our monthly bargain books visit our website: **saperebooks.com**

www.ingramcontent.com/pod-product-compliance
Lightning Source LLC
Chambersburg PA
CBHW052026240626
47153CB00006B/1978